A Former Person

Daniel Fludgate

(The first in the Dmitri Romanov series)

Copyright ©Daniel Fludgate

Cover image by kaczor58, through Shutterstock

Cover font of Aprille Display Caps SSi, through wfonts.com

The author asserts their moral right under the Copyright, Designs and Patents Act, 1988, to be identified as the author of this work.

All Rights reserved. No part of this publication may be reproduced, copied, stored in a retrieval system, or transmitted, in any form or by any means, without the prior written consent of the copyright holder, nor be otherwise circulated in any form of binding or cover other than that in which it is published and without a similar condition being imposed on the subsequent purchaser.

I
Scottish Borders, 1932

HE FELT, rather than saw, the gun. He hadn't heard the person enter the first-class train compartment over the puffing of the engines and clacking of the rails.

Prince Dmitri Andreevich Romanov, great-grandson of a tsar, wasn't scared; the Bolsheviks had pointed many guns at him during the revolution fifteen years before. Whilst not afraid, the thirty-one-year-old playboy was concerned. His assailant could be a jealous husband, an outraged father, or a bad loser from the gambling tables; the list was long.

When his attacker spoke, the exiled Russian prince wasn't shocked to hear a female voice.

"Do you know," she said, "I have a revolver pressed to your spine."

"No my dear, but if you hum it, I might remember the tune," quipped Dmitri.

"Put the jewellery back in the case," she instructed.

Having made the switch before being caught, the real jewels were already in his pocket, so the situation was not entirely without hope of success. The replicas he held up would look enough like the real ones to not raise the young woman's suspicion.

"You cut short your breakfast," remarked Dmitri. "I thought I had another ten minutes at least before your return."

"It's lucky I never take breakfast, only coffee," she said. "Now sit down."

"Not so lucky for me it would seem," said Dmitri, slowly seating himself on what had recently been a sleeping berth, but which the porter had converted back to being a seat moments before Dmitri had broken in. "And the caviar omelette is a treat; you really are missing out," he added.

"You don't sound like a common thief," she said. "Nor do you look like one."

He recognised the flicker of attraction in the young woman's eyes.

"Thief, I'll accept," said Dmitri. "But common, I cannot. May I smoke?" he asked.

"No, you may not," she said, aiming the revolver closer as Dmitri reached towards the inside pocket of his jacket.

"I don't think you're going to shoot me," he said.

"Don't be so sure," she replied. "My father owns the railway company. No police will be called."

The train jolted as a bend was taken too quickly. The young woman lurched, and the gun fired. The bullet thudded into the fluffy cushions embroidered with the rail company's logo, inches from Dmitri's hip. An explosion of duck feathers filled the compartment.

Dmitri sprung forwards, knocking the revolver from the woman's grip with one hand and, with the other, slapping her hard across the face.

"I'm terribly sorry, my dear," he said. "Must dash."

Peering out into the corridor he could see it was already blocked in both directions by people curious to find out what the noise was. Dmitri closed and locked the door. He crossed the compartment, stepping over the young woman.

The train was travelling at eighty miles per hour, so when he opened the exterior door it flung backwards against the carriage, shattering the window glass.

There was now furious knocking on the compartment door, and someone was trying to force the handle.

Dmitri carefully stepped onto the thin sill along the outside of the train carriage. He hadn't planned to leave via this route, and the oxblood brogues with new leather soles were thoroughly unsuitable for the task ahead.

He shimmied along the side of the train, pressing himself tighter against the carriage each time the train passed a signal mast. His fingers were numb with cold, and it was more by luck than skill that he was able to firmly grip the window rail to pull himself along the speeding locomotive.

The vapour of his breath steamed the windows of the first-class sleeper compartments he pulled himself past. Every muscle was tense, controlled, focussed on keeping his body attached to the train hurtling along the track.

Glancing down at the connecting rod, churning over and over, gave Dmitri a moment's hesitation as he imagined himself falling under the mighty steel wheels; this was a far from sensible endeavour.

An elderly woman, finding Dmitri clinging to the frame outside her window as she opened the curtains, shrieked. This broke his momentary pause. He smiled and nodded to the open-mouthed woman, then stretched his left leg so that his foot could reach the step of the carriage doorway.

His shoe slipped.

His foot fell.

His body disconnected from the side of the train.

The sleeve of his jacket caught on a loose nail sticking out of the side panelling. The fabric tore open, slicing the sleeve from cuff to upper arm. But the padded shoulder held, and with it, Dmitri's legs stopped, barely three inches from the wheels that would slice them to shreds.

As he stretched for the exterior handrail, the shoulder pad of his jacket gave way. His fingertips touched the metal. With one mighty reach his hand gripped the pole and he hauled himself to safety on the step.

In the vestibule mirror he smoothed down his hair and inspected the ruined jacket.

"Guard!" shouted the old woman he'd disturbed moments before. "Stop that peeping Tom!"

As Dmitri swung round to plead his innocence, a gun fired. The bullet shattered the mirror he had just being using. The young woman he'd slapped earlier was pushing her way through the other passengers with the gun aimed for a second shot.

Dmitri didn't wait.

He hurried through the restaurant car. An elderly waiter was taking his time to serve breakfast, shakily laying plates down at one of the tables. Dmitri picked up the remaining dishes from the serving cart and laid these in front of the passengers at the table.

"I'd avoid the kippers," he said, then wheeled the empty trolley past the waiter, through the carriage, and left it by the kitchen. Dmitri scooped some jam onto a croissant that was waiting to be served, and moved through another vestibule into the day carriage. He weaved past milling passengers in the second-class carriages as he ate the croissant.

With each section of the train he passed through there was a realisation that he would soon run out of places to go. He hadn't expected to be caught stealing the jewels, and didn't have an escape plan. But one was now required.

Eventually, as expected, there were no more carriages.

Dmitri glanced back and saw a surge of angry train officials in pursuit.

He jumped over the gap between the last passenger carriage and the tender of the locomotive. He climbed the ladder to the top of the water tank. He could now feel the full force of the mighty wind on his face, so flattened his body and slid himself forwards. The train conductor's head emerged at the top of the ladder behind Dmitri, but he seemed reluctant to follow onto the top of the tank.

The smoke billowed back, engulfing Dmitri as he pulled himself forwards.

The coal bunker was over two-thirds empty. As he climbed down into it, he slipped on the loose pieces of coal and fell to the floor of the bunker, covering himself in coal dust. He looked down at the soot covered Saville Row suit and shrugged.

He peered over the top of the coal bunker, surprising the driver and fire crew in the cab.

"Good morning, gentlemen," said Dmitri, wiping some of the blackness from his face with his remaining jacket sleeve.

"Blimey!" exclaimed the driver. "You ain't supposed to be in there guvn'r."

"What's the next stop, please?" asked Dmitri.

"Why, Berwick-Upon-Tweed," said a fireman. "We'll be there in a few minutes."

"I'm in a spot of bother you see, gentlemen," said Dmitri. "Could I trouble you to perhaps let me off before we get there?"

"What's your game?" asked the driver.

"I'll make it worth your while," said Dmitri, extending a filthy hand in which were several pound notes.

"It's more than my job's worth," said the driver. "'sides, there ain't nothing but the bridge over the river between here and the station."

"A river, you say?" An idea occurred to Dmitri.

One of the firemen guessed what the peculiar passenger was considering.

"Don't even think about it, mate," said the fireman. "It's over a hundred-foot drop to the river."

"That does sound rather a leap," said Dmitri. "Stand by, gents." He carefully crossed back and crawled up the coal mound. One of the waiters had either been ordered, or had volunteered, to continue the pursuit; he was halfway across the water tank.

Dmitri returned to the front of the train and swung himself down into the cab to join the driver and firemen, one of whom was brandishing his coal shovel as a weapon.

"I come in peace," said Dmitri, raising his hands in surrender. "What reduction in speed might this cash bonus buy me?" He counted out pound notes.

The driver and firemen glanced amongst themselves.

"Listen, it's not worth –" as the driver spoke, Dmitri took out another bundle of pound notes and added these to the first.

"We'd be slowing down to approach the station anyways I guess," said one of the firemen to the driver.

"And who's to say what speed we'd normally be going," suggested the other, having lowered his coal shovel.

The driver took the money, stepped over to the controls and turned the brass handled lever to apply the brakes.

Dmitri peered out of the cab and saw the stone arches of the bridge approaching. The drop looked even more than one hundred feet. The impact of hitting the water might kill him. But, if he didn't jump, he'd definitely be arrested, and the real jewels discovered in his pocket. Having spent time in prison as a detainee of the Bolsheviks, both in Petrograd and Siberia, Dmitri knew incarceration was not to his taste.

He stepped to the edge of the cab as the train began to cross the bridge. The driver had slowed the locomotive sufficiently to enable Dmitri to make the jump.

It seemed an even greater distance now that it was directly below him.

"Don't do it guvn'r," said one of the firemen.

"You'll surely kill yo'self," said the other.

The waiter peered over the rim of the coal bunker. In his hand was the revolver fired at Dmitri earlier.

"Well, that does it," said Dmitri. "Thank you for a pleasant ride, gentlemen."

He grabbed the handrails either side of the cab entryway, secured his feet, flexed his knees, leaned back, then threw his body forwards to clear the bridge.

The three second fall seemed to take forever.

Prince Dmitri Romanov's body plunged into the River Tweed.

II
Tangier.

THE YOUNG dark-skinned man smiled at the crumple-suited journalist from the Daily Express. The Moroccan's white teeth dazzled Aubrey, who was embarrassed to expose his own caffeine-stained dentistry.

"I'm –" began Aubrey.

"Yes, His Highness is expecting you, sir," interrupted the attendant in a soft voice. In a street crowded with Moroccans, donkeys, and well-dressed European émigrés, the pale sweaty face of Aubrey had been sufficient proof of his identity as the expected Englishman. "Please follow me."

The large medieval wooden doors of the Moorish gateway were pushed open to reveal a sun-bleached courtyard with neat borders of red, yellow, and blue flowers. The doors that could stop a cannonball then creaked closed, shutting out the smells, dust, and noise of the Kasbah.

There followed a series of labyrinthine alleys, the final turn of which led them into a courtyard bordered by date-palm trees. Through arches carved in the stone wall

Aubrey could see the azure-blue ocean that he'd sailed across from Gibraltar earlier that day.

"Salima will take you inside," said the young Moroccan. He gave a slight bow and stepped back into the maze of small streets.

Aubrey realised he'd be unable to find his way back unaided. This gave him a peculiar sense of unease. He was trapped.

Removing his battered panama hat, he wiped the sweat from his forehead with a handkerchief. He no longer envied the foreign correspondents; the heat was unbearable.

"Ahem."

Aubrey turned sharply towards the sound of the cough.

Under an archway flanked by two impressive palm trees stood a slim woman. She couldn't be more than twenty years old, thought Aubrey. She was dressed in a tight-fitting cream-coloured kaftan with orange embroidery. Her green eyes sparkled under long eyelashes. A hand beckoned Aubrey to approach. Without speaking she walked gracefully into the building.

Aubrey followed.

The cedar doors led to a long corridor decorated with Islamic blue and white zellij tiles. Archways were surrounded by intricate plasterwork and covered with lightly fluttering thin curtains. Frankincense filled the passageway with a woody, spicy aroma.

Aubrey felt as if he were in a dream from which he would soon wake. He'd find himself back in the stuffy bedroom at the guest house in Orpington, where he'd been staying while his wife decided whether to forgive him for yet another of his career mishaps.

In a central courtyard the bubbles from a large fountain of geometric blue and green tiles made the rose petals on the water's surface swirl and bump against each other. It was a place of dappled sunlight and complete privacy, with an ethereal calmness to it. This was not somewhere Aubrey had expected to find his playboy prince.

Salima led Aubrey into a narrow salon furnished in a sympathetic fusion of the city's Berber, Arab, Moorish, and French history. A wing-backed leather armchair was the only item out of place. It was turned with its back to the door. Plumes of white smoke were wafting over the top of the chair.

Salima coughed quietly, too quietly, and retreated to the courtyard. Aubrey stood rather awkwardly in the centre of the room.

The puffs of smoke continued to rise and escape through the latticed shutters of the upper windows in the double-height reception room.

"Heavens!" exclaimed Dmitri, rising from his chair to freshen his drink. Aubrey was standing a couple of feet away in the centre of the room looking uncomfortable and embarrassed. "Who the devil are you?" asked Dmitri. "And why are you creeping up on people?"

"Um, the girl did cough," mumbled Aubrey. "But she left. I'm a journalist." This wasn't the best start to an interview. Dmitri's expression of confusion turned immediately to understanding.

"Ah! The chap from the Express. Why, of course you are." Prince Dmitri beamed a wide, welcoming smile. He walked forward, extending his hand towards the man from the newspaper. "Anthony …?" Dmitri was searching for the name contained in the letter he'd received the week before.

"Aubrey," corrected the Englishman. "Aubrey Hollebone, sir."

As they shook hands the young Russian looked directly into Aubrey's eyes, as if trying to take the full measure of the man in just this brief exchange of physical contact. The prince had a firm, confident handshake.

"Sorry about that. The bloody girl's always sneaking around like a damned ghost," said Dmitri. "Drink!" he exclaimed, more like a command than a question, as if a brilliant idea had just occurred to him. He walked over to a table adorned with what looked like a full bar of alcohol. "What'll you have?"

"Ah…not sure really…" Aubrey's voice trailed off as he spoke. He looked at his watch, noting it was still early in the afternoon.

"I detest evasiveness," joked Dmitri. "If you can't decide, then I shall choose for you. And trust me when I say, that can be dangerous."

There was an energy to Dmitri that none of the pictures in the press had been able to convey. The journalist felt a mesmeric pull, as if Dmitri were a magnet drawing him closer.

"I suppose I'll have a gin and tonic?" said Aubrey in the tone of a question. He wanted to please the prince but was unsure why.

"An excellent choice. Now comes the hard part, as your work is not done there. Do you want German, Scots or English gin?"

"I didn't even know there was a German gin," said Aubrey.

"Ah, then this will be an education indeed. Let me introduce you to a cheeky little number from Prussian juniper berries. It's a great starter for the uninitiated." As Dmitri mixed the drinks, Aubrey moved from where he'd been standing and inspected the photos on the nearby piano. They were of the most famous celebrities of the day, pictured in Tangier, and all with the Russian prince.

"Quite a gallery?" remarked Dmitri, handing across the drink. His accent was unique. A perfect English vocabulary, but spoken with a timbre that couldn't easily be placed; French mixed with his native Russian, guessed Aubrey.

"Certainly a decent collection of who's who, sir," answered Aubrey. "Although not many who'd make it into Debrett's."

"Quite so," said Dmitri. "Rogues one and all, and me first among them! Now I absolutely refuse to call you Aubrey, ghastly name, and you simply must stop with this 'sir' nonsense." Dmitri had already finished his drink and reached forward for Aubrey's glass, which was still half full. "Catch up," he joked. "I say, what did your chums at school call you?" Aubrey drained his glass, balking slightly at the unexpectedly generous proportion of gin to tonic.

"Well, it's been a while since…"

"I can't believe those fellows in the press room call you Aubrey all the time. Makes you sound like someone who plays bridge with his landlady of a Saturday evening." Dmitri was already back at the drinks table. Aubrey, having spent the previous Saturday evening doing just that with the widowed Mrs. Cathcart, felt ashamed of his prematurely middle-aged life and Dmitri's disdainful account of it.

"Well, at school I was mostly called 'Bones', on account of my surname," suggested Aubrey. Dmitri took a second to recall the journalist's full name.

"Aubrey Hollebone…Bones…of course! Then Bones it is." He handed Aubrey the second drink of the afternoon. "Assuming that's all right with you of course?" Aubrey nodded his approval as he cautiously sipped the drink, forewarned to the strength of the gin this time.

"The family have always called me Mitya," said Dmitri, taking his second drink almost in one gulp.

"Do you see your family often?" asked Aubrey, bringing himself back to the task in hand of interviewing his subject.

"Straight in with the interrogation, that's the chap," joked Dmitri. "I suppose you mean what's left of the family, the imperial family that is?"

"I'm sorry, that was rather clumsy of me to ask right off the bat, just habit I suppose. If this is too…" Aubrey regretted starting with a question that would be so obviously harrowing for the orphaned prince to answer.

"Not a bit of it." Dmitri waved away the journalist's apology. "Of course, things have been more difficult since the dowager empress died."

"That was four years ago, wasn't it?" asked Aubrey for clarification.

"Quite so, the early winter of 'twenty-eight." Dmitri paused to take a second gulp of his drink, one large enough to drain the glass. "All that business with Uncles Kirill and Nikolasha made things very ugly." He seemed reflective for a moment. "I don't put much stock in being a prince of Russia, but others take it terribly seriously. I mean what's the point of being an emperor of nowhere? The 'former people' is what the Bolshies call us back in Russia, seems about right to me."

"Do you mind if I…" Aubrey put down his drink and reached in his pocket for a notebook.

"I'd rather you didn't if it's all the same," said Dmitri. "Plenty of time for that later." There was authority to the younger man's voice. A verbal power. It was a reminder to Aubrey that he was in the company of a tsar's great-grandson who had, until the age of fifteen, been a member of Russia's ruling family. The interview Aubrey had been granted may have been held in the smoking room of a Tangier nightclub, but a royal audience it nevertheless was. Aubrey slid the notebook back into the pocket of his plaid sports jacket, which was now considerably creased from his travels.

"Ah, here's the girl with the refreshments," said Dmitri. "Let's take a seat." He walked barefoot over to an area of large floor pillows adorned with pompoms and tassels. He fell into one such seat with considerably more grace than Aubrey, who almost rolled off completely as he lost his balance trying to squat down onto one.

A dark-skinned woman started serving the two men with tea, poured from a considerable height into small glass cups. The large collection of horn bracelets on her wrists clacked together as she then passed around a selection of sweets and snacks.

"Thank you for the hospitality," said Aubrey, sipping the Chinese gunpowder tea infused with fresh mint leaves.

"Not a bit of it," replied Dmitri, plunging a fork into one of the honey-glazed poached pears. "How have you found the exotic Orient so far?" he asked, quickly adding, "Oh, by the way, I hope you're all right with spice, might want to give the orange segments a miss if not, they're sprinkled with something that can carry quite a punch."

"I only arrived in Tangier earlier this morning," replied Aubrey. "And it's my first trip outside of Europe to be honest with you." He hoped this didn't make him seem unqualified to interview a man who had seen the world twice over, despite being nearly ten years younger than the journalist.

"Where are you staying?" asked Dmitri, drinking the tea with the same urgency as he had the gin; he didn't seem like a man who did anything by small measures.

"The Velazquez," replied Aubrey.

"Absolutely not!" exclaimed Dmitri. He tried to jump up, but winced with pain and fell back. "You'll have to give me a hand up, old chap," he said. "Would you believe I jumped off a moving train recently?"

"It isn't all that easy to get up from these, is it?" joked Aubrey. Once upright himself, he helped Dmitri.

"We shall get you in at the El Minzah," Dmitri said. "I'm lodged there this season. We'll have someone send your things over post-haste."

"I'm not sure my editor will go for that plan," said Aubrey. "The paper's quite particular about expenses you see."

"You can tell Bax Baxter I needed you close by at the El Minzah." Dmitri adjusted the fashionably high-waisted, wide-legged tan trousers he was wearing, and looked around for his hat and shoes. "Any quibbles and we'll dash a letter off to the Marquis who owns the joint. Come on, Bones." Dmitri picked up his shoes and grabbed Aubrey by the elbow, pushing him out of the door.

THE TWO-SEATER 6C Alpha Romeo 1750 Gran Sport shot through the ancient streets of Tangier, being driven by Dmitri as if he'd just stolen it. The supercharged engine of the little dark-red open-top sports car was a thoroughbred, as was its driver. Dmitri handled each tight bend and human obstruction in the road with effortless precision, positioning the long bonnet to make every turn seem graceful. At no point in the high-speed drive through Tangier, lasting not more than ten minutes, did Aubrey feel in fear, quite the opposite – he was sad the ride was over when the vehicle pulled up outside the hotel.

"I won it in a bet with Enzo Ferrari," said Dmitri, launching his long frame out of the driver's seat. "He claimed his driver couldn't be beaten. In a time trial against his champion I was the fastest by four hairs off a frog's back, so Ferrari said I could have the car if I won the Coppa Ciano that year for him."

"And did you?" asked Aubrey, trying to uncurl himself from the passenger seat. He succeeded, but with much less grace than the vehicle's driver.

"I'm driving it aren't I?" asked Dmitri, with a mischievous twinkle in his eye. "I couldn't get to the front on the narrow hill roads with those damn stone walls, but I eventually took the hard-charging Bugatti on the Via Aurelia at the final circuit. Only eight finished from the thirty-two that started."

"And Signor Ferrari presented you with this?"

"I didn't ask him, old chap. A bet's a bet. We split the seventy-five thousand lire prize money, and he had his picture taken holding the cup with Princess Maria Ciano, so he can't have been too sore about losing this little baby." Dmitri tapped the bonnet of the sports car. He swept back his dark-blonde hair, which even the liberal amount of hair cream had not managed to keep in place during the drive.

"Things are a bit raw around here today," whispered Dmitri as he walked with Aubrey into the lobby, "on account of a soldier of fortune from your part of the world having disappeared mysteriously yesterday, name of Willoughby. Rumour is he'd been in the service of the Sultan and fallen foul of his master."

"Gosh, sounds juicy." Aubrey instinctively reached for his notebook but stopped himself for fear of losing the trust of his interviewee.

"Only if you believe in rumours, which I don't," said Dmitri. He slid two cigarettes out from a tortoiseshell case. "Dull matter off *cherchez la femme* if you ask me. The fellow was a terrible cad, so there's probably a jealous husband somewhere in Tangier with one less bullet in his service revolver."

The hotel attendants circled around Dmitri. He held the two cigarettes in his mouth and lit them both with his gold-plated Dunhill spin-wheel lighter. Speaking with difficulty due to the obstruction he said, "Trust someone who knows a little about that sort of thing." He turned and winked at Aubrey, handing the journalist one of the lit cigarettes directly from his own mouth. "Damn swine owes me money, though. Don't suppose I shall see that packet now."

"My word," coughed Aubrey after the first drag, "that's strong!" The peppery taste of the cigarette was intense.

"Sorry about that, should have warned you," said Dmitri. "It's Syrian. Most use it as a blender, but I ask my little man to serve it straight for me." He patted Aubrey on the back. "Hakim, would you send for Mister Hollebone's luggage from the Velazquez? His editor made a terrible mistake, which I'm correcting. You'll find space for him, won't you? He's a particularly important journalist from London." The hotel attendant, dressed in the uniform of baggy knee-length breeches, black stockings, a short jacket, and traditional plum-coloured fez, nodded his understanding. "And send up some coffee, would you?" The attendant hurried off to execute the instructions. "I'll play host while we wait for your kit to arrive," suggested Dmitri to Aubrey, leading the way up the stairs to his room.

"I'm afraid I'm really not that important of a journalist." Aubrey didn't want to feel as though he was misleading the prince. His newly demoted position as features writer on the Daily Express, whilst perhaps not quite the gutter press, placed him amongst those on the kerb at best.

"It used to be the case that being an Englishman was enough for these chaps," said Dmitri. "But rogues like that Willoughby fellow have queered the pitch somewhat. All officials here are incorrigible snobs."

The two of them walked along lattice-lined loggias with Burmese silk curtains and wrought-iron balconies.

"How do they feel about Russians?" asked Aubrey.

"We're the worst. Don't let Hakim's servility fool you. He makes me deposit money with him each season before he'll give me a suite."

The Arabesque woodwork, studded doors, oriental carpets, upholstered divans, and arched doorways of Dmitri's suite were combined with modern touches. The room was a very serene space with a distinct Andalusian flavour to the decor. The view through the carved sandstone portal over the bay of Tangier alone was worth whatever price the Russian prince was paying, although Aubrey suspected there was a rich woman somewhere in the city whose husband would be unknowingly meeting the cost.

Almost immediately, a waiter arrived with a tray of coffee and almond biscuits. He struggled to find a space to set the tray down as the entire room was littered with the contents of Dmitri's suitcases and trunks. It was the room of someone used to having others tidy up for them.

Aubrey, noticing the difficulty for the young boy holding the tray, attempted to move some of the prince's papers from the hammered-metalwork coffee table. Dmitri was already tapping out a second cigarette as the one held loosely in the corner of his mouth burned to a stub. He showed no embarrassment at having someone he'd just met clearing up his mess.

"Shall I be mother?" asked Aubrey, taking hold of the ornate brass coffee pot that resembled an Aladdin's lamp.

"Um, yes, super," replied Dmitri somewhat distracted. He was flicking through the calling-cards and letters that had been brought for him with the coffee. His behaviour changed suddenly. His easy charm dissipated, replaced by agitation as he checked the time on his silver Rolex Oyster wristwatch. He crushed the cigarette out in one of the many ashtrays and tucked the unlit one behind his ear. He hurried towards the door.

"You don't mind amusing yourself for a bit, do you, old man?" he asked. "I've a quick errand to run." Before Aubrey could answer, Dmitri was already out of the door, almost at a running pace.

Left alone in the Russian prince's room, Aubrey took a sip of the coffee he'd just poured, enjoying its sweetness and good flavour. He was used to the foul soluble coffee powder at the newspaper office, which he was sure came from a Great War surplus that was still being used up fourteen years later.

He looked back towards the door, wondering whether he could get away with having a rummage through the prince's things before he returned. This would help to build more of a picture of the man he'd come to interview, but about whom he'd yet to write anything in his notebook.

Had the items been in any kind of order, there might have been value in a quick snoop, but Aubrey knew he'd be more likely to tidy things up than dig for useful information. But journalism had become a habit of his, not just a profession. Something instinctively told him that he was missing an opportunity for a good story.

Instead of looking through the contents of Dmitri's luggage, Aubrey, who'd been moved six months before from a promising career at The Times to the gossip section of the Express due to a serious error of judgement, put down the coffee cup. He peered cautiously into the corridor to make sure it was clear, then he hurried off in pursuit of Prince Dmitri. Whatever the prince had received in the day's post had galvanised the young man of easy charm into a burst of panic. Aubrey was prepared to lurk in the shadows of this mysterious and decadent city to find out what that pressing matter was.

III

HAD DMITRI glanced back on his way to the rendezvous mentioned in one of the letters received, it would have been hard to miss Aubrey following rather clumsily a short distance behind. The labyrinthine passageways of the city did not lend themselves easily to following someone discreetly. But Dmitri was in too much of a hurry to concern himself with checking for a shadow. He didn't notice Aubrey, who ducked into the American Legation as Dmitri came to a halt outside the building opposite.

Tao Chen was not surprised when Dmitri stepped through the crooked doorway into the courtyard where the Chinaman had been waiting for some time.

Tao's wizened old body leant forwards on the knobbly walking stick that he'd now carried for several years since his spine started crumbling. The degeneration was a painful reminder of his time spent as a servant at the Forbidden City in Peking, being beaten almost daily by senior palace eunuchs, and even the Dowager Tzu-hsi herself.

"I knew you'd be late," said Tao.

The old man's voice was like a child's. He, like the other palace eunuchs, carried his manhood in a vial around his neck. But it was only the foolish who mistook Tao's severed masculinity as a sign of weakness. His father had been a rebel Chinese warlord. When captured by the Imperial Guards, and moments before his death, Tao's father had witnessed his eleven-year-old son's castration and initiation to a life spent as a slave in the service of his father's enemy, the Emperor.

The testicles in vinegar gave Tao more, rather than less, strength. After twenty-five years of servitude, he'd tried to burn down the palace in 1910. His punishment was expulsion from the Forbidden City. Being thirty-five years of age at the time of his eviction, Tao Chen had been young enough to start a new life, and old enough to make a success of it, which he'd done over the last two decades.

Upon his dismissal from the Forbidden City Tao had joined the Hongmen, the secretive Triad organisation he now led. The group had, in its recent history, become associated with organised crime with branches all over the world, even in Tangier.

Tao's small, hunchbacked body was dressed in the full-length silk changshan robe made in the black fabric associated with burial attire. The choice of colour was an acknowledgment that he'd never expected to live as long as he had. Tao was a man ready for death. A rounded black hat covered his hairless head, below which the intense eyes, like two black onyx gemstones, defied the soft, almost feminine face his castration had cursed him with. These eyes were capable of conveying both ruthlessness and friendship in a flicker, depending on the audience.

"I have something slightly different for you this time," said Tao.

"My debt will soon be paid," said Dmitri. There was a rare deference to his voice. Tao was one of only a few people still alive the Russian prince would cede such obedience to.

"The Red Army would have killed you in that prison camp, were it not for us," reflected Tao. Dmitri cast his eyes to the floor in respect. The old man hobbled over to him, the wooden stick thumping against the cobbled floor of the courtyard. "Two years of being their prisoner in a Siberian labour camp could easily have become a lifetime." Tao glanced at Dmitri. "But I'm glad we did rescue you."

"What's different about this mission?" asked Dmitri.

"It requires your return to Russia." Tao walked past Dmitri, who's expression was one of disbelief at the prospect of returning to the country which had betrayed him and his family.

Tao sat on a bench, and Dmitri joined him.

"The Communists are worrying us," said Tao. "And Mao Zedong is gaining loyalists. We predict he's likely to replace Zhou Enlai as leader, which cannot be allowed to happen. Some warlords are now refusing to support Peking. They're scared of the Chinese Red Army."

"They should be," commented Dmitri. Any mention of the Red Army, whether Soviet or otherwise sparked a visceral feeling of grief and hatred in him.

"The Hongmen need the Red Chinese to stay fragmented, and Moscow cannot be allowed to take on an assertive posture in world affairs. We need a new Civil War in Russia and in the East."

"And you need a burst of derring-do from me? I understand that, but what can I achieve alone?" asked Dmitri.

"We trained you to be the equivalent of twelve men," exclaimed Tao, angered by Dmitri's defeatism.

"I think you need a few more than a dozen for this. You're asking me to take on the Soviet and Chinese Red Armies, Tao."

"Mitya." Tao's use of Dmitri's nickname reminded them both of the closeness of their relationship. "We have others to help you." His smile revealed a mouthful of teeth turned rotten by opium. He patted Dmitri affectionately on the knee, and continued, "There's a brigade of two-thousand White Russian émigrés which the Hongmen are funding. They'll be gathering in Manchuria soon, at Harbin."

"Many in the White Armies don't like Romanovs such as me any more than the Reds do. And I'm to join them?" asked Dmitri. There was a tone of dissention in his voice.

"No." Tao rested both hands on the top of his walking stick and shook his head to emphasise the point. "Nobody can know about your relationship with us."

"Then what?"

"You're to go to the Crimea." The mention of this location made Dmitri shudder; it was a place of particularly cruel memories for him. "Do you know Konstantin Izvolsky?"

"The man they call the White Baron?" asked Dmitri. "He's part of the Russian All-Military Union of émigrés, isn't he?" Tao nodded. Dmitri added, "Last I heard he was in the South of France."

"Not anymore," said Tao. "The Soviets kidnapped him six months ago. But the Russians gathering in Harbin say they'll only fight under his command. So we want you to get him back."

"Is he even still alive?" asked Dmitri. He was trying to find a reason to refuse Tao. He would prefer to march outside the Lubyanka in Moscow wearing the Imperial Crown, than go back to the Crimea and the memories that haunted him from there.

"We think so," replied Tao. He sounded embarrassed by his lack of certainty. "Some Tartar smugglers in the area have reported as such."

"Surely, one of the White soldiers would prefer to be the one to liberate their commander?"

"They've tried. And failed."

"Well, I'll be even more conspicuous to the secret police," said Dmitri.

"The previous attempts failed because the general didn't trust those whom we sent to free him," said Tao. "The OGPU has been setting traps for those they call the 'former people' who are still in Russia. We're of the opinion that you, someone from the imperial family, are about the only person the White Baron will trust to rescue him."

"So, you want to send an exiled Russian prince into Soviet Russia to help someone escape? A man who has repeatedly refused similar opportunities. And this is all to prevent an alliance between the Soviet and Chinese Red Armies?" Dmitri sounded incredulous.

"You refuse?" asked Tao. He was aware of how preposterous the task was that he'd expected the young man to accept.

"Absolutely not! Sounds just my sort of sport." Dmitri jumped up. His face beamed with a smile beneath his perfectly trimmed, pencil-thin moustache. His show of enthusiasm was an attempt to disguise his emotional hesitation, but all demons needed to be confronted eventually, he thought. His debt to Tao outweighed his reluctance to return to the Crimea. The bravado was his defence against any doubt.

"But I have to make a quick stop beforehand," added Dmitri.

AUBREY DUCKED back into the American Legation building just as the wooden door opposite opened. Dmitri hurried out and headed back towards the hotel. Aubrey was about to follow him when he saw a small Chinese man walk uncomfortably out through the same doorway. The Chinaman turned in the opposite direction.

The London journalist knew where Dmitri was heading, and who he was, so there was little immediate mystery to be solved in following him back to the El Minzah. He waited for Dmitri to walk out of sight, then Aubrey followed the elderly Chinaman.

The going was slow. Aubrey felt for sure that the hunchbacked old man would soon realise he was being followed. Once on the wooden jetty of the port, Aubrey was just about to catch up to the man he was tailing to ask him some inconsequential conversation starter, when he felt an object being thrust forcefully into the small of his back.

"Vite!" commanded the voice in his ear. The aroma of expensive Gauloises cigarettes, a pack of which cost Aubrey two francs fifty back in mainland France on his recent journey, indicated to Aubrey that he was not being mugged by a Tangier street thief. The command was accompanied by a firm grasp of his elbow. He was wheeled around back towards the city. Aubrey caught a glimpse of the Chinaman, who smiled as the English journalist who'd been following him was led away.

"Now look here…" Aubrey tried to free his arm from the firm grip, but there were two men escorting him. The man without the gun made a painful swipe to Aubrey's ankle, causing him to lose his step.

Within a short space of time, Aubrey was launched headfirst into a dusty and dilapidated office in the customs building. One of the men who'd forced him into the room was of a dark, swarthy complexion. He'd have assumed this man to be Spanish were it not for the

Gauloises smell, so most likely Marseilles or Corsican French, assumed Aubrey.

The other, younger, man had a military haircut. He lurked in the background and let the first man take charge.

Whether the men were spies representing *le Deuxiéme Bureau* from Paris, or some illicit cartel, Aubrey only cared about getting away from them and back to the safety of the hotel before news of his stupidity reached Dmitri, who would then surely cancel the interview. Sylvia would never take Aubrey back in the family home if he also got the sack from the Express.

"I'll have you know," began Aubrey, "I'm a highly respected journalist." He remembered Dmitri's advice about officials in Tangier being snobbish about such things. "This sort of behaviour will simply not do," he added. Neither man indicated a change in their demeanour. "I shall tell my paper," insisted Aubrey. "Do you know who Lord Beaverbrook is, Messieurs?"

The younger of the two kidnappers kept the small revolver, a Smith and Wesson preferred by plainclothesmen due to its short barrel, aimed at Aubrey. The other man set to work on the journalist with a few well-placed fists to the body. It seemed they disliked respected journalists even more than lowly ones.

Aubrey was soon doubled over on his knees on the dusty floor, and suitably softened up by the working over he'd received.

"*Reste ici*," barked the man who'd assaulted him. Both laughed as they left. Aubrey heard the key turn in the lock.

He wasn't usually one for heroics, but it wasn't for nothing that Aubrey had been mentioned in dispatches as a keen twenty-six-year-old lieutenant with the Fourth Army at Amiens way back in 1918. He searched the ramshackle office for what he needed, then set about freeing himself.

Jamming the cylinder of a dismantled pen into the base of the upper door hinge, Aubrey used his pocket handkerchief to muffle noise as he bashed at the pin from below with an old, disconnected telephone he'd yanked off the wall mount. When the pin would move up no further, and with it still wedged in the hinge, he put the edge of his cigarette case against the lip of the pin and continued the upward taps until it was loose enough to remove. Repeating the process for the lower hinge, he had a removable door in a matter of minutes.

Aubrey freed himself from the room and replaced the door. He wished he could wait until the goons returned, just for the amusement of seeing the door fall to the floor at their first touch, but he wasn't that foolish.

He reached the hotel at a run, after several wrong turns and dead ends. He hurried up to Dmitri's room, taking the stairs three at a time. The prince's luggage was being packed by two maids. Aubrey recognised Hakim, the attendant from the lobby earlier.

"Has Prince Dmitri returned to the hotel, yet?" he asked, still out of breath.

"His Highness returned a while ago, sir. And it's good to have you back, Major Willoughby. The police have been looking for you. We were all very worried."

"I'm not Willoughby. Hollebone...Aubrey Hollebone's the name." His bruised ribs were beginning to hurt more than before. "I was with the prince earlier today."

"But of course you were, sir. I understand completely." Hakim's tone indicated that he didn't believe Aubrey, who was in too much pain to argue. No doubt all Englishmen looked the same to a Moroccan hotelier, thought Aubrey. Nevertheless his journalistic instinct made a mental note that the misguided assumption of the hotel assistant indicated that Dmitri and the missing Englishman were much closer than had been indicated when the subject was mentioned earlier.

"I'll wait here for the prince." Aubrey walked towards the balcony as he started to light one of his own cigarettes.

"I'm afraid you can't, sir," remarked the assistant, blocking Aubrey's way to the terrace.

"Now look here," exclaimed Aubrey. He was losing his patience with Tangier, and those he'd encountered. "I'm not chasing all over the hotel looking for him, while the prince is doing the same looking for me."

"You misunderstand me, sir. His Highness checked out. He's en route for the Gibraltar ferry, and asked for his luggage to be sent on."

"Sent on? The luggage is going to Gibraltar as well?" asked Aubrey.

"It's not for me to say, sir. I'm sorry." Hakim returned to the task of overseeing the packing of the prince's things.

"Damn it!" exclaimed Aubrey. He hurried off to the lobby in pursuit of the prince once again. He couldn't go back to London without a feature written about the world's most famous playboy. His own luggage, which was just arriving from the Velazquez, was still strapped on the tired mule. Aubrey ordered it be taken down to the port. He knew the two French attackers would still be looking for him, but he hoped they'd assume returning to the jetty would be the last destination their escaped prisoner would choose.

Once at the ferry terminal, Aubrey pushed his way through the passengers who'd recently disembarked from the latest ship. He had to navigate through the swarm of Moroccans who'd emerged from the shade to sell trinkets to the new arrivals.

A musician banging a frame-drum loudly, and with no apparent talent for it, pursued Aubrey through the crowd. Also in eager pursuit was a man carrying snakes in either hand. He was shouting at Aubrey in barely coherent French about his power to tame wild animals.

Aubrey arrived at the wooden jetty just in time to see the stern of the evening ferry, the last of the day, passing the end of the dock heading out on its fifty-mile journey across the Strait of Gibraltar.

If Aubrey wanted his interview, he would have to follow Prince Dmitri's luggage instead of the man himself.

IV
Paris

DMITRI WAS lying naked on a white chaise longue designed by Le Corbusier. He rolled on his side and propped his strong cleft-chin on his arm. He watched Sable, the twenty-year-old daughter of an American financier, applying her make-up.

Sable's father had embarked on a transatlantic cruise in October of 1929 as a millionaire, but disembarked in Cherbourg the day after the Wall Street Crash having to borrow cash from his valet until his wife's jewellery could be sold. It now fell to Sable to replenish the family coffers through marriage. Such a responsibility over the last three years had given the innocent-faced beauty an inner toughness that attracted Dmitri.

"Love and loving are two very different things, darling," said Dmitri.

"You're always so beastly to me, Mitya," rebuked the young American. She looked appreciatively at her reflection in a silver-backed embossed hand mirror. She was wearing Dmitri's white shirt, and nothing else.

"Then why ask if I love you?" queried Dmitri. "Anyway, you're practically engaged to what's-his-name from Germany. Surely you love *him*?"

"Oh, that's just an arrangement daddy has made," said Sable.

"And a pretty good arrangement." Dmitri's was a statement, rather than a question. "It's paying the eight hundred dollars a year rent for this Parisian penthouse."

"I shan't take accusations of extravagance from an aristocrat of Imperial Russia," said Sable.

"*Former* aristocrat," corrected Dmitri.

"I've heard the rumours, Mitya. Your family were wealthier than the tsar's."

"Exile has taught us the price of everything," said Dmitri.

"Maybe," said Sable, "But perhaps not the value." She glanced at him in the mirror. "You, Prince Dmitri, are a rogue."

"And you, Miss Nash, have expensive tastes." He held up an empty bottle of champagne from the ice bucket by the bed to emphasise his point.

"Watch the drips!" exclaimed Sable. She shrugged. "Heinz has been very kind to me."

"And I suppose the kindness of Heinz extends to your completely new wardrobe from Schiaparelli for this season?"

"He loves me very much and wants me to look my best. Not *all* men are brutes to young women."

"Meaning me, I suppose?" Dmitri asked the question, pretending to be angry. Sable simply nodded that she had meant him. She continued to admire her own reflection in the mirror. "In which case, I shall leave you alone," said Dmitri, "but I'll need my shirt back, please." He stood up and held out a hand, pretending he expected to receive the garment, but guessing Sable wouldn't leave herself as naked as he was.

Sable Nash was not one to be shy.

She put down the mirror, unbuttoned and removed the shirt. She then walked across the room to hand it to Dmitri, wearing nothing but her immaculately applied make-up and a pearl comb in her hair. Dmitri stepped forward to kiss her, but Sable pushed him back. She draped the requested shirt around the back of his neck, glanced down with a smile at his hardening manhood, and walked off to the dressing room.

"Stay for the evening," she said over her shoulder, "it's going to be a swell party."

SABLE HAD redesigned the main salon, ensuring that everything was white; she called it her own 'White House'. Not allowing the designers to use suburban shades of cream and dead-white, everything was in tones of ivory, oyster, parchment, and pearl. From the quilted satin curtains to the horsehair upholstery, velvet lampshades, and alabaster vases, everything was the same colour.

The gleaming chromium-plated tubular steel furniture and peach-mirrored screens were the only items that broke-up the starkness of the room. The apartment had a modernist flavour. Dmitri had commented that it looked like an operating theatre, but Sable shrugged off his criticism, commenting that his lack of taste was no doubt the real reason for him being exiled from Russia.

The hostess herself complemented the entirely white décor of the room, not just because of her short wavy platinum-blonde bleached hair, but also being dressed in a floor-length bias-cut ivory gown that hugged every curve of her body. This dress would have been mercilessly revealing for someone not in possession of the Junoesque figure that Sable Nash had.

Even her jewellery, specially commissioned from Van Cleef and Arpels, was made of white gold and carved coral. The only hint of colour came from the turquoise wings of the *Plique-à-jour* dragonfly brooch which accentuated her own complex-coloured green eyes.

The penthouse was now full of those from Paris high society. Dmitri entertained the guests at the piano, which was white of course, with a selection of jazz and swing hits. The Russian prince was an accomplished classically trained pianist. When alone, he would lose himself in the magical worlds of Mahler's middle period. But in public he chose only to play those pieces which amused others from his fast social set.

The decadence of Sable's guests was a drug that disguised the destructive effects of wealth given to the young rich with no sense of responsibility who had swarmed to Sable Nash's apartment that evening. Dmitri was not one of them, even if perhaps in his childhood he had been set on that course. But he pretended to still be so, as he enjoyed a good party every now and then.

He saw the despair of the wasted generation for what it was, but he felt himself due some compensation for what had been taken from him as a youth. So Dmitri played the piano, seduced the sexually bored wives, and stole back jewellery from his own family's history that had been acquired by the new nobility of Europe and America. It was a life of wonderful nonsense but born of a darkness that Dmitri understood well.

Taking a break from the piano, Dmitri joined Sable on the roof garden. Even this she'd designed with the help of emerging surrealist designers. The box hedges could slide apart mechanically to reveal Paris below, and the open-air space had been made to look like an interior room with a real fireplace, a rug-like patch of grass, and even a chandelier on a frame.

"You were right, it is a swell party," said Dmitri.

"Thank you, Mitya," replied Sable. She kissed him lightly on the cheek. "I can hear someone else has taken your spot at the piano."

"A poor replacement, even if I do say so myself," joked Dmitri.

"Dance with me, Mitya," requested Sable. She drained the champagne left in her glass and threw this behind her. Dmitri obeyed the instruction and embraced her satin-covered delicate body. The music echoed up to them from the salon below.

"Are you staying in Paris for long?" she asked, adding quickly: "I should like it if you were."

"I'm only here to visit papa in the morning, then off again."

"I'm just providing accommodation for the night, then," replied Sable disconsolately. "You know I've got you under my skin, don't you?" Dmitri said nothing, so she added, "Or perhaps that's just venereal disease. I follow your sexual exploits in the gossip columns, Mitya."

"Don't be like that, darling." Dmitri pulled away from her to lean on the balustrade. He gazed at Paris by night. Sable linked her arm through his.

"I'm sorry for being silly, Mitya. I know you father's condition is a worry for you."

Sable was the only person outside of the imperial family who knew that Dmitri's father was still alive. She also knew his whereabouts in a Paris sanatorium, and about his condition of catatonia. It was a mental state the grand duke had been in ever since hearing of his wife's murder by the Bolsheviks as he fled Russia.

"Your Heinz fellow is a tad shorter than me," said Dmitri, tugging at the borrowed dinner suit. "But otherwise this is a decent fit." Dmitri was keen to change the subject. His nightmares too frequently replayed the scene he'd witnessed of his mother's assassination. He had no wish to discuss it during the waking hours.

"I like my men broad," said Sable. She adjusted the wide shoulders of the jacket. "I'll be sure to pass on your thanks to Heinz," she joked. Sable snuggled her body closer to Dmitri's to reaffirm that she was there to support him. She ran her hands across the front of the six-buttoned double-breasted dinner jacket, smoothing out the creases. "And he's not *my* Heinz," she added.

"If he knows his onions, that Prussian lover will make you his, and pretty darn quickly I'd suggest." Dmitri sipped his drink. His comment was not one of jealousy, but of genuine hope that Sable would find happiness and security, something he knew she could never get by waiting hopelessly for him. "I always forget how much I love Paris," he said wistfully, glancing across the city skyline. There was a hint of regret in his voice that he would have to leave the following day, after only one night in the vibrant city with someone he held in such great affection.

Dmitri was a man of impressive strength, a notorious cad with all women but her, and someone who kept his own counsel. Only Sable was allowed to see a chink in his armour.

"Your ice is melting," noticed Sable. The comment hinted at a metaphor. "Shall we re-join those making whoopee downstairs?" she asked.

"I'll see you down there," he replied. "Nature calls me to iron my shoelaces first, far too much of this expensive giggle-water." He handed his empty glass to Sable as they both made their way back inside to the party.

V

DMITRI TOOK a taxi from outside Sable's apartment to the sanatorium on the outskirts of western Paris. Sable had offered to come with him, even though Heinz was due back in the city that morning, but Dmitri wanted to see his father alone.

Grand Duke Andrei Sergeevich Romanov had been a patient at the sanatorium for thirteen years. He'd been transferred there directly from Malta when the British cruiser docked in the safe port fifteen days after having left the Crimea in April 1919. He'd neither spoken, nor acknowledged any of the few visitors that knew of his whereabouts during that time.

An anglophile, who'd spent much time in England with his family before the Revolution, the last thing Andrei had said was, in perfect English: 'how is Grand Duchess Xenia Nicolaievna?'. The regretful answer received from the ship's captain, informing the grand duke of his wife's brutal murder, had plunged the imposing Russian prince, the grandson of a tsar, into a state of mental and physical disablement he was yet to emerge from. It was doubtful now that he ever would.

Even the re-emergence of his only surviving child, Dmitri, having been rescued from the gulag by the Chinese Hongmen in 1921, had not brought the grand duke out of his paralysis. Dmitri's younger sister, Anna, had already been reported dead to her parents in 1918, the year before her mother's assassination. Anna was amongst the many Romanovs murdered during that bloody year after the Bolsheviks had taken over the government.

The grand duke had been admitted to the sanitorium under the inconspicuous Anglo-French name of Andrew Durand. The pseudonym had been chosen by the dowager empress because of its translation as 'steadfast'. To some in the émigré community Andrei would be a rival claimant to the title of emperor-in-exile, were his faculties restored to him. This was a further reason why the grand duke had been kept a secret from the émigré Russian nobility who had known him as he had once been, and the Soviet spies who might seek to return him to Russia for public humiliation; the grand duke was, after-all, a cousin of the assassinated tsar.

It had been nearly two months since Dmitri's last visit. Nevertheless, he found his father sitting in the same chair by the window of his private room where Dmitri had left him several weeks before. It was as if Dmitri had only stepped away for a minute or two since last being there.

His father looked considerably older than his sixty-two years. Whilst his impressive beard was being maintained by the nursing staff, it was now completely grey and hung from slack jowls. His dark sunken eyes, pallid wrinkled skin, and wizened body gave him a ghost-like quality; he was a living corpse.

"Hello, Papa," said Dmitri. He kissed his father's bald head. There was no response from the old man, who stared blankly out of the window across a formal garden, upon which peacocks roamed amongst manicured topiary and artistic stone features. Dmitri had made one brief stop en route to the sanatorium to collect a box of Charbonnel et Walker milk marc de champagne truffles. These had been his father's favourites. Dmitri left the box on the Rosewood chiffonier, knowing they would remain uneaten until the staff took them for themselves rather than throw the delicious expensive chocolates away.

He took his father's cold, bony hand. It was unresponsive to the warm touch of his son's. On every journey across the city to see his father, Dmitri hoped that he would find a miraculous improvement in the patient upon his arrival. The doctors had assured him that there was nothing physiologically deficient with his father, and that he could start to gradually emerge from his catatonia at any moment. He might be miraculously restored quickly with no memory of the lost years, but he could just as likely remain forever entombed in the tortured mental world he now inhabited alone.

Each visit, seeing his father's condition unchanged, felt to Dmitri like a new grief. He blamed himself for not being able to bring his father back to the real world, as the presence of a son should surely do. But the visits also renewed the incredible loss of his mother and sister felt by the almost-orphaned son.

Thirteen years before, his mother had been killed in front of her son by the sadistic Red Army soldiers. They'd treated the capture of a grand duchess like sport. She had been the only adult Romanov many of the Soviet soldiers, themselves recently peasants under the yoke of monarchy, had ever met. In Grand Duchess Xenia, a woman who had been amongst the progressives in the imperial family urging the tsar to give meaningful power to the Russian people, these men mistakenly saw in Dmitri's mother the embodiment of the many Romanov terrors.

On that road in Yalta where the two Romanovs, mother and son, had been captured, she hadn't begged for her own life. She'd pleaded with the rough young men who pawed at her body only that they spare her son, a youth too young to be complicit in the Romanov crimes they held her accountable for. Dmitri was restrained by the soldiers as he fought against them. Xenia's screams were slowly silenced by twenty wounds from bayonets and the butt-ends of rifles. He hadn't been able to stop her death, but Dmitri was alive because of his mother's sacrifice.

Dmitri had been the only male offspring of Andrei and Xenia's to survive beyond childhood, something which had already laid a substantial foundation of sorrow for his father a long time before the tumultuous year of revolutions. That year, the death of his only daughter and wife built the fortress of grief which now held the grand duke its mental prisoner.

Dmitri glanced through the collection of books in his father's hospital room to see what new ones had arrived from Hatchards of London, where he had an account. Amongst the recent arrivals was Gene Stratton-Porter's 'The Keeper of the Bees,' a story chronicling a war veteran's road to recovery aided by a beekeeper, and Zane Grey's 'The Mysterious Rider', a bestselling western novel from ten years before, but one which he hadn't yet read. The plot of the war novel seemed to have too much similarity with his father's own predicament, so Dmitri selected the western to read to his father.

"A September sun, losing some of its heat if not its brilliance, was dropping low in the west over the black Colorado range…" Dmitri pulled his chair closer to his father's and continued to read aloud.

DMITRI HAD one more stop to make in Paris before starting out on his mission for Tao Chen, and his rescue of the White Baron from the clutches of the Soviets.

The nineteenth-century villa within the Bois de Boulogne had been leased to an elderly grand duchess, now one of the executed tsar's closest living female relatives. It had been granted to her by the city of Paris at a nominal rent, following the family's escape from the Crimea.

After having been admitted by a footman, Dmitri was greeted by the grand duchess' equerry, a formidable veteran of the Great War. He was a man who stood over six feet five inches tall, and an aristocrat in his own right. He was one of the few members of the royal household who had fled with them into exile.

The equerry maintained an insistence on formality. He still wore the gold court uniform he'd escaped Russia with so many years before, even if it did now show significant signs of fading and over-wear. Dmitri and the count had always liked each other.

Dmitri had stolen a polo shirt from Heinz's wardrobe to wear that morning, something he was sure wouldn't be missed from the wealthy German's collection of clothes he kept at Sable's apartment.

"Perhaps His Highness would like to change before meeting Her Imperial Highness, who is expecting him?" Count Mishukov tactfully reproached the young prince for his rather casual attire.

"Has my luggage arrived from Tangier yet, Sergei Vasilyevich?" asked Dmitri.

"It has, sir. The footman will show you to one of the guest bedrooms where the luggage has been placed. He can help you to dress."

A few minutes later, and now clothed more formally in a dark grey double-breasted woollen suit, Bastille shirt, sombre coloured tie, and highly polished toecap Oxfords,

Dmitri was admitted to the main drawing room. The grand duchess rose from an eighteenth-century cane-backed chair positioned next to the red marble fireplace. Dmitri stiffened his posture and nodded his head in a respectful bow.

The grand duchess was of a small, but regal stature. Her large eyes held a powerful gaze capable of flashes of defiance, a character trait which she shared with the distant relative now kissing her hand in greeting. She had become like a wild animal trapped and uncomfortable in circumstances not of her choosing. The opulence of her surroundings disguised the precarious financial situation she was perpetually in. Almost everything was on loan from wealthy friends, or those Russian émigrés who'd managed to flee with some of their fortune.

Her most valuable possession was hanging in a gilt frame on the pale *eau-de-Nil* panelled wall above the long banquette of gold brocade, it being an informal painting of the tsar and his family. The scorch marks of damage from the revolutionary soldiers' attack on the palace at Tsarskoe Selo were clearly visible. The grand duchess refused to have the picture restored, insisting that any visitors should see the evidence of betrayal for themselves.

The painting was one of the first items Dmitri had managed to liberate from its new owners after his return from the gulag a decade before. Only Dmitri and the grand duchess knew of his role as thief, someone who sought out the most personally important Romanov treasures from greedy international collectors. These wealthy opportunists showed no sensitivity in buying up such items whenever the Soviets sold more of the confiscated plunder at a knock-down price, something happening with increasing regularity since the death of Lenin eight years before.

The European aristocrats and wealthy American collectors knew the provenance of the items they were purchasing, and the circumstances under which the items had been seized. For this reason, both Dmitri and the grand duchess considered his clandestine activities constituted a noble liberation and return of misappropriated family heirlooms, rather than a theft from their new owners.

Dmitri's elevation to the status of international playboy now gave him even closer access to the international set who shamelessly acquired the personal Romanov family items. He and the grand duchess ranked the items according to sentimental value when news reached them of yet another off-loading from Russia.

One minor British earl even had the audacity to ask for Dmitri's assistance in confirming the authenticity of a piece of Fabergé jewellery frequently worn by the tsarina in the years immediately prior to her execution. Whenever possible, Dmitri would replace the items he took with counterfeit copies to reduce suspicion, sure that, if ever discovered, the new owner would blame the Soviet sellers for skulduggery rather than look around for any other explanation.

"My dear Mitya, it's always such a pleasure to see you back in Paris. How is your papa?" asked the grand duchess. When her great nephew visited, she saw him alone, not wanting any of the few remaining household staff present during her meetings with Dmitri.

"Much the same I'm afraid, Aunt." Even though he and the grand duchess were only related somewhat distantly, she permitted him to call her 'aunt' because of the affection the tsar's own family had for him. This fondness for Dmitri was something which she too had developed during the long years of precarious exile during which the unlikely pair had become friends.

"Count Mishukov brings Andrei Sergeevich from the sanitorium to the Bois in a rolling chair for a day out occasionally. I always spend some time talking to him, hoping that one day he might once again answer me."

"I'm quite sure he's grateful, Aunt, as I am."

"Nonsense, Mitya, it is I who am grateful to you for all you've done for the family, even if that great service must remain between us." She tapped her wrinkled nose conspiratorially.

"Speaking of which, I have the latest plunder." Dmitri took out a chamois cloth from his jacket pocket. He unwrapped it on the gilded marble-topped side table to reveal three items of jewellery.

"However did you manage it this time, Mitya?" The grand duchess lightly picked up the emerald and diamond choker necklace, as if this item, thought lost forever, might easily break now it had been returned. Such items, whether of high monetary value or not, couldn't replace the people lost, but their return nevertheless satisfied some small sense of justice. "There are some scars that can't be seen, Mitya," mused the grand duchess reflectively. Her arthritic fingers delicately caressed every part of the necklace, as if the touch were connecting her to the associated memories.

"I'll spare you the details," whispered Dmitri, "but there's an English railway heiress with three items of jewellery that weigh considerably less than those originally purchased whilst in Europe. They might even leave a green hue to her porcelain skin when worn to dinner with her wealthy father." They both laughed, but it was a gesture tinged with sadness, as always was the case when the grand duchess was reunited with items which reminded her of their legitimate, but long dead, owners.

"This belonged to Catherine the Great," she announced, "and was presented to your grandmother on her marriage. It was a favourite piece. She would be glad it is back with the family."

The grand duchess took the choker with her to the mirror over the fireplace. Dmitri moved to follow, but she waved for him to remain seated. She held the necklace in place herself without fixing the clasp. She stared at her own image with a longing expression.

"I remember her letting me borrow it once. 'It looks much better on you, Mimi', she said generously." The grand duchess swept her greying hair out of the way for a better view. "There's no one left who calls me Mimi," she said. She quickly removed the piece from her sparrow-like neck, as if a memory too sad to dwell on had flashed into her mind.

"These other two pieces aren't on the list, but I thought perhaps they could be used nevertheless for financing our endeavour. They were part of the same lot sold by the Soviets' representative to the Englishwoman." Dmitri laid out a set of earrings and a pearl bracelet.

"I'll arrange for one of the household staff to take them to our usual friend in Le Marais."

"Broken down and sold separately the stones won't make anywhere near their actual value I'm afraid, Aunt. But we can't risk them being traced."

"The money will help pay the sanatorium fees, Mitya, as the dowager empress made me promise before her death. There will be a little extra left over perhaps. I never did like these amethyst pendants anyway; they have something funereal about them." She wrapped everything back in the chamois and placed them in the drawer of a nearby Louis XV ormolu-mounted marquetry bureau.

"I've done a little repatriation of my own," she said. The grand duchess took a small, framed oil painting out of a cabinet and held it up so Dmitri could see.

"Seventeenth century?" he asked.

"Try again," said the grand duchess.

"Sixteenth? Holbein?"

"Very good, Mitya," she said. "It used to hang in the tsar's study at the Kremlin."

"And how did you come by it?" he asked, walking over to admire it more closely.

"An elderly art dealer who was infatuated with me in my younger years happened to mislay it. Fortunately, it was fully insured." She laughed like a little girl. "Aren't I terrible?"

"Some would say criminal," suggested Dmitri, holding the miniature towards the light from the window.

"How long are you staying, Mitya?" The grand duchess locked the painting back in the cabinet. "You could accompany me to the country this weekend perhaps?"

"Alas Aunt, I'm not even able to stay for supper."

"That's terrible news. What could possibly keep you so busy, or perhaps I shouldn't ask. I do worry about you."

"There really is no need to." Dmitri kissed the hand of the grand duchess. He straightened his posture, ready to excuse himself from her presence.

"I don't believe you," she said. "I read the newspapers you know. You're what they call a playboy I believe."

"Everyone needs a hobby," said Dmitri, who then gave a small bow. The grand duchess acknowledged the gesture and remained standing as the young man left the drawing room.

"I need to make a few calls, Sergei Vasilyevich. Shall I use the phone in the study?" asked Dmitri.

"Of course, sir." Count Mishukov opened the door of the study to let the prince past. "Would you like your luggage sent on anywhere?" He'd been listening at the door, and knew Dmitri was not staying.

"I'd be grateful if it could be stored here, at least for a month or so. I'll take a few things that I'll need with me today."

Thirty minutes later, a green Renault Monasix taxi was hailed down outside the villa by a footman. The same servant then carried out two suitcases.

Dmitri soon followed. He'd changed into a Glen Plaid check suit with cuffed trousers, and a pair of two-toned brogues in brown and cream. The outfit was finished by a fedora worn angled over one eye. He had a topcoat over his arm as it was too warm to be worn.

From the drawing room window, the grand duchess saw the taxi collect its passenger. The footman stowed the prince's luggage in the vehicle.

Count Mishukov approached the grand duchess carrying a silver tray, on which was a cup of tea freshly poured from an ornate silver samovar engraved with the imperial Russian double headed eagle.

"You overheard him make reservations through to Belgrade, you say?" she asked, taking the cup and saucer.

"He did, ma'am," replied Count Mishukov.

"Then contact Bogdan Timofeyevich."

"Of course," said the equerry.

"One more thing Sergei Vasilyevich," added the grand duchess. "Make sure we don't lose him this time." Without turning away from the window, the grand duchess sipped her tea and watched as the taxi drove off.

VI

AUBREY HAD been waiting in the café opposite the Bois de Boulogne mansion since Dmitri's luggage had arrived there earlier that morning. The journey from Tangier, following the many trunks and suitcases belonging to the Russian prince, had involved bribing the captain of a Portuguese cargo ship, a mad dash through Spain and France on a third-class train ticket to Paris, and then a panicked taxi ride across the city trying not to lose the vehicle carrying the bags.

As he was tired, Aubrey had paid for one of the guest rooms above the café. For a few extra francs, the café owner's son had agreed to wake him if anyone matching Dmitri's description should arrive at the villa. Neither the owner nor his son knew to whom the mansion belonged when asked.

After barely three hours sleep, Aubrey received a firm shove from the child, and the news that the man described had now arrived at the mansion. Aubrey settled the bill with the café owner and stood outside watching the grand house through tired, bleary eyes. In three days the journalist had crossed Europe from north to south, and back again. He was still wearing the same clothes he'd left London in, and had barely slept.

As he waited, Aubrey considered his options. He wanted to knock on the door of the mansion and ask for the prince, to angrily demand the promised interview, and then return to London. But this might seem too much of an invasion of Dmitri's privacy, and be counter-productive to Aubrey's goal of securing an interview with the young man whose antics filled the gossip columns of the European press, but who had only consented to one formal interview, Aubrey's. Common sense told Aubrey to wait, to continue his pursuit until a more appropriate moment presented itself for him to approach the prince and ask for what had been undertaken, but not honoured, in Tangier.

Just over an hour after arriving at the mansion, Dmitri left. As the taxi carrying Dmitri and his suitcases departed, Aubrey hailed a taxi of his own in pursuit. As Dmitri was leaving with suitcases, Aubrey assumed the destination would be one of the main train stations. He was quite surprised when the vehicle drove through central Paris and followed the road for about six miles north east of the city.

The destination was Le Bourget aerodrome, a hub for diplomats and businessmen who didn't have the time for leisurely rail travel across the continent. Aubrey had never flown before, and was not keen ever to do so. Nor would the stipend given him from petty cash for expenses cover such a ticket.

All seemed lost.

He would have to explain to his editor why there had been no interview with the Russian playboy, and no money left from his expenses. Sacking seemed inevitable, and that made the chances of his wife allowing him back into the family home even more remote. Aubrey's unfortunate life had, once again, failed to give him a win.

As a younger man, when he was up at Oxford, the Classics don who'd inspired Aubrey to consider a career in the written word frequently quoted Levy. The eccentric professor reminded his students that sometimes the boldest measures are the safest.

Aubrey watched the diplomats and businessmen dashing from taxis and limousines into the aerodrome's ticket hall. These men were all intrepid. They had achieved in life. They were tenacious. Deciding he had nothing to lose, and in a spirit of daring, Aubrey paid the taxi driver, picked up his suitcase, and followed Dmitri into the building.

He recognised the grand aviation hall from the pictures taken of Charles Lindberg, who'd landed here five years before after the first solo transatlantic flight. He glanced at the two sides of the room, one marked with the word, *arrivée*, the other, *départ*. Would Dmitri be here to leave for somewhere new, or to meet someone, he thought.

A uniformed gendarme wearing a circular flat-topped dark blue kepi approached Aubrey.

"Excuse me, sir, may I see your ticket, please?"

Aubrey's schoolboy French took a moment to translate the officer's request.

"I haven't got a ticket," said Aubrey in badly phrased local language. "I'm seeing someone off."

"Ah, I see," said the officer. "And which flight is that?"

"Well…I'm not sure…you see..."

"Please come with me, sir," said the officer.

Aubrey was led into a side office. This was the second time that he'd been detained at a transport hub whilst trying to get an interview with Dmitri Romanov. He cursed his bad luck.

"This can't be a coincidence," said Dmitri as Aubrey stepped into the office. "Thank you, officer, that will be all," he added to the gendarme. The military police officer saluted the exiled Russian prince, and left the two men alone.

"I don't think very highly of your espionage skills, Bones," said Dmitri. "My driver noticed you as soon as we left the Bois."

"I'm not a spy," replied Aubrey defensively. He was embarrassed that he'd been caught following Dmitri.

"Well that seems evident. Which begs the question, what the devil are you doing here?" Dmitri continued to puff on his cigarette. He waited for Aubrey's explanation.

After a pause, the journalist said, "I'm here to interview you."

"I don't believe it!" exclaimed Dmitri with a guffaw of laughter. "You've tracked me across continental Europe just to finish an interview for a newspaper feature?"

"Well, yes," stumbled Aubrey. He realised it did all sound like madness now. "I tried to catch you in Tangier, but I missed the Gibraltar ferry."

"Well, you're certainly tenacious, I'll give you that, sport." Dmitri offered Aubrey a cigarette as a sign of no hard feelings. "But I'm afraid your pursuit has been for nothing. I shall be on a plane that leaves in about ten minutes, and I'm not sure when I'll next be back amongst the civilised."

"I'll come with you," suggested Aubrey. He spoke before he'd had time to think about what he was saying.

Dmitri, about to get angry at the impudence of the journalist's reply, stopped himself, and took a second to get the measure of the man now in front of him. It had been an unexpected suggestion, and just the sort of thing that appealed to the playboy prince. Perhaps he'd misjudged the Englishman's character during their first meeting in Tangier. He'd assumed Aubrey to be one of the stuffy conservative types, handicapped by manners, and the sort of Englishman who can only show affection to dogs.

"Impossible, I'm afraid," said Dmitri, after considering the idea. "And dashed impertinent of you too." Despite the admirable boldness of Aubrey's suggestion, Dmitri had an arduous, sensitive mission to carry out. He couldn't have someone tagging along with him. He expected an apology from the journalist and would then offer a handshake. He'd promise to contact him upon his return from Tao Chen's mission.

"Would you have let Signor Ferrari out of your arrangement with him over the sports car so easily, just because it was inconvenient?" asked Aubrey. He surprised himself by the continued show of brazenness. "A deal's a deal I believe you said." He stiffened his back and stomach to anticipate a hard-thrown fist, but instead the Russian prince smiled in admiration.

"I'm on a flight through to Budapest, with stops for refuelling at Strasbourg and Vienna. There are four spare seats. We'll do the interview on board and, once you feel I've honoured my deal, you can bail out at the next stopping point. You can then make your own way back to London. How does that sound?"

"Thank you, sir. I didn't mean to…" Aubrey was stopped from completing his sentence.

"Don't you dare apologise," interrupted Dmitri. "Hold your ground, man. You bested me good and proper, don't gloat about it, but by God don't snivel either."

"I wasn't snivelling, but I may have misrepresented my financial situation somewhat. What's the cost of the ticket please?"

"More than your editor will pay, that's for sure." Dmitri laughed. "But I'm in funds, and I've no doubt already put you to some considerable expense dashing away from Tangier as I did. Let's consider this part of me settling my account with you."

The Bernard 190T cantilever monoplane of the *Compagnie franco-roumaine de navigation aerienne* had arrived on the parking apron just outside the departure building. Porters loaded the cases onboard, and the steward lowered the steps and welcomed his passengers. It would take the pilot about two and a half hours to get to Strasbourg.

"I take it you've never flown before?" asked Dmitri in a shout. He'd noticed Aubrey's pale complexion. The take-off had rendered the thirty-nine-year-old journalist paralysed with fear. Aubrey was clinging to the arms of the wicker chair, a seat that faithfully transmitted every vibration from the plane through to his sweat-soaked body. Dmitri lit a cigarette for his companion. He had to lean across the aisle and put it to Aubrey's lips.

The steward made a brief announcement through the megaphone, being the only way his words could be heard over the deafening noise of the engine, to the effect that motion sickness bowls could be found on the floor under each chair. He also reminded his passengers that cigarette buts and other debris should not be thrown out of the window, especially not when flying above populated areas. He then distributed ear plugs and magazines to each passenger, along with an offer of coffee.

The cabin was decked out like a Pullman rail carriage. There was wood panelling around the picture windows, velvet lampshades, and cushions to try and mitigate the vibrations through the wicker seats, which were bolted to the floor along either side of the cabin. The altitude started to affect the cabin temperature, so the passengers wrapped their overcoats tighter around themselves.

As they were flying below the clouds, the turbulence soon started to shake the plane around until it became like a fairground ride for the passengers. Each series of bumps and drops made Aubrey turn from a complexion of white to green. Eventually, the journalist had to unbuckle his belt and stagger back to the cloakroom.

"I'd advise you use the bowl under your seat for motion sickness," shouted Dmitri. Aubrey couldn't hear him and was too British to entertain the idea of being sick in public anyway.

The cloakroom only loosely fitted the description of being such. The metal can set into a ring looked more like farm equipment for livestock than a receptacle for a gentleman's toilet needs. Aubrey lifted the lid, only to find the plumbing constituted a hole in the bottom of the bucket which aligned with a hole in the floor of the fuselage. Staring into the can, the first-time flyer had an uninterrupted view of the Picardy countryside below.

His stomach and throat momentarily closed. His body was in synch with his mind, and he found himself unable to be sick in the bucket. As he turned to exit the cloakroom and attempt the remainder of the flight in silent dignity, a small bump followed by a large drop released whatever muscles had contracted. Aubrey just had time to lift the lid on the toilet, before spraying the contents of his stomach out through the hole to fertilise the French farmland below.

The descent into Strasbourg offered Aubrey no respite as the plane heaved and dipped trying to manoeuvre towards the runway in heavy winds.

"I'm not sure you're up to the next leg of this adventure, my dear fellow," suggested Dmitri once they had stepped off the plane at Strasbourg airfield. Aubrey had no such doubt, despite the extreme discomfort. He'd been unable to ask even one question for his interview with the prince during the first leg of their journey. The further he progressed unsuccessfully to get the information for his article, the greater the need became to persevere no matter what the consequences. The excuses for failure would sound more and more unbelievable to his editor and wife back in London. He knew he'd have to get back into the confounded machine, come what may.

"Trains are for luxury, planes are for speed," said Dmitri. He passed his new friend a flask of whiskey.

"Is it too late to choose luxury?" asked Aubrey sardonically. He was bending over with hands on his knees in case any residual bile had yet to finish its journey from his stomach.

"That's the spirit, a bit of humour!" exclaimed Dmitri with amusement. He took the flask back from his travelling companion and enjoyed a large swig himself.

"How long is it to Vienna?" asked Aubrey.

"Best not to know, I'd say." Dmitri lit himself a cigarette, but didn't offer one to Aubrey, realising it wouldn't help the other man's nausea. "Just take things as they come."

"Why in God's name would anyone sanction such an inhuman contraption for the carriage of passengers?" asked Aubrey, somewhat rhetorically. His senses were slowly returning to him.

"Governments heavily subsidise the carriers to encourage passengers. They need to support an air industry, maintaining the technological and manufacturing capacity in case there's another war." Dmitri answered Aubrey's question, even though he knew it had been asked out of complaint rather than genuine enquiry. "It also means I can cross the continent in a matter of hours rather than days by train."

"Why are you heading to Budapest?" asked Aubrey. He felt as if he'd earned the right to start his interview with the prince. Before Dmitri could answer, the pilot, having checked the plane over, accepted a nip from Dmitri's flask with thanks, and signalled for the steward. The passengers assembled by the plane to return on board.

Aubrey was the last to approach the machine which promised him a fresh round of torture.

The steward checked the floor bolts on the wicker chairs. He tightened those that had worked themselves loose. He then swept up the remains of the coffee cups and saucers that had not survived the turbulence of the flight's initial leg. Welcoming the passengers back on board, the steward punched their tickets to show the first portion of their trip was complete.

Aubrey could feel his stomach unsettling itself once again, even though the craft was still motionless on the concrete apron.

The steward checked his watch and then the railway timetable that all crew were expected by the airline to carry with them. Should there be any issues with the plane as it attempted the second journey, the steward needed to make sure he was familiar with the train schedule to get his passengers to the station and on their way to Vienna by other means; this wasn't an unheard-of eventuality.

Just as the steward was about to close the door, he was hailed by the controller, who was hurrying from the hangar with two other men, neither of whom had luggage with them. Dmitri noted this and considered it peculiar.

The two new passengers boarded. Both glanced at Dmitri for a fraction longer than they did the others, as if they recognised him, or that he should recognise them. Everyone said their welcome to the new travellers, apart from Aubrey, who was concentrating on keeping control of his constitution.

Once airborne, the steward rolled down a screen at the front of the cabin, and set up a projector at the rear of the plane to play the in-flight movie. It was a silent film due to the noise inside the cabin. He handed out chicken salad and coffee to all but Aubrey, who had now abandoned the formality of using the cloakroom. Instead the journalist sat with the motion sickness bowl on his lap, even though there was nothing left in his stomach to be brought up.

Whenever he could do so without drawing attention to himself, Dmitri glanced back at the two men who had joined them in Strasbourg. After the initial lingering look they'd each given him, neither man paid any attention to the Russian prince. Their deliberate lack of eye contact with him increased Dmitri's sense of unease.

Despite having boarded at the same time, the two men didn't appear acquainted. The younger man - Dmitri guessed his age as being around twenty-five - was so nondescript that he could easily be a national of any continental European country, from the Nordic nations to the Iberian Peninsula. He had a haircut that was of a military style. He was ill at ease, and overly polite to the steward, as if unused to finding himself in the role of master rather than servant. He spoke so quietly that Dmitri didn't get an opportunity to try and place his accent.

The older, dark-haired man could only have been a national of the Slavic countries. He had large features and a somewhat broad flattened face. His complexion was pale, almost jaundiced. When he spoke, his formal phrasing of French highlighted that he was not a native of that land. His loud voice had a distinct accent, and one which was familiar to Dmitri, placing the man in the eastern Slavic region. As the Russian Imperial Court had spoken mostly French rather than Russian, it was easy for Dmitri to recognise this passenger as a fellow countryman of his. This realisation increased Dmitri's anxiety at the appearance of the two men. The Slav was at ease with himself and his surroundings, even chuckling at the slapstick comedy of the movie.

"I don't think I can go on," said Aubrey once they'd all disembarked for a further refuelling in Vienna. He was lying flat on his back on the warm concrete of the taxi apron, no longer having sufficient energy to stand for any length of time. He waved away the steward, who was trying to apply a cold cloth to the travel-sick patient's forehead.

"The interview seemed rather important to you back in Paris," replied Dmitri, calling down to his companion. Dmitri was enjoying a second glass of apricot schnapps, which had been brought out for him and Aubrey on a tray. The other passengers had gone inside to wait in the lounge.

"Hang the blasted article!" exclaimed Aubrey. He rolled on to his side in the hope that this might relieve the nausea. The steward gave up trying to help and returned inside to his other passengers. "Let them fire me! Let Sylvia divorce me! Just don't make me get back on that infernal contraption. Leave me here to either recover or die."

"Ordinarily, I'd be happy to accept your surrender, after all you have put up a brave fight against the turbulence. I'd even be willing to put in a good word for you with your editor. The wife might be more troublesome." Dmitri crouched down and patted Aubrey on the shoulder. He checked that no one was in earshot. "However, I don't think we are in a normal situation here, my dear fellow."

"Nothing is normal about feeling such as I do!" Aubrey had lost any sense of decorum. His thoughts were now being consumed with one goal, and one goal only – not getting back on the plane.

"That's not what I mean. I don't think I can leave you here," said Dmitri.

"I can find my way back from…where are we?"

"Vienna. But our situation may have taken a turn for the worse."

"How so?" asked Aubrey. As he began a slow recovery, his natural journalistic inquisitiveness was piqued by Dmitri's uncharacteristically furtive behaviour.

"I know you're having a devilish time of things, Bones, but I need you to get back on the plane." Aubrey groaned loudly at this suggestion and gripped his stomach as if the idea alone were enough to unsettle him once again. "It's terribly muddling, but I'm sure those two new passengers aren't on the same flight as us by chance. Don't you find it odd that neither of them boarded with any luggage?" Aubrey made no comment, so Dmitri continued, "When I spoke to the steward a few moments ago, he confirmed that both men had purchased tickets at the terminal in Strasbourg. Neither had a prior reservation."

"Good luck to them, I say," groaned Aubrey. "They can even have my chicken salad!" The mention of food made him retch once again.

A new pilot surveyed the plane and signalled for the steward to assemble the passengers once again.

"Listen, I'll explain more later, but I can't leave you here, it really is for your own good." Aubrey tried to resist Dmitri's attempts to get him upright. "It's only an hour or so to Budapest, then you can ask me as many questions as you like for your article, and I'll put you in a first-class sleeper train back to Calais."

Aubrey groaned insensibly but was too weak to continue his struggle against Dmitri, as the younger man pushed him up the steps and into the cabin once more.

"Did either of the passengers who joined us in Strasbourg make any phone calls?" Dmitri asked of the steward, before the passengers from the lounge arrived at the plane. He slipped a few francs into the steward's top pocket.

"Both gentlemen made use of the telephone, sir. Long distance calls I believe." He tapped his pocket to show thanks for the extra tip and descended the steps to welcome the remaining travellers back on board for the final leg of their journey to Budapest.

HAVING ARRIVED at Budapest, Dmitri was glad to have the excuse of Aubrey's condition to take seats in the lounge. He settled Aubrey there with their luggage, rather than make their way to the exit for onward connections by rail or vehicle, as the original Paris passengers had. While Aubrey slowly recovered from his sickness, Dmitri toured the terminal building.

He found the Slavic man waiting near the information desk, perched by a candlestick telephone, perhaps waiting for a call from someone. When a full reconnoitre of the building drew a negative to the nondescript younger man, Dmitri was ready to accept that his concerns might have been misplaced. Perhaps his suspicions that the two Strasbourg men were following him had been nothing more than fantasy.

Whenever he went to visit his father, Dmitri usually allowed himself a day or so in Paris to let his emotions return to equilibrium. On this occasion, due to Tao Chen's mission, he'd forsaken that recovery period. He was willing to admit a misjudgement, no doubt due to still feeling unsettled after his visit to the sanatorium. He would spend the night in Budapest, provide Aubrey with the promised interview, and be back at the airport ready for his reservation on the morning flight to Belgrade.

As he walked down the stairs to the ground floor lounge, he saw the younger man emerge from the rear of a car, which had been parked by the entrance. The vehicle didn't look like a taxi. As he began to walk into the building, the young man was called back to the car. Something was passed to him through the window, after which the car drove off. The young man returned inside the building.

Dmitri made a deliberate point of walking past the Slavic man near the information desk. As had happened when first seeing each other, this passenger held his gaze on Dmitri for longer than would be expected by a disinterested stranger.

"I'm afraid my plans are subject to a last-minute change," said Dmitri to Aubrey. He was glad that the colour had returned to Aubrey's cheeks. "I believe I'm being followed by those two chaps who boarded in Strasbourg."

"Why would they be following you?" asked Aubrey.

"Well, you did," replied Dmitri. This seemed the most evasive response he could give in answer to Aubrey's reasonable question. The journalist's expression did not seem satisfied by the reply he'd received, so Dmitri tried another explanation, "Jealous husband, angry father of a defiled daughter, hotelier in possession of an unpaid bill? The list of possibilities is quite long I'm afraid." This seemed to persuade Aubrey more convincingly.

"Just ask them. They're hardly likely to cause a scene here at the airport," suggested Aubrey. He was sipping a carbonated drink. It was slowly settling his empty stomach.

"I'm not concerned for myself, you goof. I don't want to embroil you in whatever this matter's about. That's why I needed you to stay with me until we arrived here. I didn't want them to do anything to you in Vienna, considering the state you were in."

"And now what?" asked Aubrey.

"This is where we say goodbye," said Dmitri, offering his hand in farewell. "And we hope they follow me, and forget about you."

"But the interview?" asked Aubrey, still not appreciating the danger to himself that Dmitri was indicating. He refused Dmitri's hand.

"I can promise to look you up next time I'm in London, but that's the best I can do I'm afraid."

"My editor is –"

"You editor is not my problem, I'm afraid," interrupted Dmitri. He was watching the two men from Strasbourg. "I have two problems of my own at the moment. Take a taxi to the train station and get the hell out of Budapest, that's my advice."

"But -"

"Best of luck," said Dmitri. He then hurried off, leaving Aubrey to finish his drink.

Dmitri found a vantage point in the lounge from where he could watch the men from the flight. They were still waiting for someone or something. Their lack of onward travel suggested to Dmitri that their presence was an ill-omen. Both men took notice of Aubrey's departure. The younger man went straight to the telephone and made a call, while the Slav wrote down the license number of Aubrey's taxi.

"Blast!" said Dmitri to himself, realising that Aubrey was not safe. He had to act quickly. He dashed down the marble steps, taking two at a time. He sped across the lobby, glancing behind, and seeing both men hurrying to follow him.

As Aubrey's taxi started to pull away, Dmitri leapt in front, banging on the bonnet of the grey 8-cylinder Ford. He flung the door open and hurled himself into the back seat next to Aubrey.

"*Vezess tovább!*" shouted Dmitri to the driver, repeating, "*Vezess tovább!*"

The taxi driver understood, and threw the vehicle forward at speed.

Dmitri spun round in the seat. The Slav and the younger man both emerged from the terminal building. The Slav waved his arms to hail forward a taxi, while the younger man ran across the road to a parked car.

"What happened?" asked Aubrey.

"Oh, I just fancied a tour of the city," joked Dmitri. He leant forward and instructed the driver to loop once around the airfield and return them to the terminal building.

AUBREY AND Dmitri ran across the airfield to an adjacent hangar where a plane was waiting with its engine already whining. The last of the air freight was being loaded as the two men carrying their own suitcases arrived.

"Well, who *is* going to fly the damned machine?" asked Aubrey.

"I am," replied Dmitri with a smile. "The scheduled pilot was only too happy to take the cash I offered him, and the opportunity to spend the night in Budapest with his mistress. We'll be doing the evening mail delivery to Belgrade for him."

"Can you even fly?" asked Aubrey.

"Can you?" asked Dmitri.

"Of course not."

"Then you'd better hope I can," said Dmitri. "Unless you fancy your chances with whoever those chaps are back in the terminal."

Aubrey waited on firm ground while the last of the freight was loaded onto the Junkers tri-motor monoplane. He was undecided which option was favourable: the discomfort of getting airborne once again, with the cavalier carelessness of Dmitri as pilot of his fate; or the unknown interrogation awaiting him on land at the hands of either or both men who'd followed them from Strasbourg. He'd already been assaulted in Tangier by two other men, and had found the experience was not to his liking.

He didn't believe that either of those now pursuing Dmitri would take such an expensive and arduous journey just to redress some sexual misdemeanour of the Russian's; there was a story here. Aubrey was a nervous air traveller, but he was also a journalist who needed a break.

Moments before the chocks were about to be pulled away from the wheels of the mail plane, the engine of which was straining against the impediment to forward motion, Aubrey made his decision, more out of journalistic than personal safety considerations. He boarded the plane and fastened himself into the co-pilot's seat harness, triple checking that the catch was secure.

The wheel chocks were removed. Dmitri pushed the throttle forwards, and the plane vibrated with the effect of 1825 revolutions. A green flare was sent up into the darkness of the early evening sky by the controller, signalling that Dmitri had permission to take off.

"As my Latin tutor used to say, 'hold on to your *membrum virile*'," said Dmitri.

"Mine used to say, *stultus est sicut stultus facit*," replied Aubrey.

"You'll have to translate for me, Bones. I was a terrible student."

"Stupid is as stupid does," said Aubrey, whose hands now gripped the side of the seat.

Air was pushing against the rudder as Dmitri guided the aircraft forwards along the runway. Aubrey glanced sideways and noticed that his pilot's expression had changed to one of deep concentration, and his body had tensed.

The propellers were trying to catch against the air, and the engine roared with energy as they sped along the closely mown grass. There was no headwind. Aubrey could feel the accelerations increasing. The plane rose then bumped back down.

"Blast!" said Dmitri, whom Aubrey noticed was frowning. One at a time, Dmitri quickly dried the palms of his hands on his trousers, then leant forwards and stared into the darkness, as if hoping to get the plane airborne by his will alone.

They lifted clear off the ground once again, the plane straining to fulfil the task Dmitri was directing the instruments to carry out. Again, the plane returned to the grass with a bump.

"For God's sake, stop!" urged Aubrey.

"We're committed now, Bones," replied Dmitri, not taking his eyes off the blackness ahead of him. "We're going too fast to abort."

Aubrey turned and looked forwards to where his pilot's eyes were fixed. He now saw the forest of trees and the end of the grass strip of runway.

For a third time, the plane left the ground. Aubrey realised this was their last chance; they'd either continue to rise, or plough into the trees and, most likely, explode upon impact.

The wings lifted and the plane stayed in the air. The ground disappeared beneath them, but they weren't rising quickly enough.

"Turn! Why don't you turn?" exclaimed Aubrey as he watched the wall of trees getting closer.

"Can't," said Dmitri through gritted teeth. "Need more altitude, or we'll just plunge back down."

"Christ man!" bellowed Aubrey. "We're going to -"

"Hit them," interrupted Dmitri. "Yes, I know. Brace yourself, Bones. If you have a God, now might be a good time to say a prayer, but better make it a quick one." Dmitri made the sign of the cross over himself.

The undercarriage of the plane whacked against the treetops. Aubrey now gripped the co-pilot's steering wheel, as if this would somehow help them to gain altitude. He stiffened his muscles, ready for imminent disaster. He squeezed his eyes closed.

The sound of the tree branches hitting the plane stopped, the propellers continued to whir, and Aubrey felt the plane rising into the night sky. He opened his eyes and braved a cautious look out of the window. The lights of Budapest glittered below.

Dmitri laughed and, in a German accent, said, "Up, up, and away in good old Iron Annie." He patted the instrument panel of the plane in thanks, then his body relaxed into the pilot's seat. Aubrey took his hands off the co-pilot's wheel, leaving behind damp patches on the wood.

The loop aerial searched for a strong signal, and the steady continuous hum confirmed the plane was 'on the beam' and heading in the right direction for Serbia. It was too dark to follow rivers or roads, so Dmitri had to rely on the instruments in the cockpit.

"How's the stomach?" asked Dmitri.

"In more knots than a bo'sun's bow line," said Aubrey. He took the notepad out of his pocket, knowing from recent experience that his subject might not be available for long once they landed in Belgrade, or whatever cow pasture they might be forced to ditch in en route. "Now, about that interview," he added.

Between moments using the torch to help check the various gauges, Aubrey was able to ask his companion various questions for the much-anticipated interview. Dmitri's answers were surprisingly candid; it was only those questions about the reason for them travelling across Europe that Dmitri refused to answer.

When the green Ford beacons of the landing field at Belgrade's Dojno Polje Airport came into sight, the two men had used the circumstance of their escape from Budapest to develop the foundations of a friendship. Aubrey could relax knowing that, whatever happened once back on firm ground, he had enough for an article which, combined with an explanation of the circumstances in which the interview took place, he was sure would restore him in the opinion of both his editor and wife.

Aubrey's new sense of relaxation lasted only until Dmitri started the descent into Belgrade. From four thousand feet, and at ninety miles an hour, Dmitri twitched the stick and banked left.

Aubrey gulped, trying to control his nausea, which wasn't helped by the smell of exhaust fumes that filled the cockpit.

"Shine a torch on the gauges, there's a good chap," said Dmitri.

Dmitri squinted to read the gauges in the dim light from Aubrey's shaky torch beam, then made a descending turn. Aubrey noticed the strength of Dmitri's grip on the controls and the careful movements of his legs and feet on the rudder pedals.

Dmitri dipped the left wing and took the monoplane into a skidding spiral that quickly reduced their altitude.

"Be careful," said Aubrey, who then clasped a hand over his mouth to stop himself from vomiting as his stomach weakened.

"That is the general plan, old chap," replied Dmitri.

With the ground approaching fast, Dmitri throttled up slightly as the warm air from below caught them. The parking apron, hangars, and administration buildings were clearly visible now as the plane continued to lose altitude.

"We're coming in too damn fast," said Dmitri, adding, "and bloody high."

The ground rushed up towards them. Aubrey was holding his breath and his hands gripped either side of the torn leather seat. Aubrey really did hate flying.

VII
Belgrade

DMITRI'S EXPRESSION was one of deep concentration. They were coming in to land too quickly.

"Go around again," barked Aubrey.

"Fate doesn't always give us another attempt," said Dmitri. "And I've run out of second chances in this life I'm afraid." He pushed the throttle forwards, committing to his course of action.

The nose was up, but they were still coming in too fast, so Dmitri had to hold the nose off. The ground was almost upon them. Both pilot and passenger mentally prepared themselves for disaster.

"We're not going to make it!" said Aubrey.

"*Fornulum pani lolo*," said Dmitri.

"What?" demanded Aubrey.

"Another bit of Latin to give you courage," said Dmitri. "Here we go, Bones."

Aubrey concentrated on translating the Latin phrase.

Dmitri eased the stick forwards as carefully as he ever had done, and the wheels touched ground. He forced the nose down, anticipating catastrophe. The wings wobbled as if they were deliberately trying to catch on the ground to teach their pilot a lesson for every dastardly deed he'd committed, every married woman seduced, each cocktail-too-many drunk, and every society bore he'd insulted.

Dmitri pulled the throttle back, tapping the rudder pedals.

The speed reduced.

The wings steadied.

The plane stopped.

They were safe.

Dmitri turned the magneto switch to off, and the blades slowed their rotations. There was a loud creak, a strong smell of hot metal and petrol, but no fireball. Aubrey at last took a breath, saving himself from imminent suffocation.

"I don't want a toaster," said Aubrey.

"Eh?" asked Dmitri as he removed the leather flying gloves.

"*Fornulum pani lolo*. It's got nothing to do with courage, it means, 'I don't want a toaster'."

"I know, but it took your mind off the landing, didn't it?" asked Dmitri. He turned to Aubrey and added, "Welcome to Belgrade."

As Aubrey's senses returned to him, he had a sudden flash of inspiration and announced, "You know, I'm sure one of those goons from Budapest, the younger one, was in Tangier."

Dmitri took a second to think about this.

Aubrey continued excitedly, "I thought the two that worked me over were probably French."

"One of those on the plane was definitely a Slav," said Dmitri, shaking his head.

"Either way," said Aubrey, "I felt for sure, whoever they were, they'd have the advantage over us by the time we arrived."

"I should hope not," replied Dmitri, returning to the familiar demeanour of daring cad. "Especially as I was supposed to land this baby at the old Pancevo airport on the other side of the city. I'd say that means we have the advantage, old man, wouldn't you?" He winked at Aubrey and offered a hip flask of liquor to his companion.

"I LOVE this city," said Dmitri. Both he and Aubrey had arrived at the train station in Belgrade city centre on the banks of the Sava river. "I'm sorry you won't be able to see it."

"Now we're here safely, and undetected, I could stay a day or so," said Aubrey. "If that doesn't interfere with your plans?" Aubrey asked this, not so much because he wanted to sightsee around the Serbian capital, but he felt that, in his new friendship with Prince Dmitri, there was scope for more than just a brief biography piece for the Daily Express. The Russian was clearly caught up in something intriguing, and circumstances which, documented in print, might restore Aubrey's name to the columns of Fleet Street broadsheets.

"I'm afraid it would muck things up rather," replied Dmitri. "I'm not looking for a Passepartout, and I'm certainly no Phineas Fogg."

"What business is it that you have in Belgrade? I don't think we covered that in the interview?" Aubrey took his notepad out again.

"No, we didn't cover it." Dmitri was still giving nothing away about his mission. "Good luck, old man," he said. "The Arlberg Orient Express locomotive will be coming through here from Athens later. That will take you right through to London." He handed over a ticket. "I think you earned it," he joked, extending his hand as a farewell. "Or I could exchange it for a plane ticket."

"I shan't ever fly again!" replied the Englishman. He put his notebook back in his jacket pocket, accepting that he would get nothing further from the prince. "Goodbye, Your Highness." They shook hands.

"Call me Mitya," said Dmitri, adding, "Don't follow me this time, there's a good chap." He walked back out towards the vibrant city.

Having dispatched the journalist, Dmitri could now continue with his mission for Tao Chen. He was ahead of schedule due to the earlier than expected flight from Budapest, but getting from here into Russia undetected would not be an easy task.

He'd chosen Belgrade as his access point, not just because of the geographical proximity to Russia, but because no other city in Europe had as many spies. Where there were government agents, he could also find mercenaries, smugglers, adventurers, crime syndicates, and vice of every description. This wasn't his first time in the relaxed city, one which had the best nightlife in South Eastern Europe, and where he knew to find the help required.

He stepped into the nineteenth century Orthodox Church at the southern end of the main city park, Kalemegdan. The cathedral had an imposing bell tower and grey façade; it was not the most beautiful example of a place of worship. As he entered the chapel, Dmitri felt the power of the religion he'd always been a follower of. The smell of the incense, the weight of the silence, and the beauty of the intricately carved iconostasis took him back to his childhood, worshiping with his family alongside that of the tsar.

Dmitri had been born on the same day as the tsar's youngest daughter, Anastasia. This coincidence had been seen by the religious and superstitious tsar and tsarina as a happenstance of great importance. It brought the lives of the immediate imperial family and that of the tsar's cousin, Grand Duke Andrei, much closer than would otherwise have been the case for distant relatives. Many at the Imperial Court had muttered about the eventual marriage between the young second cousins who shared a summer birthday.

The tsar and tsarina gave Grand Duke Andrei and his wife Xenia the honour of being their son's godparents. In doing so, Russia's emperor and empress had made themselves answerable to God for the execution of that solemn spiritual duty towards Dmitri.

On his seventh birthday, the age Dmitri became responsible for his sins, his godparents placed a simple silver seven-point Slavonic crucifix on a chain around his neck. Dmitri then made his first confession to the palace priest, prior to receiving Holy Communion.

He still wore that cross around his neck, but his commitment to the sacrament had waned. Whether he was still reconciled with God would be for others to judge, thought Dmitri. Prayer, fasting, self-examination, and chastity had not been high on his list of priorities since the Hongmen freed him from the Siberian prisoner of war camp, where he'd taken exceptional measures to not have the crucifix confiscated by his Red Army gaolers. He was not yet penitent, but faith still mattered. His religion had become a symbol of identity and defiance against the secular Soviets.

Having crossed himself, and lit a candle for his mother and sister, Dmitri stepped back out into the liveliness of the Belgrade morning. He was now ready to arrange his return to Russia, into the territory of those who still sought to destroy him.

Opposite the cathedral was a tavern that he knew of. It was somewhere he expected to find those likely to help him.

The wood-framed Turkish-Balkan kafana was a well-known centre of economic, political, and social life for the city. It was a place in which vice, plotting, and arrangements of a discreet nature could be made. It was a location that embodied the spirit of Belgrade, a city where excess was normal. The kafana promised singing, drinking, crying, fighting, and debates. It was somewhere only for men of courage.

It only seemed correct that Belgrade, physically positioned at the confluence of the Danube and Slava rivers, would have become a crossroads where every aspect of life could mix. Serbs are vigorous adventurers, with a history of being conquered and fighting back. Those Dmitri had met previously were able to be brutal and tender in equal measure. They had a love of dangerous undertakings, and respected men of courage. Being delicate was for diplomats, not buccaneers. Dmitri knew this particular kafana was where he could mingle amongst others like himself.

After several rounds of Šljivovica plum brandy, drunk directly from a leather-wrapped bottle being passed around, Dmitri was singing with a group of thick-necked men. Each man was as broad as he was tall, and with bushy black moustaches worn proudly like medals of bravery. An abundance of food was brought out to be eaten communally. Bread was covered in lashings of salty karmas cheese. There was also a banquet of grilled spiced mince ćevapčići, salads, and jellied pork pihtije. The meat was greasy, and with enough garlic to frighten any vampires back across the border to Transylvania, but Dmitri proved himself worthy of the Serbs' company.

This was an investment which eventually paid its dues.

One of his new friends, Toma, enquired as to Dmitri's reason for being in Belgrade. When a few vague hints and cautious replies seemed to be losing Dmitri the trust of his new acquaintance, he swigged more plum brandy and boldly told Toma he needed to find passage into Russia that didn't involve tickets or official checkpoints.

"Well, why didn't you just come right out and say that?" joked Dmitri's new acquaintance. "Leave it to your new friend, Toma."

As Dmitri continued to enjoy the company in the lively tavern, Toma hurried off, leaving the Russian prince wondering if his show of trust would be betrayed or respected. A few moments later, Toma returned, and gestured to Dmitri that all was in hand. After another round of grilled meat, singing, dancing, and drinking, a waitress dressed in an embroidered blouse and peasant skirt leant in closely as she picked up empty tankards from Dmitri's table.

"*Kod konja*," she whispered. She then hurried back into the crowd of revellers. Dmitri knew this to be a popular phrase in Belgrade, meaning 'meet at the horse'. It was usually exchanged between friends and lovers in reference to the equestrian statue of Prince Mihailo Obrenović in the square opposite the national theatre.

He stayed in the kafana a little longer, joining in the revelry to not raise any suspicions from those in the tavern who were being paid to monitor the activities of its patrons, especially new faces. Dmitri raised a glass to Toma from across the room. The gesture of thanks was acknowledged.

It was early afternoon by the time Dmitri stepped out of the fug of smoke, noise, sweat, and alcohol from the kafana. He caught a bus down to the square. A copy of the New York Herald Tribune had been slipped into his jacket pocket, folded in such a way as to make the title clearly visible. He realised this must be part of Toma's arrangements. Catching the bus, Dmitri made sure that no other patrons from the kafana boarded with him; this was not his first covert mission.

He soon disembarked from the bus and took a circuitous route to the statue that celebrated the city's liberator from the Turks. Obrenović's depiction had been positioned pointing south towards the Ottoman threat.

A young woman waved at Dmitri from across the street. There was no one else standing immediately next to him, so he waved back. Either she was part of Toma's plan, or she was short-sighted and signalling to the wrong man. Either way, she was young and beautiful, so Dmitri saw no harm in an introduction. She crossed the road and embraced Dmitri. She gave him three kisses on alternate cheeks.

"God helps three times," she said. It was a traditional Serbian greeting. Dmitri was unsure whether this was a trigger phrase that required a coded response. Before he could explain any misunderstanding, she'd looped her arm through his and led him back to the centre of the city.

"I believe we have a mutual friend in Toma," said Dmitri, once they'd crossed the road. He needed to ensure he hadn't misinterpreted events.

"You'll find details for your journey at the Roman Well in Kalemegdan Park. Do you know it?" she asked.

"The park, yes," he replied. He slowed down to match her casual walking pace. To any onlookers they seemed like a happy couple browsing the craft stalls that sold embroidery work and handmade pottery in the afternoon sun of central Belgrade.

"The well is on the opposite side of the park to the zoo. You'll find it easily," said the young woman. Dmitri offered her a cigarette, which he lit for her. She seductively blew a controlled plume of smoke from her full lips. "Take one-hundred steps down the well, there you'll find a loose brick which will have your instructions behind it."

"What time am I leaving?" he asked.

"I've not been told the exact arrangements." She stopped at one of the stalls and pretended to take an interest in what was being sold. Dmitri bought a bag of peanuts from the stallholder. "Smugglers will take you with them, that's all I know." She spoke English very well, and without a Serbian accent. She sounded Austrian. As an afterthought she added, "It's best I don't know."

"Then can you see any reason why we shouldn't stop for a drink first?" asked Dmitri.

"I really shouldn't." She blushed with embarrassment.

"All the more reason to then," he joked. They crossed the street to the Art Nouveau edifice of the Hotel Moscow, where Dmitri knew there was a decent bar.

TWO GERMAN tourists were visiting the Roman Well at the same time as Dmitri. He had to descend the full two hundred and eight steps, thirty-five feet down, to avoid them. On his way back up he stopped where Claudia had indicated. He moved his hands across the brickwork, feeling for a loose stone. None moved.

He returned to the top, then carefully counted out one hundred steps as he walked back down. He stopped where he'd been before. Despite being sure of himself, he worked with his hands slowly and methodically around the stonework. None came free, let alone there being any sort of instructions to be had for his onward journey. He'd have to return to the tavern and hope that Toma was still around to correct the girl's error.

Returning to the surface, he found the iron door locked from the outside. He checked a clock on the wall, but the tourist attraction was not due to close to visitors for another hour or more. He tried the door again. The obstacles to his journey were frustrating. None of them made him feel auspicious about completing Tao Chen's task. Being in Russia was supposed to be the tricky part, not this. He tried the door again, pressing his weight against it.

"Mister Romanov?" asked a voice from the other side of the metal barrier.

Dmitri was surprised by the question as he hadn't disclosed his real identity to anyone he'd met in Belgrade. It was also very unusual for anyone who might know him to use a name so unfamiliar. Only the Bolsheviks called members of the royal family by their surname. He decided not to answer and to see how the situation developed.

"I know who you are, Dmitri Andreevich," said the stranger.

"Then why ask?" replied Dmitri.

"Quite so," replied the questioner in a tone of defeat.

"So, you managed to get a flight from Budapest then?" asked Dmitri. He now recognised the voice as belonging to the confident Slav who'd boarded the plane in Strasbourg.

"If we unlock the door, will you behave?"

"I haven't behaved since I was a small boy," joked Dmitri, "so I can't make any such promise I'm afraid." He lit a cigarette.

"Do you know how many people have been cast down that well shaft you're standing by?" asked the man from the airplane. "It's become an oubliette for many traitors. I don't suppose one more will perturb the Serbian authorities."

"Unless you expect me to hurl myself in there," replied Dmitri, "you'll need to open the door first." He looked around for something to defend himself with. "Maybe there's room at the bottom of the well for more than one traitor today."

He picked up a wooden chair and smashed it against the wall. He held a chair leg in each hand and braced himself for the door to open.

"What was that noise?" asked the Slav.

"Me committing suicide," replied Dmitri. He assumed the man was not alone, and that things would get rough when the door was opened. "So you can clear off now, OK?"

After a long pause the Slav warned, "I have a gun."

The key turned in the lock. Dmitri positioned himself by the wall.

As the first crack of daylight shone through the opening door, Dmitri smashed his shoulder into the metal, and emerged outside. He was in a fighting stance with the two chair legs ready to club anyone who made a move towards him.

The woman who'd turned the key had been knocked off her feet but was otherwise unharmed. The man from the flight, along with Toma and two Serbs prevented Dmitri from running away.

"I'll shoot if I have to," warned the man from the flight.

One of the Serbs, taking a dislike to the prince's show of resistance, charged forward. Dmitri managed one hard swipe across the upper arm of his attacker, but the man was the size of a bear, and twice as strong. He launched himself onto Dmitri.

"That's enough!" commanded the Slav. By the time the Serbs had restrained their friend, Dmitri had been disarmed and bruised, but was otherwise able to stand.

"This jacket is from Cifonelli," said Dmitri. He dusted himself off and checked for tears in the fabric with comic exaggeration. "Arturo will never forgive me; he really does work exceptionally hard to get the cut of the shoulder just so." He smoothed down his hair.

"Do we need to handcuff you?" asked the Slav.

"My dear fellow," replied Dmitri. "I don't think any of you appreciate how hard it is to find a good atelier in Paris?" Dmitri knew his deliberately foppish behaviour would irritate his captors, as he intended. "You look like the sort of chap who goes for mousquetaire cuffs," he added. He reached over to the Slav's sleeve, but his hand was brushed away as the man stepped back.

Dmitri was outnumbered, and in a city where he was a stranger. His immediate goal was to subtly resist and dominate, as he was doing. When an opportunity for escape presented itself, he would be ready to take it.

"Don't do anything stupid," advised the Slav.

"To disrespect one's tailor is the height of stupidity, and precisely what I'm trying to avoid," said Dmitri. He adjusted his suit and pulled the shirtsleeves down from underneath the jacket. "Anyway, isn't this whole thing rather dramatic?" enquired Dmitri. His voice was as haughty as possible to further antagonise his aggressors. "Coded messages, seductive women, and a false treasure hunt down a well?" At the mention of the girl, Toma's expression turned from disinterest to outrage. "Somebody's been reading too much Robert Louis Stevenson I surmise."

"It was Toma's suggestion. It was supposed to disorientate you," said the Slav. His tone and body language suggested he was embarrassed by the unnecessarily elaborate scheme he had not been responsible for.

"Toma looks more like an Alice in Wonderland fan," said Dmitri, glancing at Toma. "And the whore was on his payroll too I assume?" Dmitri knew he'd touched a raw nerve with his drinking partner from the tavern, and he knew angry men made mistakes. The Serb raised a fist, which was stopped by the man from the airplane.

"She is his…I think the polite term is niece," advised the Slav. He nodded to show it was time to leave as the Russian prince was controlling the discussion and the Slav didn't like that. Toma took a firm grip of Dmitri's upper arm and pushed the Russian prince forwards.

"You're with the Bolsheviks I assume?" asked Dmitri of the Slav. "Do you have a name?"

"Let's go with Vladimir," he replied.

"Oh well, if we're making names up, then I'd prefer to call you Fëdor. We had a parrot called Fëdor when I was a boy. He did everything his master asked. The similarity is uncanny, wouldn't you say?"

When Dmitri slowed his walking pace or turned his head to look for an opportunity to escape, either the barrel of Fëdor's gun was jabbed into his lower back, or Toma tugged his arm, forcing him to hurry up.

They walked up the cobbled path across the fortress. The citadel complex had been subjected to two thousand years of war, siege, damage and reconstruction, so many of the structures were now just piles of rubble, whereas others still seemed capable of withstanding cannon fire. They walked past a hexagonal building that was clearly left over from the Turkish occupation. They continued through arched stone gateways towards two rounded towers. A heavy door was opened, and a firm shove encouraged Dmitri to enter.

"A dungeon, really?" he asked. "The rest of you will man the ramparts and prepare for a jousting tournament I suppose? I'm not suitably dressed for playing at knights and damsels."

"It's just temporary," replied Fëdor. "The Soviet Embassy has to make certain travel arrangements." One of Toma's men searched Dmitri for weapons. "We didn't expect to catch you this easily, or quickly."

"Seems a bit ungentlemanly to leave a chap without his cigarettes," suggested Dmitri, as the Serb searching him pocketed the tortoiseshell cigarette case. "Or are you collecting booty also?"

"Return it," ordered Fëdor. "*We're* not thieves."

"A communist with honour," said Dmitri.

The wooden door was locked behind him. The only light was coming from the bars in the door, otherwise the mediaeval cell was dark, damp, and cool compared to the warm late afternoon beyond the thick stone walls. Dmitri ignited his gold-plated Dunhill lighter to survey his new confinement.

"Hello Dmitri."

The shock of someone speaking his name from the shadows caused him to drop the lighter, plunging him back in near darkness.

VIII

"IT'S AUBREY," said the voice in the dark.

"What the devil are you doing here?" asked Dmitri. "I suppose I should be flattered that you like my company so much." He found the lighter and illuminated them both. Aubrey stepped forward from the shadows.

"They took me off the train just before it left the station," explained the Englishman.

"Are you hurt?"

"No. There's a bench over by the back wall if you'd like to sit."

"Well, we may be here for a while."

"And where are we exactly?" asked Aubrey. They found the bench, and each then smoked a cigarette. Dmitri shut off the lighter to save the gas.

"The fortress is an old citadel in the north of the city," explained Dmitri. "I'm assuming this is one of the dungeons the Turks used to keep their Christian prisoners in." The two men sat next to each other on the small bench, in the dark of the cell, two orange glows coming from their cigarettes.

"Any ideas what to do?" asked Aubrey.

"Dungeons tend to be pretty secure," replied Dmitri. "There's a lock pick hidden in my cigarette case, but I had a quick look at the door catch and it won't work."

"Sounds like this isn't the first time you've found yourself in a cell," suggested Aubrey.

"It isn't. But I've never had to escape from a dungeon before. No, we're in a pickle for sure."

"The men from the plane are Soviets I assume?" asked the journalist.

"One of them at least. I'm still not sure they're connected. You said the younger one on the plane might be French. You remembered him from Tangier?"

"Yes, but I haven't seen him since. Why are they after you?"

"That's assuming they're after me, old chap. Is there anything you're not telling me, Aubrey Hollebone of the Daily Express? Perhaps you've been caught with your grubby fingers in the petty cash?"

"Certainly not! I'm exactly what I appear to be," exclaimed Aubrey.

"Well then, I must be the object of their interest I suppose." Dmitri took another drag on his cigarette. "Sorry, old boy."

"Why *are* you in Belgrade?" asked the journalist. Despite their dangerous situation, he was unable to contain his professional curiosity.

"I don't see the harm in telling you now, especially as we seem to be chummed up together for the foreseeable." As they smoked a second cigarette Dmitri, speaking in a hushed voice, brought Aubrey further into his confidence, "I was en route to Yalta. There's something important I need to do there, and someone I need to rescue."

"Into Russia! But why, and who?" asked Aubrey. His was just a voice in the darkness.

"Shh, keep it down, there's a good fellow," warned Dmitri. "No need for you to know why. It seems the mission's a damp squib now. That snippet isn't to make it into print, should we get out of here. You do understand?" Dmitri flicked on his lighter and shone it close to his companion to emphasise the point through eye contact with Aubrey. "I'm afraid I need your word on that."

Aubrey nodded. He looked nervous and uncomfortable. The journalist's hand was shaking as he took a long drag on the strong Syrian tobacco.

"I'm sorry," said Aubrey.

"There's no need for you to apologise," replied Dmitri. "Just keep that bit about me heading back to Russia out of the papers, there's a good chap."

"I really am sorry, Dmitri," repeated Aubrey. He walked across the flag-stoned floor and knocked on the cell door.

"You have the information?" asked Fëdor.

"Yes," replied Aubrey. The cell was unlocked.

Dmitri exploded across the room once he realised what had happened. The door was flung open, and he was beaten back and restrained by the Serbs, as Aubrey was safely extracted. Dmitri was still shouting oaths so offensive that a sailor would have been shocked when the door was closed and relocked.

"I have a family!" called Aubrey, by way of excuse to Dmitri, as he was being escorted away. "I'm sorry!" he added.

Dmitri composed himself as best he could. Fëdor came to the cell door, opened a small shutter, and peered through the bars into the darkness.

"Exactly what you appear to be, you said!" hollered Dmitri, but Aubrey was already beyond its hearing. "Was he in it from the very start?" he asked, retreating into the gloom at the back of the cell.

"We're not that good!" joked Fëdor. "We gave him two choices when we took him off the train here in Belgrade earlier today. He chose freedom rather than prison in Siberia. You can hardly blame him."

"Collaborators always have an excuse," replied the prince. "No man thinks himself a villain, even Bolsheviks like you manage to pretend what you've done is heroic or justified."

"Overthrowing an autocrat is heroic," insisted Fëdor.

"Abusing and killing women in front of their children isn't." Dmitri almost spat the accusation at Fëdor. "And anyway, the Provisional Government got rid of my family for you in the February. All your comrades did in the October was destroy one of Europe's first democratic liberal governments."

"The car will be here shortly to take us to the Embassy," said Fëdor. He closed the shutter and walked away from the door. He was unwilling to engage in political debate with a Romanov.

AFTER ANOTHER attempt to fight against his captors when the cell door was opened to take him to the Embassy, Dmitri's wrists were tightly bound with rope.

Two Serbs either side of him each took an arm and forced Dmitri across the wooden bridge over the old moat, on the other side of which a large green Duesenberg limousine was waiting. Neither Fëdor nor Toma were there. Dmitri assumed this would be in case the vehicle was stopped by the Serbian police, and the Soviet ambassador could then claim it had been stolen. Dmitri was gagged and forced onto the floor of the car so that nothing would appear out of place to any onlookers as they drove to the Soviet Embassy.

After barely five minutes, the limousine stopped behind a covered truck which was waiting in the large square in the city centre. The driver pressed the horn to encourage the truck to move off.

A young man holding a map approached the driver of the limousine and stepped up on the vehicle's running board. He was dressed like a Roma gypsy.

"*Kako mogu da dodgem do…*" Before the gypsy had finished asking for directions, he'd produced a knife from under the map. He swiped its blade across the limousine driver's throat. The powerful car jolted and crashed forwards.

A group of other young gypsy men exploded out of the truck that had been hit. They had with them a collection of shotguns and pistols. In the back of the truck a Thompson sub-machine gun was pointing at the limousine. The Serbs in the car put their hands up in immediate surrender.

A nurse standing by the nearby lilac bushes with two young children under her supervision gave a scream of horror.

Dmitri was dragged from the floor of the car by a pair of strong hands. He looked up at his assailant.

"Bogdan?" asked Dmitri. He was unsure whether to trust his memory. He hadn't seen the imperial family's Cossack bodyguard for nearly ten years, not since the Donbass soldier had returned to Russia to help rescue stranded members of the imperial family. He had not been heard from by the young prince since.

"Hello Your Highness. In trouble again, I see?" asked Bogdan. He easily cut through the thick bindings on Dmitri's wrists with a bejewelled kinzhal double-edged dagger. He returned it to the equally ornate scabbard on his belt next to the leather holster of his pistol. His warrior-like appearance, dressed as he was in full Cossack uniform of scarlet tunic and black fur cap, made for an imposing figure. It would have been a dishonour in his mind to meet the young Romanov prince in anything other than full military dress, regardless of the peculiar circumstances of their reunion.

"This can't be a coincidence," said Dmitri.

"Count Mishukov wired me on behalf of the grand duchess," said Bogdan. "I was told to expect you."

"And here I am, old friend!" exclaimed Dmitri.

Bogdan helped Dmitri into the truck. It pulled away from the scene at speed once all the gypsies, Dmitri and Bogdan were on board. The only victim was the driver of the car. The other kidnappers had been left alive. It would have been insensible to ignite a war between the two Serbian ethnic groups with unnecessary violence. This was a rescue not a massacre.

After several turns the truck stopped and everyone disembarked.

"This is Pesha, trust him," instructed Bogdan. An athletic man, not much younger than Dmitri, stepped forward.

"Will I see you again?" asked Dmitri.

"I expect so," replied the Cossack.

Pesha tugged at Dmitri's sleeve. Bogdan issued instructions to the other gypsies for the dispersal of their weapons, themselves, and the hiding of the truck.

Pesha led Dmitri into the narrow cobbled leafy streets of the Skadarlija district. This was the area of a Roma site in the early nineteenth century, but more recently had become home to the bohemian artists, musicians and actors of the Serbian capital. Pesha led Dmitri into a small apartment above a handicraft shop.

"We need to change clothes," said Pesha. He was already getting undressed. "Then they will follow me until they realise the mistake."

"I'm afraid not," replied Dmitri. "This is my fight, not yours. I can't put you in danger."

"It's no danger," said the young man. "This is my city. They'll never catch me." He smiled in anticipation of the inevitable chase he would lead the Soviets on. "Here," said Pesha, passing Dmitri a razor. "You need to remove that." He pointed to Dmitri's pencil-thin moustache, something the Russian prince had meticulously cultivated. It was a small price to pay for freedom, he thought as Pesha started drawing something similar on his own bare upper lip with a stick of charcoal.

Dressed in the weather-worn mid-length leather jacket, woollen trousers, and flat cap of Pesha's, Dmitri looked at himself in the mirror. He then realised why Bogdan had chosen Pesha for this task. The two men were identical in size and bore a remarkable likeness. After checking the alleyway, Pesha returned to collect Dmitri. Waiting in the handicraft shop was a large man, introduced as Djordji. He was wearing an embroidered shirt, sheepskin jacket, and traditional leather sandals with upturned toes.

"Djordji will take you across the river," advised Pesha. In a broken mirror he was admiring himself in the tailored Cifonelli suit from Paris. Dmitri had left money in one of the pockets, which he hoped wouldn't be found until later. Under the circumstances, he would have been embarrassed to receive any thanks or refusal of payment from those to whom he owed such gratitude.

The young man checked the narrow street.

"It's clear," said Pesha.

"Thank you, Pesha," said Dmitri. "And good luck." Pesha gave a broad smile and hurried off to lay a false trail while Djordji escorted Dmitri down to the river for a ferry ride across the muddy-brown Danube.

THE ROMA site on the opposite bank of the river was not somewhere a Soviet agent would dare to enter in search of the Russian prince.

Dmitri felt confident the immediate threat had passed. Toma's men would soon lose interest in the endeavour and, like the Roma, they would not want to incite a local war over something as trivial as a foreign hostage. The Soviet ambassador in Belgrade would be unlikely to make representation to the court of King Alexander, not being sure whether the monarch would side with the Soviet government or the Romanov prince.

After an hour or so at the riverside settlement, Dmitri was passed from courier to courier and taken further into the Serbian countryside.

As evening settled in, he found himself in a village that was just a muddy street with a few log-framed houses. Pigs roamed freely. There was the occasional sound of a cart rolling along being pulled by an elderly horse. At a small inn he was provided with ale and greasy sausages.

With a chance to rest, Dmitri began to consider Aubrey's betrayal, and whether the disclosures he'd been duped into providing would have fatal consequences for the mission, which he now felt once again could be resumed. One of the characteristics Dmitri's father had so admired about England, enough to send his son there for some of his education, was their gentlemanly character and supposed honour. Prince Andrei would have been angrily disappointed by Aubrey's cowardice, as was Dmitri.

The information he'd accidentally revealed would alert the OGPU secret police officers to his destination. His safety whilst in Russia was always going to be dependent on remaining undetected anyway; it would just be more difficult to hide now that people were specifically looking for him. He hadn't told Aubrey who was to be rescued in Yalta, nor whether that was his final destination. He hoped there was still sufficient uncertainty to make it worth his while carrying on with Tao Chen's mission.

The stakes had now been raised, and not in his favour, but he was not one to quit so easily.

Luminitsa, the young girl who'd been bringing Dmitri his food and drink, tugged at the sleeve of his battered leather jacket. She smiled and indicated to Dmitri that he should leave now that he'd finished his meal. He left some money for the food on the table, put the flat cap back on, and followed Luminitsa outside.

There was a large group gathering, and more people walking out of the darkness of the night towards a fire which had been lit. Flecks of orange were dancing above the flaming logs and burning themselves out in the moonlit late summer evening sky. For a moment, Dmitri wondered if this was a lynching by people unhappy that a former Russian aristocrat had attempted to hide himself amongst them. When the first few notes from the band silenced the hum of approaching voices, Dmitri realised his presence was being celebrated.

Brass, drums, clarinet and fiddle erupted into a frenetic čoček, a musical performance that soon had the villagers forming up in a line that spiralled around the fire.

"Dance or die!" exclaimed an elderly woman dressed in a pleated peasant pinafore dress, and with a headscarf covering her grey hair. She was joking, but Dmitri played along with the order and joined the line. Holding hands at shoulder height with the people either side, the group danced back and forth, then sideways, tightening and then expanding the spiral as the music quickened.

The folk dancer at the head of the line waved a handkerchief in her free hand, which seemed to be conducting the small orchestra, occasionally commanding the dancers to jump in the air. It was an infectious expression of community solidarity and happiness. The women who'd come from the forest to join the festival in Dmitri's honour, swayed their hips and concentrated their attentions on their handsome guest. The young men competed with their friends to holler the loudest and steal the eyes of the women away from Dmitri with a show of dancing prowess.

The Russian prince learnt the shoulder, hip, and leg movements quickly and was soon being praised by the older members of the community for his willingness to join in with this group of poor Roma villagers. For his part, Dmitri was glad of the distraction and expression of friendliness. Aubrey's betrayal had shaken his faith in the trustworthiness of recently made companions; this dance went some way to restoring that faith.

A man playing bagpipes made from a sheep's stomach stepped forward to bring the music to a crescendo. As he did so, some of the young women broke away from the group and twirled in a frenzy. Their pleated skirts billowed as their bodies obeyed the music. One of the young women, wearing a scarlet headscarf, caught Dmitri's attention. As the band brought the music to a final note of high energy, and the women fell to the floor, the one in the red headscarf held Dmitri's gaze.

IX

"DON'T TELL us who you are," said the man in the car's passenger seat. His accent didn't sound native to Serbia. "We'll take you across the border to Romania."

Dmitri had been bundled out of bed before sunrise, leaving Simza still asleep and with the red headscarf covering her otherwise naked body.

"Thank you," replied Dmitri. He was trying to get dressed in the back of the small car. "How much?"

"Everything's been paid for," replied the same man as before. The driver started the engine and turned the rusting vehicle onto the muddy track leading out of the village.

From the village, the car drove directly east. Apart from the red tint to the earth, the landscape of eastern Serbia reminded Dmitri of the Scottish Lowlands, where he'd spent one summer a few years before in the company of a British friend. He remembered how his friend's debutante sister, only recently having come out into society at Court, was determined to hook herself a prize catch during her first season. It was an uncomfortable weekend where the man-hungry and rather horse-like debutante worked her way sexually through most of her brother's friends with little discrimination. Dmitri, being one of those she rode, had not been invited north of the English border again.

Peasants in the Serbian countryside took notice of the rare sight of a motor vehicle cutting through the scenery of water-meadows, willows, streams, vineyards, livestock, and ramshackle villages. There was evidence everywhere of fighting, but the structures were so old it was impossible to determine whether this scarring was from a recent skirmish or an historical testament to resistance.

When they stopped for food at one village, a young girl offered Dmitri a rose-pink tamarisk bloom as a gift. The coin he gave her as reward for her kindness immediately attracted a larger crowd of children. The car, and now Dmitri's show of generosity, were making him conspicuous and memorable. These were two things which a man trying to escape should avoid. But he was also a fugitive with few options. He'd intended to find someone who could take him all the way through to the Crimean Peninsula in Russia, but for the moment his fate was in the hands of others, at least until there was some distance between him and Belgrade.

They crossed the border into Romania just south of Vatin. At a nearby monastery his two companions, neither of whom had engaged with his attempts at conversation, indicated that this was as far as their duty to whoever had retained their services extended. Dmitri assumed this mysterious benefactor to be Bogdan.

"Do you know if anyone else is to collect me from here?" asked Dmitri.

"We were paid to get you across the border," replied the driver. This was one of only three comments he'd made during the drive from the Roma village that morning. "We don't care where you go now."

"I understand," replied Dmitri. "You have to see a man about a dog," he joked.

"Dog?" asked the driver's companion.

"Never mind," said Dmitri. He closed the door of the car and waved them farewell.

The car turned back towards the Serbian border and drove off at speed. Dmitri was under no illusions that whenever they crossed the path of Fëdor, in exchange for a similar amount of cash paid to them by Bogdan, these two smugglers would unhesitatingly disclose where they'd left their human cargo. He couldn't remain where he was for long. Apart from the monastery, there was neither a village nor a train track in sight.

Dmitri approached the monastery door. A sign announced that the cloister was dedicated to Saint Christopher, someone he remembered to be the patron saint of bachelors, travellers, and toothache. Dmitri satisfied two of the three criteria, so took this as a good omen, and entered the unlocked door.

Dmitri was stared at by the black-clad monks tending to the garden. He was left to wait for someone of authority to deal with him.

"We're not used to visitors here," said the abbot. "This is somewhere to leave the world behind and live in prayer and contemplation."

"It wasn't my intention to disrupt you, Father. My being here is as much a surprise to me as to you."

"My role here as elder is to give direction to the novices, and tenured monks."

"It's less spiritual direction I need, Father, more earthly assistance." Dmitri considered revealing who he was. As a member of the Russian imperial family it would guarantee the loyalty of any member of the Orthodox Church, but he neither wanted to abuse his family connections nor put the monks in further danger than his arriving at their door already had.

"You're Russian?" asked the abbot.

"Yes," confirmed Dmitri.

"It's not easy to wear that in your home country." The abbot looked at the Slavonic cross Dmitri had made sure was on display around his neck.

"It was given to me when I was seven years old. I've managed to keep it so far." The abbot seemed impressed by Dmitri's show of faith.

"Take some refreshment and tell me what you need." The abbot led Dmitri through the cloister to a kitchen where monks were working. Over a cup of milk and some fresh bread, Dmitri explained that he was fleeing Soviet agents in Belgrade and needed to get across Romania. He'd learnt his lesson from Aubrey, and was only going to give away sufficient information required to enlist the support of others.

"I don't want to put you in danger," said Dmitri. "I hadn't expected those helping me escape to leave me here. I have money to pay for my passage if you can point me to the nearest village where I might find transport please, Father."

The abbot considered what he'd heard. He encouraged Dmitri to eat and drink, even though neither he nor the other monks were. Nevertheless, from previous tricky situations Dmitri had found himself in over the last decade, he knew that food and drink needed to be taken when offered as it may not be available again for a while. As Dmitri tore at the flatbread, the abbot ran his hands down his long white beard, as if that aided his thought process.

"There is a village nearby," he said eventually. Dmitri expected more, but the old man continued to think. A few moments later he continued, "But the arrival of a stranger would be noteworthy." Dmitri nodded his agreement and waited patiently for the next thought to be verbalised by the softly spoken holy man. "You really need to disappear, and for that you need a new identity." Again, Dmitri nodded, unsure how he would know when the thought process had finished and required an answer from him. "We may be able to help." The abbot stood up and walked out of the kitchen to the cloister. Dmitri followed.

They walked slowly and in silence for some moments. The monastery was on the edge of the Carpathian Mountains, so the air was cool, and Dmitri was glad of the leather jacket he was still wearing. He was worried about the delay to his escape. He was losing time, and unsure that the abbot would ultimately be able to offer any assistance. Fëdor would not be far behind, and Dmitri's trail from Belgrade was easy to follow.

"It occurs to me that there's more you haven't told me about you journey," said the old priest. Dmitri was about to offer some vague addition to his reasons for being there, but he was stopped by the abbot. "I'm not asking for a confession, at least not yet." He smiled at Dmitri. This was an encouraging sign. "There is more about you which is restless than this current trip you're making." This was a statement, not a question. The staretz, as such holy men were called, may have anticipated a denial from Dmitri, but the young Russian prince didn't offer one. His silence was an acknowledgment that his life was far from settled. "What's been your experience with the Church?"

"My godparents were devout," replied Dmitri. It seemed wise not to identify them as the former tsar and tsarina. "So, I received a lot of religious instruction. When I was last in Russia, I spent time with Patriarch Tikhon, but that was some years ago now." His disclosure would be sufficient for the abbot to deduce that the young man he was talking to was an exile from a noble family.

"That's good," muttered the abbot. "And the people looking for you are likely to be here soon?"

"I imagine so."

"Then it would seem imprudent to think you can get sufficient a head start on them. It is many miles to get down from the mountains, and the nearest village is unlikely to be able to offer you much more than a daily bus ride to a train station. You must stay with us."

"I can't hide here, Father. I'm unwilling to put you all at risk."

"I'm not suggesting that you hide here, quite the opposite." The old man sat down on a bench that faced into the cloister garden where several monks were tending to the vegetable beds. "I'd like you to consider remaining here as one of us. We occasionally receive young men interested in taking holy orders. Some remain with us for a few hours, others never leave."

"I'm afraid the life of a monk is not for me," replied Dmitri. He resisted the urge to be amused by the idea. "And I must be honest, my journey is not one I shall abandon. I made a promise that cannot be broken."

"You cannot outrun those pursuing you. If they catch you, the promise will be forfeit anyway. And it doesn't hurt one of the faithful, however lapsed he may be, to spend some time in contemplation. I hold you to no expectations. I will happily escort you to the village nearby myself if you prefer." He stood up and walked a few paces forwards. Turning back to Dmitri, he added: "Consider it, young man."

FËDOR AND the Bolsheviks arrived at the monastery the following morning.

Dmitri, now dressed in a long, collared, black cassock that reached down to the top of a pair of borrowed sandals, had been awake with the other novices in his dormitory since four o'clock. After a communal wash in cold water, he'd helped light the icon lamps, prayed, cleaned the chapel, and baked bread with the other brothers. His hair had been cut down to the scalp and covered by a skufia, the black fez-like hat with straight sides worn by all Orthodox monks.

"Brother, only you can betray yourself," advised one of the other monks, seeing Dmitri agitated by the arrival of the Soviet agents. Dmitri only recognised Fëdor, so the other two men were less of a risk as they wouldn't have seen him before. These two might have been shown a photo of Dmitri from a glossy Sunday magazine supplement, but he looked far unlike a playboy prince now.

The abbot was welcoming, but deliberately vague. He told Fëdor that the only people at the monastery were monks, thus not lying, since Dmitri had been accepted as a novice the day before. The abbot offered the cloister as a rest stop for the three men, suggesting they remain for a while before continuing with their journey. He even offered them lodgings, knowing they'd decline. He encouraged them explore the rest of the monastic complex at their leisure, showing the Soviets he had nothing to hide.

Dmitri knew he would not be betrayed by any of the monks. The persecution of their brothers in Russia had shown these monks what Bolsheviks were capable of. The desecration and confiscation of the churches, and even the abuse of the nuns, were still fresh scars for the Orthodox Church.

Feet crunched on the gravel path and stopped next to Dmitri, who was kneeling down turning over the soil in what would become a new vegetable patch. Not glancing up would seem suspicious but, if the feet belonged to Fëdor, he might recognise Dmitri and the monks would be in danger.

In one hand Dmitri gripped the trowel he'd been using. In the other hand he picked up the small garden fork. If he had to kill Fëdor then he would, monastery or not.

"Put that gun away." It was Fëdor's voice, albeit in a whisper, that Dmitri recognised. Another pair of shoes, much less well polished than the others appeared alongside the first.

"They're only monks, just parasites," said a voice Dmitri didn't recognise. "Article thirteen states it is our duty to assist the liberation of the working masses from religious prejudices."

"Are you really quoting Central Committee guidelines to me?" asked Fëdor, adding, "To *me*?"

"Sorry, comrade commissar."

"That same article warns us to avoid insulting the feelings of believers as this only leads to a hardening of religious fanaticism," said Fëdor. "And, what's more, we are not in Russia. Now search every room for the traitor, but do so respectfully."

"Yes, comrade."

The scruffy shoes hurried off. Dmitri tightened his grip on both tools, but the polished shoes, assumed to be those of Fëdor, turned and walked away.

Almost without thinking, as Dmitri stood up, he looked over at Fëdor. Their eyes met for a fraction of a second. Dmitri looked away first. He looked back and saw Fëdor glance over at him a second time before turning and walking back towards the kitchen.

X

"HE RECOGNISED me," said Dmitri. He was taking the bundle of Pesha's clothes out from behind the cupboard where he'd hidden them.

"Don't worry," urged the abbot, having found Dmitri in the dormitory. "They're getting ready to leave. You're quite safe here."

"I'm sorry," said Dmitri. "I've put you all in danger. They have guns."

The sound of pottery breaking echoed across the cloister.

Dmitri and the abbot looked through a window into the courtyard.

Fëdor and his two accomplices were roughly knocking off the headgear of the monks on the opposite side of the quad.

"Come this way," urged the abbot. He realised he'd been mistaken in his assessment of Dmitri's safety, and did not delaying in reacting.

"You must let me surrender," said Dmitri. He uncovered his head ready to reveal himself to the Soviet kidnappers.

"I can't let you do that, Your Highness," replied the abbot. "It will be worse for us if they take you."

"You know who I am?" asked Dmitri. He allowed himself to be taken through a door into the meadow.

"Bogdan Timofeyevich told us to expect you," said the abbot. He lifted the black cassock to allow his pale thin legs to move more freely. "He hoped you might stay with us and give up whatever this journey is of yours."

"I can't."

"Perhaps," replied the abbot walking quickly through the first line of trees at the edge of the pristine forest.

Dmitri checked behind.

Fëdor emerged from the monastery. His two henchmen were pushing one of the young monks in front of them.

The elderly abbot quickened his pace.

"I must go on my own from here," suggested Dmitri. He was keen that the abbot should not be with him if the Soviet agents caught up with them.

"You'll never find your way through this forest alone," advised the abbot. He waved for Dmitri to catch him up. The abbot was more interested in where they were going than what was behind them.

They hurried on for another fifteen minutes. The abbot stopped occasionally to check his sense of direction and look for a landmark in the claustrophobic forest of spruce fir. They passed openings to caves, and eventually found a cliff edge that dropped away hundreds of feet. The abbot seemed satisfied to have found this geographical feature and began to follow it.

"I can hide in one of these caves," suggested Dmitri. He'd noticed the old man was getting out of breath.

"With the bears?" wheezed the abbot in reply.

"I have an idea," said Dmitri. He stopped and removed the black robe. He untied the bundle of clothes given to him by the Roma smugglers.

"We haven't time," urged the abbot.

"They'll follow this," replied Dmitri pointing to the discarded cassock. The abbot immediately saw the logic of the prince's plan.

While Dmitri finished getting dressed, the old man carefully picked his way down a slope of loose rocks towards one of the cave openings. He positioned the garment just on the edge of the darkness so that a portion of the fabric could be seen.

"Let them find the bears instead," he said. He took Dmitri's hand as he was aided up the unstable incline back to the cliff path. "God forgive me," he added. He crossed himself.

They walked back into the thick forest until the sound of rushing water could be heard. When the tree canopy broke and the sky once again became visible, they had reached a gorge cut through the rock. A glacial river was swirling and rushing some distance below. Above it, on the opposite side of the crevasse, was an almost deafening torrent of water bursting down over the edge of the ridge.

"It's a steep climb down," said the abbot. He was shouting over the noise of the waterfall. He'd taken the first steps onto the descending ledge of mud and rocks. "Be careful, Your Highness."

"No," insisted Dmitri. He took hold of the abbot's wrist to emphasise the firmness of his refusal. "I must go on alone from here." There was little resistance in the abbot's eyes staring up at him from the gorge path.

"Is your journey really this important?" asked the old man.

"I hope so," answered Dmitri. The abbot took a few seconds to consider matters. He then stepped back up to a safer footing.

"Climb down carefully," advised the abbot. "There's a settlement at the bottom, and you can ask for directions to the town from there."

"Thank you for what you've done," said Dmitri. "I hope no harm comes to you and the others."

"Your family has lost so much more than us," said the elderly monk. He reached forwards and held the Slavonic cross hanging from Dmitri's neck in his wrinkled hand.

"It was given to me by my godparents," said Dmitri. For clarification he added, "The tsar and tsarina." With tears forming in the corners of his cloudy blue eyes, the abbot leant forward and kissed the icon that had once been in the hands of the martyred leader of his faith. Dmitri began to lift the chain from the back of his neck, but the old man realised what the Russian prince was about to do. He stopped Dmitri and tucked the cross back under the shirt, patting the cold metal against the skin of Dmitri's chest.

"That's where it belongs," said the abbot. "Now you must go." He knelt in the mud and pressed his hands together in front of himself. Dmitri knelt next to the abbot and raised his own hands, also clasping them together in prayer.

"Our Father. Thou art in Heaven …" Dmitri began to recite the prayer that had once been so familiar to him. He spoke in a soft voice and saw the abbot's lips moving in sync with his own words. Neither could hear the other as the waterfall overpowered all other noise apart from its own cascade of water.

THE PATH was treacherous and only wide enough at some points to be navigated sideways with his back to the rock face. Branches and exposed roots made slimy from the constant spray provided Dmitri with some extra support to hold on to as he slipped and slid on the wet ground. The river charged downwards through the valley below him.

The sound of a gunshot, muffled by the surge of falling water, reached Dmitri as an echo several moments after the weapon had been discharged. When the young prince looked up, holding firmly to the branch of a shrub as he did so, the body of the elderly abbot was just stumbling over the edge of the cliff. It looked like the monk was walking off the verge of solid ground, stepping forwards into air, rather than falling backwards.

Whether he'd been forced off the edge by the power of a bullet, or the abbot had chosen to escape the horror and humiliation of being caught by the Bolshevik kidnappers, Dmitri couldn't be sure. The body, twisting into different positions, and with the black cassock flapping wildly with the wind, fell past Dmitri close enough to make him press his own body back against the side of the gorge.

There was no sound of screaming.

It was a final journey, lasting only a couple of seconds to the river below, and one taken in silence.

Dmitri started to climb back up the path without realising what he was doing. An anger from inside his soul screamed at him not to run away from Fëdor, but to confront the assassin and avenge the death of the monk; too many of Dmitri's people had been killed by beasts like Fëdor.

This wasn't Dmitri's first experience of such foolhardy willpower.

The first time he could remember such an urge was when he was six years old, and aboard the tsar's imperial yacht, *Standart*. His own family had joined that of the tsar's for a few days as part of the royal family's usual summer cruise around the Finnish coast.

Life aboard the ship was informal, with royalty and crew mixing freely. Their parents frequently encouraged the young Dmitri, dressed in a nautical outfit, to play with the little grand duchess who shared his birthdate.

Anastasia would hide behind the polka-dot skirts of her older sisters rather than play with Dmitri. She only emerged to carry-out a practical joke on the boy, and then quickly run away. At that age, Dmitri had little interest in the grand duchesses anyway, and was more intrigued by the crew and the workings of the ship.

Each of the children were assigned to a specific sailor, who remained vigilant to any prospect of his young ward falling overboard. Dmitri tried to hide from his sailor-nanny as often as he could. During one such game of evasion, Dmitri was in a well-chosen hiding place polishing the collection of coloured rocks he'd found on the beach when walking that morning with his godfather.

He'd heard the call to afternoon tea but remained hidden sorting through his pieces of quartz. The ship jolted violently as it struck a rock in the narrow channel through which it was trying to navigate. Dmitri remained hidden despite the siren and the shouting, but when he heard the gushing of water bursting through the hull nearby, he decided to reveal himself from where he'd been so well concealed. As he ran along the passageway towards safety Dmitri heard panicked voices calling for the three-year-old tsarevich, who had apparently not been found.

Dmitri turned quickly and, without thinking of the risk to himself, ran back towards the part of the ship slowly sinking into the cold water.

He found Alexei, the blue-eyed, auburn-haired infant, in one of the hiding places the older boy had shown to the heir to the Russian throne during a previous game. Dmitri, damp to the waist from the rising seawater, carried the younger boy out on deck, but his heroism was only greeted by a telling off for having taught the tsarevich where and how to hide.

The two boys had established a trust between themselves that day that would last for the remaining ten years of the tsarevich's life. Despite the lack of acknowledgment from his parents, Dmitri knew he'd done the right thing, and that instinct had remained with him ever since in moments of danger.

A bullet struck the mud a few feet ahead of Dmitri. He continued to grab forwards at whatever support he could find to pull himself along the ascending pathway, looking up to see if Fëdor had started to climb down to meet him.

A further bullet hit a small outcrop inches away from Dmitri's head. It splashed him with mud and shards of splintered rock. Instinctively, Dmitri put both hands to his face in protection but, in doing so, he lost his balance. He quickly repositioned one foot to stop his body from falling, but the boot slid on the wet mud and simply accelerated the motion towards danger.

His foot lost contact with the ledge and propelled the rest of Dmitri backwards into the gorge.

His hands grasped but fixed on nothing.

He felt controlled terror during the freefall. Time seemed to have stopped. Dmitri prepared himself, expecting to smash into the river. He tightened his muscles, wrapped his arms around his head as a shield, and covered his nose with the crook of his right elbow. He clamped his legs together and tightened his buttocks. With his eyes and mouth closed, he was water-tight and ready for impact.

It was a smooth descent. He didn't thrash around or jerk in panic. Every muscle in his body tightened. He expected not to survive, and that calmed him. Dmitri discovered that mortal fear was exhilarating.

When it came, the collision felt as if he'd been smashed on the rocks instead of into the river. But his limbs uncurled and seemed to work. The water at the base of the waterfall was mixed with so much air that the bubbles made swimming impossible. The dark, turbulent whirlpool spun Dmitri's bruised body around until he was utterly disorientated. He relaxed his limbs, resisting the water no longer, and let the tumult push him to the surface.

After the first desperate gasp of air, Dmitri was thrust back below and carried into the rapids.

The water was freezing cold. He could feel his heart nearly exploding in his chest.

A second gulp of air was taken, and he thrust his legs upwards in front of him, spreading his arms out to the side to manoeuvre through the chaotic foaming water. Trying to keep his head above the rapids and his eyes forwards, Dmitri frantically propelled his arms to steer his body away from the mighty boulders which he was approaching quickly.

His mind started to shut down, mini blackouts preventing him from seeing clearly. Remembering his training with the Hongmen after his release from the Siberian prison camp, Dmitri forced his thoughts back into lucidity and to focus on survival as the cold water battled to claim its prisoner.

As the riverbed began to flatten, calm sections appeared. Dmitri steered his body towards these but kept missing their edge. The swirling water swept him back into its grasp. His energy was draining fast when a flat section of river appeared in front of his path. Dmitri flipped his body over on to its front and swam aggressively, knowing this would use up the last of his energy. He hoped the river would release him if he showed it some courage and determination.

Having miraculously survived the fall, Dmitri promised that he would not let himself drown. He gritted his teeth and powered his arms through the water. He could feel himself being dragged further away from the chance of safety towards the riverbank. It felt futile, but he swam harder.

The water began to calm.

XI

TAKING A series of rickety local buses and barely serviceable trains, Dmitri made his way across the lofty Carpathian mountain range.

The granite schists eventually gave way to the gently folding hills of the sub-Carpathians. These looked like Alpine villages. They reached down to the marshy Danubian plain. Here rivers and streams flowed across the flat landscape to the famous river circling the southern border.

Dmitri was still weak and bruised, but the villagers of the settlement the abbot had spoken about had dried his clothes, let him rest, and helped him find a path out of the mountains.

Dmitri's journey was undisturbed by any hint of the Soviet agents. Even so, he resisted the urge to remain for a night in Bucharest, the 'little Paris' of eastern Europe.

He crossed the city via the unpaved side streets rather than the broad boulevards. If they were in the city, the Soviets would be searching hotels in the main district for any trace of him.

Smuggling himself aboard the mail train when it stopped at the eastern station near the Malaxa metal works, Dmitri settled in for the final leg of his Romanian journey with mail bags as a makeshift bed. The train was due to arrive at Constanta, the main seaport on the Black Sea coast, several hours later.

It hadn't exactly been a Cook's tour, but eventually Dmitri made it to the last land footing on his journey across Europe. On the other side of the Black Sea was the Crimea, and there, hopefully, was General Izvolsky - the White Baron - waiting for rescue.

Dmitri strolled around the port checking whether any of the commercial trawlers were suitable for him to work his passage across the sea. He'd considered being honest about needing covert entry into Russia and asking to pay for his trip as a passenger. But there was no way to be sure how connected to the Soviet secret police many of the ship's captains were, even the Romanian ones, so he dismissed the honest approach. He knew his way around a ship well enough to pass any initial competency test, so Dmitri decided to ask for work on any vessel bound for Sevastopol; he would then abscond once in Russia.

The set of clothes he'd swapped with Pesha were now beginning to show signs of several days wear. He hadn't shaved for a couple of days, his hair had been roughly cut down to the scalp by the monks, he was battered and bruised from his fall, and more tired than it seemed possible to be whilst remaining conscious. The combination of these factors gave him the appearance of exactly what he was now pretending to be. It was only the significant bundle of money still in his pocket that set him apart from any other out-of-work trawlerman.

He made it known at the harbourmaster's office, and at the nearest inn to the port, that he was looking for work aboard a ship. He then settled into a chair at the inn and ordered himself a beer and a meagre meal. Despite being famished, a man eating a hearty dinner looked less desperate for work than a man nibbling on the scraps that he'd negotiated for small change. He left a few coins in front of him on the gnarled wooden table, as if this were all he had left to spend.

"You're the stranger looking for work?" asked another customer. The man brought his own drink with him as he approached Dmitri's table.

"I am," replied Dmitri. He tried to disguise his educated voice as much as possible by saying little.

"Any trawler experience?" The man sat down at the table. He didn't ask Dmitri's permission to do so.

"Two years aboard the Amundsen out of Tromso," replied Dmitri. He was gambling that no one here would be familiar with North Sea fishing. His appearance also seemed more plausible as being of Baltic or Scandinavian origin than South-Eastern European. This story would also cast less suspicion if his accent seemed out of place.

"The North? What're you used to?" asked the stranger.

"Schooners," replied Dmitri. "Mostly under canvas, but some steam or diesel too. Catch mostly of haddock, pollock, and cod."

"Why are you here?" asked the interviewer. He seemed satisfied by the answers so far.

"The weather." Dmitri's answer was deliberately elusive; no other trawlerman would be happy about being questioned.

"And nets? How are you with a needle and shuttle?"

"Better lace work than your grandmother." Dmitri's reply was belligerent. Timid or polite men were unlikely to be offered a position aboard any of these ships, where the work was hard graft. He also realised this was a middleman, a landlubber who made a small commission on finding crew for vessels short of numbers. A captain would appreciate obedience, this agent would admire guts.

"Wait here," advised the go-between. Dmitri was feeling hopeful, so he spent the remaining change in front of him on another drink.

Half an hour later the man returned.

"The *Khartoum*, bound for Sevastopol and Istanbul," said the ship's agent. "Ask for Captain Yilmaz."

"Is Sevastopol the first port?" asked Dmitri. He couldn't afford a further delay, nor the opportunity of being found out and put ashore in Istanbul if that were first for the *Khartoum*.

"Why? You got holiday plans?" asked the agent. If Dmitri were on board when the ship left in the morning, the agent would get his commission payment. What happened after that was of no concern to him. "Name?"

"Makinen." This was the surname of the only Finnish person Dmitri knew. "When does she leave?"

"Before sunrise. It's gonna be a fair day to get out to sea. All she got last time was fog, which you can't sell at the market. Cap'n'll be keen for her to not stay here any longer."

"Can I board tonight?" asked Dmitri.

"If the Cap'n'll have ya." The man made a note of Dmitri's false name in a small pocketbook. He then left to find any others seeking work.

HALF THE crew of the *Khartoum* were, like its captain, Turkish. Dmitri tried to ally himself with them. The mix of international crew included men from various European nations who would be more likely to ask questions about who he was. The language barrier made the Turks a safer cohort.

Dmitri knew the rudiments of sailing, albeit not on such a large vessel. Luckily, the *Khartoum* was a diesel trawler, so the engineers would take care of the ship's progress. The basics of being a trawlerman on such a ship were easy to grasp relatively quickly, albeit perhaps not to become a master at them.

Dmitri was out of his bunk at the pre-dawn call and dressed in a set of old oilskins he'd managed to buy in the harbour before boarding. He sorted out the large nets with the others on deck. By sunrise they were underway into the brackish waters of the Black Sea.

The winches controlled the vast nets being dragged at two-hundred-and-fifty fathoms along the sea floor. The engineers maintained the ship's course and speed, and Dmitri followed every instruction shouted at him obediently. In spare moments he was tasked with repairing the reserve nets, using a large needle, shuttle, and fresh rope to mend the holes. He had no idea what he was doing but hoped no one would take notice if he gave the impression of competency, which he did. The repaired nets could unravel once he was off the ship for all he cared.

As the first set of nets were reeled in by the industrial winches, he followed the commands shouted over the noise of the old engine chugging along at four knots. He looped a rope around the end of the bag, brought this over the side to the deck, loosened the ripcord, and tried to stay standing as the whole catch cascaded onto the slippery wooden boards. He re-tied the net, lowered it back over the side ready for the winch to deploy once again.

Working at a furious pace with the rest of the crew, Dmitri then cleaned and sorted the catch of goby, jack mackerel, Pontic shad, turbot, dogfish, and even Black Sea sharks. The cleaned fish were cast down into ice bins in the hold whilst the oil man sorted out the valuable livers from the other fish-waste on deck. The crew had to clean the ship of the remaining offal and blood, ready for the next full net to arrive an hour-and-a-half later. Thousands of pounds of fish made it into the ice bins, until, after six hours of hard, physical, fast-paced work, Dmitri and his fellow trawlermen were fed a meal of mussels or shrimp taken from the catch. They were sent back to their bunks, which were still warm from the next shift who now took their places on deck.

By his second shift seabirds were swarming all around for any scraps. The decks were beyond returning to a state of perfect cleanliness based on the limited time available between catches; the blood and oil could only now be removed by a deeper clean when in port. The crew were in a race to get the ice bins filled before the earlier catches of fish at the bottom of the ice bins started to rot, then the captain could give the order to the engine room to make for port at top speed.

There was nowhere to escape on board for a few minutes of solitude. Eating, sleeping, working were all communal endeavours. But this closeness led to a feeling of camaraderie, sharing equally in the difficult conditions, each only expecting the smallest of pay packets when back in Constanza some days later.

Whilst Dmitri was sharing a cigarette with some others on his shift, the alarm suddenly went up. All hands, even those sleeping in their bunks, rushed on deck as the ship's engines cut out.

Orders were screamed from captain to mate, and from mate to crew. There was a problem with the drag, possibly a broken sweep or wire. If the second sweep also broke, then the net and its valuable contents could be lost. As the crew carefully worked to bring the net in slowly, it became apparent it had snagged on something, the force of which had torn through a cable completely. An engineer used a spare length of cable to reattach it, and the others worked furiously to repair the torn net. Dmitri, watching those next to him, was able to improve his sewing skills. Everyone was too busy with their own tasks to pay him much attention anyway.

Tired, wet, physically wrecked, Dmitri and his new acquaintances eventually managed to empty the net of its catch and recast it fully repaired back into the depths. There was immense satisfaction in working with others to achieve such an outcome. The Russian prince was a long way from either of his two former lives whilst aboard the *Khartoum*, and he felt the vastness of that distance in his aching muscles.

The relative isolation of the encircled Black Sea from any oceans, its anoxic depths, and low salinity, made the waters rich with a varied fish stock. This kept the ports, such as Constanza, Istanbul and Sevastopol, busy with vessels. This was a feature which Dmitri hoped would allow him to escape unseen off the *Khartoum* and into his native Russia. This would be the first time back there since his rescue from Siberia eleven years before.

The demands of the work aboard the ship distracted his thoughts, stopping him from dwelling on those nightmarish memories of the final days spent in Yalta. It was only when the coastline of the Crimea came into sight that Dmitri began to feel trepidation about the next stage of his mission for Tao Chen.

XII
Sevastopol

AS EXPECTED, the port of Sevastopol was congested with fishing boats trying to unload their catch whilst still fresh.

Dmitri knew the Soviet OGPU security agents would be looking for him. He hoped the chaos of the busy port would provide him with an opportunity to evade them. Also in his favour, the agents would be paying attention to passengers, rather than crew. He no longer resembled the physical description those agents would have been provided with. If the captain, or other crew members of the *Khartoum* were asked about a Romanov fugitive, Dmitri was sure they wouldn't identify him as being such.

He knew his presence in Russia would be detected at some point. Belgrade had shown him how unreliable people he confided in were. If he could just have a head-start and get to General Izvolsky - the White Baron - in Yalta quickly, he might be able to evade detection before his presence was confirmed.

Some crew members aboard the *Khartoum* were restless to go ashore, and the captain eventually released a few to do so. Dmitri stayed behind. He knew the first group to disembark would be under more scrutiny from the Soviet customs officials. He remained behind to help document and unload the cargo of fish. Whilst Fëdor, if he were here in Russia, would be diligent in his inspection of every visitor to the port, Dmitri hoped the other Soviet officials would not be as meticulous, especially as there were so many ships. The captain was not happy with the congested port, as the competition would reduce the price of the catch, but Dmitri considered the cover and chaos these other ships provided as a good omen.

He'd gone down to the dock and back up to the ship so many times as part of the unloading, and had made conversation with the Russian port officials so that, when the *Khartoum* was empty of its catch, and the captain gave the rest of the crew permission to visit the town, Dmitri passed by unstopped at the dockside with other crew members. His absence back on the *Khartoum* when she set out for Istanbul later that day would not be remarkable as he was not likely to be the only man not to return. Many of those too drunk or under arrest for some public order offence would remain in Sevastopol for an extra few days until they were able to find work on another ship.

Dmitri was not as familiar with the large town of Sevastopol as he was with the small resort of Yalta, his next destination. He exchanged his leather coat for a tattered lighter-weight suit-type jacket with a peasant who was glad of it, despite the overwhelming odour of fish. Dressed in the threadbare jacket, collarless shirt that was overdue for a wash, and burlap trousers, Dmitri looked more like a Soviet worker and less like a guerrilla fighter, which the leather coat had given him the appearance of.

He spent time in each of the inns nearest the docks, where he was most likely to find someone who could help him with the next stage of his journey. Several times he was approached by middlemen recruiting for ships, as had happened to him in Constanza. But Dmitri needed a different service this time, and he had to be careful who he asked for assistance.

He noticed a man in one tavern sitting in the corner, receiving visitors, rather than going from table to table himself looking for business. He had the complexion and clothes that identified him as a Tatar. He behaved like a makler, a broker for the black market. He was the type of person Dmitri had become more familiar with whilst in exile from Russia, occasionally trading in stolen jewellery that needed to be sold off discreetly.

"What?" asked the dark-skinned man. He didn't look up from his drink. His corner of the inn was gloomy and filled with the fug of tobacco smoke. Dmitri stepped forwards. The man cast his eyes over the figure in front of him, as if his knowledge of men were such that he could take the measure of someone simply by their appearance and demeanour.

Dmitri saw no need to continue pretending to be a peasant. The service he now required would cost serious money, so he needed the man to believe him capable of paying. The young Russian prince straightened his back, and spoke in his normal accent, revealing himself to be someone of education, despite his clothes. Since the revolution, outward appearance in Russia had become less reliable as an indicator of character anyway; former aristocrats wore rags, and former peasants drove around in limousines.

"I'm looking for help," said Dmitri.

"Lots of people need help," replied the man. Such exchanges were like a dance, and each person needed to play their part. Declaring your hand too early would make you look like a security agent out to entrap someone as part of a black-market crack down.

"There aren't many who can help with what I need," said Dmitri.

"So?" The Tatar returned to his drink.

"And you look helpful." Dmitri sat opposite the man. He slipped the equivalent of fifty American dollars in francs under the tin mug he'd brought over with him and slid the drink across the table. The dark-skinned man dragged this towards himself, letting the money drop into his lap as he raised the cup to his lips. The money was a significant amount, demonstrating that Dmitri was not trying to buy some new shoes or extra meat ration instead of using the state stores. It was also more than an undercover Soviet agent would be likely to use to try and trap someone, such a result could be achieved with as little as fifty roubles.

"Come back in two hours. Wait for me outside," instructed the Tatar. Dmitri nodded his acknowledgement and left.

TWO HOURS later, and after an almost inedible meal at one of the ship workers' cafeterias, Dmitri was waiting outside the tavern as instructed. There was a strong chance that it would be OGPU agents that arrived instead of the dark-skinned man. His chances of escape now that he was in Russia were remote; he would have to rely on bribery.

The two hours came and went. He considered whether the cash incentive given to the Tatar had been too much. The broker might consider that any request from someone with such funds was likely to be too risky.

Moments before giving up, Dmitri recognised the man on the opposite side of the street. With a glance and a nod of his head the broker discreetly indicated for Dmitri to follow him.

The route taken around the docks was deliberately circuitous. It was designed to flush out any shadows that either of them might have picked up. Apparently satisfied that things were safe, the dark-skinned man waited for

Dmitri to catch up. They descended steps to a cellar below a warehouse.

"Come in, please." It was a female voice that bid Dmitri enter. The room was almost bare. It was clearly not somewhere that would be used more than once for such a meeting. Behind a table sat a woman. Traces of bright red dyed hair reached down to her shoulders. She was dressed in a black and gold embroidered anarkali lehenga dress. A loose veil covered her face, as was customary for Muslim Tatar women indigenous to the area.

"I understand you're looking for friends?" she asked.

"No," replied Dmitri. He stepped further into the dark room. "I'm looking for help. I have enough friends."

"I often help people," she said. Her voice was croaky. A leathery-skinned hand indicated for Dmitri to sit opposite.

"I need to get to Yalta, and quickly."

"But you don't need help with that," she replied. "There are trains, cars, and boats that go there regularly."

"I need identification papers and somewhere to stay when I get there." Dmitri held his breath. He was waiting either for a Soviet agent to burst through the door to arrest him, or for the woman to dismiss his request as too dangerous. She took her time to consider what he'd said.

"Such help is expensive," she said.

"You already know I can afford it," replied Dmitri.

"Come back tomorrow."

"I can't wait," urged Dmitri.

The woman stared at him through her veil for a few seconds. She then got up and left the room without saying anything in reply. The sound of her robe swishing across the dusty floor echoed around the large empty room. A sweet balsamic scent from her amber perfume lingered after she'd left.

Dmitri became worried. There was only one door, and Dmitri tried the handle. It was locked. There was nothing else in the room apart from the table and chairs. There was no window. He tried the door handle again, pulling down hard to make sure it wasn't just stuck. He was locked in.

When the door opened again, Dmitri swung round.

"What you need is possible," said the veiled woman, returning on her own. "But it's not easy, especially as you can't wait." She'd brought a tray with some dark Turkish coffee for them both.

He waited for her to open the negotiation. She knew he was desperate, something which would push the price up even further.

"Twenty thousand francs," she said. Dmitri knew it was a preposterous amount, most likely to test how serious he was.

"One thousand seems more reasonable," he replied.

"Reasonable can be unreliable." She sipped her coffee. "And slow."

Dmitri and the woman watched each other. Dmitri tried to indicate through a confident posture that there was a chance he might refuse and try his luck elsewhere.

"Try again," she suggested.

"A further one thousand when I arrive safely in Yalta." He'd doubled his offer. His need to get to Yalta was greater than that to save money.

She shook her head. She didn't make a counter proposal. The service he requested was simple and inexpensive to arrange. But it was highly risky, and Dmitri was desperate. Both factors favoured her.

Dmitri took a few minutes to think. He then said, "Double?" It was a bold offer as time was precious.

"Five thousand francs now, and a further five thousand when you arrive safely in Yalta," she replied. Her offer was half that which she'd opened the negotiation with, but still considerably more than the service being asked for was worth. The money would make her rich.

"Agreed," said Dmitri. At the equivalent of nearly five hundred dollars, Dmitri had decided the cost was steep, but necessary. He reached in his pocket for the money. She raised a hand to stop him.

The woman poured him a glass of the sweetened coffee, which he was grateful for, and which he drank quickly.

"It will take about an hour to arrange," she said. "Wait here until then. Marin will collect you, and you can pay him."

"Thank you," said Dmitri. There was hesitation in his voice. The arrangement had been too easy to make. He was uneasy and suspicious when things were this uncomplicated.

He put the glass back on the tray, but his hand felt heavy, and the glass dropped, smashing on the floor. His vision blurred and he felt suddenly queasy. As he blinked, the image of the woman became more indistinct, but he could tell she was smiling. He felt his shoulders slope and his body start to drop, but couldn't stop himself from falling off the chair. Then there was just blackness.

XIII

THE GROWL of the small boat's engine and the impact of the bow hitting the waves eventually woke Dmitri from his drugged sleep. He checked for the money in his pocket.

"It's all there," said Marin as he steered the boat through the water. "I only took what was agreed but we couldn't have you seeing our route out of Sevastopol."

"Where are we?" asked Dmitri, sitting up.

"About an hour away from Yalta," said Marin. "Which should give you enough time to learn your new identity." He tossed a bundle of identity papers over to his passenger.

Dmitri was now Iurii Stepanovich Nekrasov, an industrial worker from the Ukraine whose hard work had been rewarded with a stay at a sanatorium in the Crimea. The set of papers looked suitably well-used to pass as authentic. Iurii Nekrasov was every bit a new Soviet man it seemed, and Dmitri would try to live up to the role his ten thousand francs had just purchased.

The coastline became more familiar.

"Hold on," said Marin. The small boat had put in at a discreet cove just outside of Yalta. The Tartar gave

Dmitri a suitcase. "You wouldn't arrive from the Ukraine without luggage."

"I suppose not," replied Dmitri.

"Good luck," said Marin. It was clear from the grave expression on his face that Marin did not expect Dmitri to make a return journey.

"Thank you," replied Dmitri as the two men shook hands.

Yalta was a place he knew well from his youth. His family had spent almost every Easter, and many summers, here. He remembered the pretty, white-washed houses on the hillside. These villas led down to the seaside boulevard and well-maintained beaches.

The Yalta of his youth had been a bright, clean place. It mixed European Russia with the interesting oriental influences of the region's Islamic heritage. In spring the fruit tree blossoms, and gardens of lilac, wisteria and violets had perfumed the sea air. In summer, the lushly dramatic landscape of the town was caught between the rugged mountains on one side and the blue and emerald waters of the Black Sea on the other.

The Yalta he walked quickly through now was not that of his youth. This Yalta was crumbling and tired.

The people he passed were dour. They were dressed in rags. Some didn't have shoes on their dirty feet, and many were as thin as rakes. Malnourished donkeys were tied up, braying in distress. The ragamuffin children looked at him with mistrustful eyes. The adults he met seemed frightened by the presence of a stranger.

He passed the post office, now boarded up, where he'd once joined the tsarina and her children to sell pieces of the tsarina's needlework to raise money for the local hospitals. When the local people cooed over the children, Dmitri and the children of the imperial family would give a small bow. Alexei, the tsarevich, had been nine, and Dmitri twelve. The two boys so impressed the tsarina with their skill at selling the embroidery that she allowed them to take charge of the stall the following day. The reward was a family picnic in their honour.

These memories seemed imagined as he hurried along those same streets now.

There was no time for journeys of reflection.

He haggled with a horse-and-carriage driver over the fare to take him several kilometres to the sanatorium the Tatars had arranged for him. The fifty kopecks agreed would buy the carriage driver two kilos of potatoes at the local state store, assuming there were any to be had. Dmitri resisted the temptation to be overly generous, as this would raise suspicion and cast doubt on his biography as a poor industrial worker from Ukraine.

After a slow journey, the landau carriage, likely confiscated from one of the noble families, turned into the grounds of the former Vorontsov Palace. The Romanov adults would often talk about balls they'd attended there. The architect had mixed English Tudor, Scottish Baronial, Gothic, and Mughal into a complex of buildings that could seem like a mediaeval castle one minute, and a grand mosque the next. Minaret chimney stacks blended mysteriously with grey stone turrets.

"Papers?" asked the sour-faced middle-aged woman who greeted him. She checked his documents. "Are you expected?" she asked.

"Yes, comrade," replied Dmitri, hoping the Tartars had not mis-sold him this new identity.

"I'll check," she warned, thumbing through the vouchers he'd been given; these tokens proved his entitlement to the week's stay at the rest and recuperation centre.

"Do so," said Dmitri with more confidence than he was feeling.

She went off to speak to someone else to confirm whether he was expected.

Dmitri uncrossed his arms, trying not to look tense. He waited to be told that the vouchers weren't valid, or that no reservation had been made in his name. Worse still, OGPU agents could arrive to arrest him.

It was a significant leap of trust in the Tartar black marketeers that stopped Dmitri from running away.

The woman returned and said, "You need authorisation to leave the grounds." She tore the vouchers and handed the receipt stubs to Dmitri.

"Noise will not be tolerated," she barked. "Don't shout, stamp your feet, or slam doors." She glared at Dmitri until he nodded his understanding of the rules. "There will be no drinking of alcohol, and no spitting." She held his gaze again, as if the average visitor could only process a few details at a time.

"I understand comrade," said Dmitri.

"Follow me to the resident doctor," she commanded.

They walked along corridors stripped of their former opulence. Faded marks on the walls revealed where expensive pictures had once hung. Stains showed where water leaks had been left to drip. Everywhere smelt of stale food.

The doctor was young and didn't appear to have any medical knowledge at all. There was no examination. He merely wrote down whatever mild ailments Dmitri made up.

The doctor looked confused that Dmitri continued to answer his medical questions even after the female receptionist had left the room.

The doctor put down his pen and stared at Dmitri.

"Where is it?" he asked in a quieter tone.

"Where is what?" asked Dmitri.

"Come, come comrade," said the doctor. He leant forward and, in an even more hushed tone, added, "You're safe."

Dmitri didn't understand. The doctor noticed his frown of confusion.

"Where is it?" asked the doctor again. His tone had changed. He stood up from behind the desk. In his hand was a gun. "Give it to me now."

Dmitri noticed the doctor's grip on his gun loosen.

Dmitri said nothing. He needed the doctor to come closer.

The doctor moved from behind the desk. Dmitri watched each step. He'd marked a point on the threadbare carpet. Once the doctor reached this, Dmitri would explode forwards and disarm him.

One more step, thought Dmitri.

The doctor hesitated.

An attendant opened the door. In one hand was the suitcase Dmitri had been given by Marin, in the other hand the attendant held a bundle wrapped in brown paper.

"Is that it?" asked the doctor.

The attendant nodded and said, "It was wrapped in this." In his hand was a khaki tunic with a red star badge of the Red Army sewn onto the sleeve. The jacket looked authentic, and well worn. Was there really a Iurii Stepanovich Nekrasov, wondered Dmitri. And if so, was that double of Dmitri's dead or just drunk in Sevastopol and missing his luggage? He couldn't think about such complications now.

"Sorry about that, comrade" said the doctor. He put the gun in a drawer. "I suppose I understand your caution. Marin told us you'd be bringing the package."

"My pleasure," replied Dmitri. His body relaxed into the chair.

"Enjoy you stay with us," said the doctor.

The attendant packed the military tunic back in the suitcase.

Dmitri was unhappy at being an unwitting courier for contraband for the Tartars, especially as he'd paid so much for his passage to Yalta and the new identity. The Tartars had put him in even greater risk than he was already, that is if the Tartars even knew about the contraband.

"Time for your bath," said the attendant.

No doubt most of the new visitors arrived in an unclean condition, and Dmitri was no exception. It was a welcome opportunity to get clean after the escape from Belgrade, the travel across Romania, and then the time spent aboard the fishing trawler.

He hadn't intended to shave, seeing value in keeping the beginnings of his beard as a disguise, but he was ordered back in the bathroom by the attendant and told to complete his ablutions properly.

He needed to escape the confines of the sanatorium to make enquiries for the White Baron, but his bath was followed by the issuance of a strict schedule of medical treatments.

The timetable accounted for every aspect of Dmitri's day. It was a programme of callisthenics, mud and oil baths, radon-water enemas, inhalation therapy, and something listed as the 'electric hot chair', which didn't sound encouraging. His mealtimes were detailed, along with a very bland dietary plan. Every minute was regulated, even to the allowance of sunbathing time at the beach. The evening schedule detailed a series of lectures about industrial methodology. It was a far cry from Baden-Baden, thought Dmitri as he was escorted across the Vorontsov estate to what used to be known as the Shuvalov Wing.

He was shown to a metal-framed bed set amongst a long row of about thirty other such beds in a corridor. There was a ceiling rail and a white curtain which could be drawn around for privacy, but none of them had been.

There were some men in their beds, but none were talking, and the silence was oppressive.

Dmitri was disappointed that the communal nature of the sleeping arrangements, combined with the detailed itinerary, restricted his freedom of movement to and from Yalta. The doctor and attendant might help him, but he couldn't be sure what exactly they were mixed up in with the Tartars. Whatever the doctor and the Tartars were involved in, Dmitri didn't want anything more to do with it.

If he absconded, then this would be reported immediately. But neither could he waste time suffering the tortures listed for him on the schedule, in case his presence in Sevastopol or Yalta earlier had been reported to the OGPU. The real Iurii Stepanovich Nekrasov might also appear at any time, looking for his missing luggage, and unhappy about the circumstances of his delay getting to Yalta.

He transferred the money he had left into one of his worn-out shoes.

The early dinner, of what would likely prove to be rather a beige and limited assortment of food, was not for another hour, so Dmitri took the opportunity of a rare gap in the schedule to wander the grounds and consider his options.

As he strolled, Dmitri imagined he might recognise one of the sanatorium staff, perhaps even a 'former person' from the nobility like himself - someone who'd either chosen to remain in Russia under a sense of hope, or who had got stuck here. The staff he'd once known at the mansion his parents rented further along the coast, or from the tsar's palace, might have remained, taking up roles under their new masters. It was unlikely that he'd recognise any of them after almost fifteen years, and he felt confident that his appearance had sufficiently changed to make him unrecognisable.

There were guards blocking all of the gates. A high fence surrounded the gardens. His only accessible escape seemed to be via the sea.

The other guests of the sanatorium walked on their own and didn't make eye contact with anyone else.

Three men walked towards him along the gravel path. Their clothes, expressions, and even posture were alike. They were clearly OGPU agents, and coming for Dmitri. Someone had betrayed him, either directly by reporting his presence, or because of the contraband he'd inadvertently smuggled here. He considered making a dash for it, but this seemed a futile gesture. He was on Soviet territory now. In his own former country there was now nowhere for him to go.

"You need to come with us, comrade," said one of the agents. He stepped forward to identify himself as their leader.

"Of course, comrades," replied Dmitri with a smile.

To escape Dmitri would need a weapon and an opportunity, neither of which he yet had. He needed to buy himself time.

None of the other sanatorium guests in the garden looked at Dmitri or his escort. Everyone knew who the men in suits were, and they were glad it was someone other than them being led away.

XIV

THE CAR sped along the mountain road. There were no other vehicles, and the horse-drawn carts got out of the way quickly.

None of the OGPU officers spoke to him, presumably being under orders to keep the interrogation for later, most likely by Fëdor. Dmitri clenched his fists, angry that he'd only managed to get this far in the mission.

The OGPU officers hadn't threatened him with any guns. This showed just how confident they were that their prey had been well and truly caught. Dmitri had complied. He didn't yet have an opportunity of escape or resistance.

As they drove along in silence, Dmitri felt a shiver down his spine. His capture took him back to a different time in the Crimea. He thought about when the Red Army had reunited him with his mother, only to then witness her murder.

Nearly fifteen years ago seemed like just yesterday.

When the February revolution of 1917 took place his parents had been at their villa in Yalta. The Provisional Government forbade them from leaving to join their children in Petrograd. During the German occupation of the region, the request was again denied. In Petrograd Dmitri and his sister had suffered raids, restrictions, imprisonment, and eventually separation. Their requests to travel south were also refused.

The family would never again be together.

After the October revolution, when the Bolsheviks took power, the siblings were sent separately further east, where the Bolsheviks tried to keep all nobles away from the reaches of the advancing White Armies. Seventeen members of the Romanov family had been reported killed during those two years of separation from his sister; she had been one of them.

Dmitri escaped from his prison and headed south, only to be caught when he was almost back in Yalta and the safety of the departing foreign ships. As the remaining members of the imperial family were evacuated aboard British and French rescue vessels the Red Army advanced on Yalta, defeating the White Army troops still there. Dmitri's father's ship had left port when rifle fire could be heard from the mountains, and just hours before the town was overrun.

Dmitri now knew that his father had departed unaware that his wife, upon hearing reports that Dmitri was en route to Yalta to escape with them, had disembarked to find her son.

These traumatic memories had haunted Dmitri ever since.

Yalta was a place of nightmares.

The mental discipline taught him by the Hongmen two years after his capture in Yalta and re-imprisonment in Siberia helped to keep such suffering out of his conscious mind as much as possible. But being back in the actual place where those events had played out, where he'd seen his mother for the last time, only to witness her being abused and murdered for the amusement of the Red

Army, the recollections took on a greater sense of reality and power.

There was nothing to be gained in letting that grief overwhelm him. Instead, Dmitri tried to stir himself to resist whatever Fëdor and the OGPU agents had planned for him. The last time he was in the custody of the Bolsheviks he had been a youth. This time he was a man, and one who would show them what resistance looked like. As a prince of Russia he would remind the Bolsheviks that the 'former people' were still a threat, able to get this close and, in future, possibly they would get closer.

Livadia Palace was much more familiar to Dmitri than the Vorontsov estate, the location of the sanatorium. He recognised the approach road as soon as the vehicle made a turn off the main road.

This had been the tsar's favourite holiday home, and a place where Dmitri had often stayed during his childhood. It seemed darkly poetic that it would now become the location of his imprisonment, interrogation, resistance and execution.

The complex of buildings was made of white Crimean granite in a Renaissance style of columned balconies, courtyards, recesses, and large ornamental stone vases. One hundred and fifty feet below the palace was the private beach and the sea where the tsar had swum every afternoon with the children. The tsarina had sat on the balcony outside her boudoir of pink chintz warning the family about getting sunburnt.

On many holidays here with his godparents, Dmitri had run freely around the grounds of the palace. He'd swum in the sea with 'Uncle Nicky', and played at being soldiers with his friend, the tsarevich, Alexei.

For the Easter of 1916, the last such holiday, Dmitri had left Petrograd aboard the imperial train. As a fifteen-year-old, and having already chosen to join his father's cavalry regiment, the Blue Cuirassiers, when he came of age, Dmitri had been fascinated by the security precautions taken. Two identical imperial trains departed at different intervals to confuse any assassins.

The tsar had stopped their train somewhere in the vast expanse of the Ukrainian steppe for his guests to disembark and enjoy a break from the heat of the mahogany-panelled carriages. Finding a steep embankment, Dmitri and the imperial daughters had taken silver serving trays from the pantry to race each other down the bank using these as toboggans.

Seeing that the unwell tsarevich had been forbidden by his mother from joining in, Dmitri gave up his own tray to a gold-braided equerry. Dmitri had remained behind to keep his young friend company. It was for just such considerate conduct that Dmitri, a distant relative, had been favoured as a guest of the imperial family.

During that last holiday with the imperial family the tsarina had asked Dmitri many questions about his plans for adulthood. It had seemed like an interview for the position of prospective son-in-law. In his answers, Dmitri had tried to demonstrate himself a suitable prospect, but it wasn't the youngest daughter, Anastasia, the girl with whom he shared a birthday, that Dmitri was seeking to prove himself worthy of marrying. It was Marie, the elder of 'The Little Pair', as the two youngest daughters were called, that he hoped one day to make his wife.

His walks through the cypress groves and vineyards with the tsarina had ended before Dmitri felt he'd made his intentions, and suitability, clear to his godmother. He would never have another chance.

Dmitri was now passing those same cypress trees. They looked as they had done then, but so much else had changed. Marie had been murdered two years later with the rest of the imperial family in the basement at Ekaterinburg.

The boxy black Lancia turned into the palace gates and parked up next to what had been the chapel. This small church was where the imperial family had gathered that last Easter in a circle of lighted candles as the priest looked into the empty church and shouted, *"Khristos Voskres!"* In reply to his call that Christ had risen, the worshippers replied with a call of, *"Voistinu Voskrese"*, after which a late-night feast broke the long fast of lent. The following morning some of the local children would receive small kulich Easter cakes from the female members of the imperial family.

It seemed inconceivable to him now that the tsar and tsarina were able to relax as much as they had at Livadia, considering the turmoil Dmitri now knew about during these early, privileged, years of his own life.

The small chapel was now being used as an office for the OGPU. Those who'd driven Dmitri here handed him over to a man who had a cruel stare and thick dark hair showing signs of greying at the temples. This guard surveyed the young man who'd been brought before him as one might size up a calf at an agricultural show. Seemingly content with his assessment, this man signalled for Dmitri to follow him as he entered the main palace building.

Dmitri again considered the benefits of fighting or running away, but there wasn't yet any hope of success, or even much opportunity for resistance before he'd be easily subdued. The grounds were full of Red Army soldiers. Despite Tao Chen's praise that Dmitri was the equivalent of twelve men, such a skill required an element of surprise and planning, neither of which he had available to him yet.

He followed the lead officer inside the main building.

It was the first time Dmitri had been inside the palace for nearly sixteen years.

The palace had over one hundred rooms, and Dmitri imagined what sort of desecration the Bolsheviks had undertaken to create somewhere to interrogate prisoners.

They walked up a staircase and turned left. The officer knocked on the door that Dmitri knew to once have been the schoolroom for the older grand duchesses, Olga and Tatiana.

"Wait here," commanded the OGPU man. He closed the door behind himself.

Dmitri was left alone.

This was the opportunity the prince had been hoping for and he reacted quickly.

It had been complacent of the agents to leave him alone thinking he wouldn't try to escape.

He turned back towards the staircase but could hear voices from below. To his left were the former bedrooms of the grand duchesses; he knew there was no staircase that way.

Dmitri ran down the opposite corridor and took the door facing him into the library of his godmother. From here he knew there was an exterior gallery with a staircase down. If he could get to the trees without raising suspicion before the alarm was sounded, he'd at least have a head start.

Where once there had been large plush sofas, a desk, and tables overflowing with books, now there were camp beds and the discarded kit of Red Army soldiers, several of whom were on the beds.

"Who are you?" asked one of the soldiers. He was lying on one of the beds and reading a leather-bound volume that once had been read by the tsarina. He stood up, as did some of the others.

Dmitri couldn't think of anything to say that wouldn't have him immediately arrested.

"Would you believe me if I said I was the former tsar's godson?" asked Dmitri.

The soldiers looked curiously at him, then at each other.

After the first one laughed, the others joined in.

"And I'm Rasputin!" bellowed a burly soldier with a bushy moustache.

"I always thought you were, comrade," joked another.

"No, no," interrupted Dmitri, "he looks more like the tsarina to me."

Amid the laughter and jokes, Dmitri stepped to his left into the tsarina's boudoir.

"There you are," said a voice behind Dmitri. It was the OGPU guard who'd escorted him. "Come with me," the guard ordered.

Dmitri was led through what used to be the imperial family's private dining room, but where more camp beds and soldiers were now billeted. He was shown into the former schoolroom.

"He was wandering around," said the guard to a bald man sitting behind a desk.

"No harm in being curious I suppose," said the bald man. "Come in, comrade." He gestured for Dmitri to come closer.

The room was dark, even with the overhead chandelier switched on. Dmitri noticed that the grand duchess's schoolbooks were still in the glass cabinets next to him.

The ugly, narrow-shouldered man got up from the desk and approached Dmitri. He had a head that was completely bald. He seemed confused as to why Dmitri was hesitant.

"Comrade Nekrasov?" he asked. Dmitri, annoyed by his failure to escape, almost forgot his pseudonym. He looked blankly at the little bald man. "You are Iurii Stepanovich Nekrasov?" the man asked. He checked the details on the piece of paper he was holding. Dmitri nodded, wondering what this latest game was about. Perhaps the lower echelons of the OGPU hadn't been informed who their prisoner really was yet. The man continued, "Good. I'm Alexander Nikolaevich Poskrebyshev. Nobody meets the *khozyain* without first speaking to me."

"The boss?" asked Dmitri. He understood the colloquial term used but was puzzled to whom it referred.

"Yes. Didn't anyone tell you?"

"Tell me what?" asked Dmitri.

"He's keen to meet you." Poskrebyshev was becoming equally confused by the exchange.

Dmitri was now sure the identity he'd been given by the Tatars wasn't fictitious, and that there really was a Iurii Nekrasov somewhere in Yalta. Perhaps the real Iurii had a prior appointment with whoever the local Communist Party boss was.

Poskrebyshev chuckled to himself.

"Don't seem so surprised. The report from the sanatorium when you arrived detailed your work as winch operator at the mine in Kiev. The outstanding results listed on the vouchers were very impressive. We need people like you to set an example to others, Iurii Stepanovich."

"Of course, comrade," replied Dmitri.

His thoughts tried to catch up with the remarkable events. The misunderstanding might present another opportunity for Dmitri to save himself and complete his mission for Tao Chen. This encounter with a senior bureaucrat could allow Dmitri to delay his return to the sanatorium and enable him to find the White Baron.

"It's only right that we celebrate our heroes, comrade," added Poskrebyshev.

"I became a hero along with the people," replied Dmitri. It seemed the sort of thing a communist would say. He was getting himself into character. Poskrebyshev seemed impressed by the answer.

"How old are you?" asked Poskrebyshev, consulting his slip of paper.

"I am thirty-five years old," confirmed Dmitri, hoping he'd remembered correctly what age was on his false identity papers, "but I have been alive for only fifteen years." He'd heard this said before by Bolsheviks, dating their existence from the 1917 Revolution. There was a risk of Dmitri laying it on a bit too thick but, if this was a screening process for an audience with someone who might permit him some freedom around Yalta, then he wanted to pass.

"And tell me about your origins. Your father, he was a shoemaker like mine?" Poskrebyshev asked, pleased by the connection.

"I was a bit of a hooligan when I was younger, comrade," began Dmitri, falling into character, "but a teacher inspired me to join the Party and I have been remade through work." Dmitri's sense of high jinks was perfect for this sort of game, even if the other participant didn't realise he was also playing.

"Our past is not an irredeemable stain, Iurii Stepanovich. Many find happiness in the collective." Poskrebyshev took a moment to reflect.

"Every member of the Party is responsible for the whole Party, and the Party is responsible for every individual," quoted Dmitri.

"Comrade Lenin? You *are* impressive, Iurii Stepanovich." Poskrebyshev walked over to the large French windows. "Come over here, please." He stepped out onto the balcony over the colonnade.

They stared out across the gardens and at the stone fountain in which Dmitri had once splashed naked as a child. It was a view very familiar to him.

"I have an idea," said Poskrebyshev.

Dmitri stepped closer.

"I see from your records that your month's territorial service with the Red Army is due to commence when you return home."

"It is, comrade," replied Dmitri, unsure whether this was the case or not.

"Stay with us instead," suggested Poskrebyshev. "Carry out your annual commitment here. Surely the surroundings are finer?"

"Much more so, comrade," said Dmitri. He couldn't resist a smile at the absurdity of the proposition. "But surely you have enough men here already, comrade?" As amusing as the idea of infiltrating the Red Army was, Dmitri needed to get away from this nest of Bolshevik troops before anyone realised who he really was.

"I shall be candid with you, Iurii Stepanovich." Poskrebyshev unfastened the two top buttons of his tunic. He felt uncomfortable being honest. "We have had many desertions."

Dmitri resisted the urge to cheer.

Poskrebyshev continued, "As collectivisation has increased many troops are going back to their villages to resist. And they're taking their rifles with them."

"I hardly think a winch operator such as myself can do much about that, comrade," suggested Dmitri.

"You are wrong," insisted Poskrebyshev. "Comrade Lenin's intention was to create a modern army, to endow millions of men with a single will. You were awarded the Order of the Red Flag in the Civil War, and your record shows you can shoot as well as Voroshilov."

"But still -" began Dmitri. It was worrisome that a senior official knew so much about the person he was pretending to be. Either the Tartars had got carried away creating a fictitious identity, or a real Soviet hero had been deliberately waylaid on his journey to Yalta. Either way, things were getting dangerously uncomfortable for Dmitri.

"No," interrupted Poskrebyshev, "we need people like you who can show the men that, in remaining here, they are still fighting for their hearth and homes, that here they are defending the gains of the Revolution. You can help us, Iurii Stepanovich by taking command of a small squad and showing them the true path."

"I'm only a factory worker, comrade," implored Dmitri. "I've no experience of leading others."

"I disagree," insisted Poskrebyshev. "Your character will inspire others. You have applied yourself energetically and with purpose to your work at the mine, as you shall do now, here, with us. With others like you we shall guarantee the continuance and intensification of the proletarian character of the Red Army."

"I'm honoured to be asked but -"

"Follow me," said Poskrebyshev. It was in the tone of a request rather than an order. "I shall prove to you how serious we are, comrade. You shall meet the *khozyain* as promised."

Poskrebyshev hurried back through the former classroom, down the stairs, and along the main corridor to the parade hall. Dmitri followed.

In the few minutes it took to walk to the main entrance of the palace, an idea had occurred to Dmitri. He needed to find the White Baron. Perhaps the easiest way to achieve this would be as a Red Army unit commander pretending to expose counter-revolutionary plots. As the old military maxim made clear, no plan survives contact with the enemy. Infiltrating the enemy at its core might be a way to recover the mission.

Having been brought to what used to be known as the tsar's waiting room, all thoughts of escape had now left Dmitri. He would play this latest twist out to its conclusion.

With him in the waiting room was a large group of smartly dressed men fidgeting, presumably also waiting for an audience with the local boss.

After five minutes Poskrebyshev came to collect Dmitri.

The White Hall of the Livadia Palace had previously been used for gala dinners hosted by the tsar. The impressive ceiling mouldings and huge windows on either side gave a very grand impression to the visitor.

The glass doors were open to the rose garden, the scent of which wafted in and took Dmitri back to those happier days when he and the other children would crawl around underneath the long table and create havoc amongst the tsar's dinner guests.

The end of that same expansive dining table was now being used as a desk. On it was a bank of telephones and a stack of paperwork. Standing off to the side was a short scruffy man with a thick black moustache. He was waving a piece of paper in the air, clasped in fingers that resembled those of a woman. He was slim-shouldered, and his face disfigured by pockmarks. His crooked left arm was held against his side.

The General-Secretary of the Communist Party of the Soviet Union only vaguely resembled the many paintings and photos Dmitri had seen, but the little man shouting at his advisers was unmistakably Joseph Stalin.

XV

DMITRI WAS transfixed with a mixture of hatred and fascination for the Soviet leader. This was all the more potent as he was about to meet the man in a place which had been so special to Dmitri and his wider family, a family which Stalin had helped to destroy.

He considered changing his mission. No other assassin would ever find himself in such a position with an unguarded Stalin so close by. He considered what his father would have done.

Stalin was angry. Poskrebyshev was embarrassed that a worker should see the Soviet leader having one of his rants, and indicated that Dmitri was to wait on the other side of the archway in the anteroom.

The feared Soviet dictator was dressed shabbily, even his boots had holes in them, and his collarless military style tunic was splattered with food stains. He unravelled cheap Herzegovina Flor cigarettes and then used the tobacco for his pipe, which he thrust under the thick black moustache.

As his advisers made apologies for the crimes of others, Stalin paced back and forth with short, creeping steps. It seemed incongruous to Dmitri that such a comic individual could be responsible for so many monstrous inhuman acts.

"Go to the Devil!" exclaimed Stalin as he interrupted his advisers' apologies. He scolded them as someone might a disobedient dog.

"Comrade Stalin, we shall make enquiries, but may I introduce —" Poskrebyshev interrupted the other advisers. He alerted Stalin to the presence of Dmitri standing a few feet away, but the Soviet leader didn't let him finish his sentence.

"Nothing about the party!" bellowed Stalin. Once again, he waved the piece of paper in the air. "Punish this captive to anti-Soviet elements. Hang him by the balls for all his present and past sins. If his balls hold out consider him acquitted at court; if they don't hold out, drown him in the river."

"Comrade Stalin —" Poskrebyshev tried again to change the conversation, but his leader wasn't interested.

"Poskrebyshev, you're a Jew, what do you think of this policy Molotov and Kaganovich have been in touch about?" Stalin was boorish, and the men standing with him cowed into the role of supplicant. His heavy Georgian accent set him apart as half foreign.

"Iosif Vissarionovich, I am not a Jew. I am a Communist," replied Poskrebyshev. Stalin gave his attendant a cold smile, as if the man had just answered correctly to a question deliberately set to test him.

Two small children burst into the room behind Dmitri. They rushed over to Stalin. It seemed peculiar for Dmitri to see children in such a place, as if he were seeing ghosts of himself and the tsar's children haunting the room where he'd once played himself. Stalin sat down and raised the children up, one on each knee. There was a change in the Soviet leader; the boorishness disappeared. The officials stepped back to allow their boss to joke with his niece and nephew. Stalin sang them a few bars of what Dmitri recognised as Orthodox chants. He was a surprisingly decent baritone.

A young woman hurried into the room in pursuit of the children, her expression one of fear and apology.

"Comrade Korchagina the children seem in good spirits," said Poskrebyshev to the young woman. He'd noticed Stalin looking over at Dmitri, standing quietly watching, and was keen for the children to be removed so that other business could be concluded, and Dmitri's presence explained.

"I'm sorry they've disturbed you Comrade Stalin," apologised the maid. She took the children from their uncle.

"Comrade Stalin, we have a visitor from Kiev." Poskrebyshev indicated for Dmitri to step forward. "He has impressed the Party with his work as a winch operator in a mine."

"Iurii Stepanovich Nekrasov," said Dmitri. He walked forwards and extended a hand towards Stalin. As he spoke these words a flash of devilment crossed his mind, urging him to announce himself as Prince Dmitri Andreevich of Russia.

"We thought a photograph with Iurii Stepanovich would be a good idea," said Poskrebyshev, "for the press."

"If we must," replied Stalin. He shook Dmitri's hand, and the official photographer took a picture.

In that moment, as the hands of the two men from different ruling dynasties of Russia met, Dmitri felt his own grip tightening in anger.

Stalin was the paladin of Lenin, a ruthless revolutionary who'd dedicated himself to settling a personal score with the Romanovs after a previous tsar had refused to spare the life of Lenin's elder brother. That decision of Tsar Alexander had led Lenin, thirty-one years later, to order not just the murder of that tsar's successor, but the entire imperial family.

Dmitri had only recently read with horror the full reports from the White Army who'd found the evidence of the imperial family's assassination at the chillingly named 'House of Special Purpose' in Ekaterinburg.

Those carrying out Lenin's order had shown an indifference to human suffering. When the firing had stopped, and with the cloud of gun-smoke not yet dispersed in the basement room, the hand of the tsarevich had reached across the floor for the lapel of his dead father's coat. Alexei, the boy Dmitri had played with and protected, had his head kicked in by one of the executioners from the Cheka, the Soviet secret police. When Anastasia, the girl who was exactly the same age as Dmitri, and who both sets of parents had thought would marry him one day, had started screaming, rifle butts and bayonets silenced her.

Stalin was an agent of Lenin, and as guilty as those who'd carried out that merciless order.

But foremost in Dmitri's thoughts, as he looked for anything nearby that he could improvise as a weapon, were his mother and sister.

It had been a ruthless logic from the Bolsheviks that extended the hunt to all Romanovs. Grand dukes, duchesses and their children were murdered during the next two years. Stalin had inherited that responsibility for merciless extermination of the 'former people', just as Dmitri now carried the obligation to avenge his family.

His free hand reached to the desk for a letter opener that was on top of the nearest pile of papers. Stalin released his hand from Dmitri's strong grip and dismissively turned back to the papers on the desk.

Dmitri wondered if he was the only Romanov to have touched one of the architects of his family's destruction. He also considered if it might have been Stalin's personal order that Dmitri's mother and sister be killed. It seemed incumbent upon him, as a Romanov prince, to seek decisive redress for those injustices.

He glanced at the back of Stalin's neck which was exposed above his sweat-stained collar as he leaned over the papers on the table. Dmitri could feel himself coiling up energy inside, preparing for a violent act, one which would be the ultimate sacrifice for him. He was ready to pay the price of death and rid the world of this vile creature. Dmitri stepped forwards to bring the small knife within his reach.

Perhaps sensing the change in Dmitri's expression, the OGPU man he'd earlier met by the chapel quickly took the visitor firmly by the arm and swung him around. Stalin moved to the other side of the table. Dmitri looked back. Stalin was now out of reach.

Dmitri knew that even the most determined of approaches on his part now would result in failure; he would be killed even before he could injure Stalin. He resisted the OGPU agent's grasp but was thrust out of the room and into the hallway.

The full force of a coward's shame disabled Dmitri.

His anger would be satisfied by the futile gesture of bursting back into the dining room, declaring himself a Romanov, and propelling his fists towards Stalin. But he knew this would be unsuccessful; it would just be vanity - a pointless conceit. He wouldn't be able to kill Stalin in a room full of Bolsheviks.

But he could still kill the system by rescuing General Izvolsky, and getting him to the army waiting in Manchuria. It would be better to rip this systemic menace to the world out by its roots rather than fail in trying to break one of its branches.

Whether due to cowardice or brave restraint, Dmitri stepped into the Italian courtyard.

"Impressive isn't it?" asked Poskrebyshev. He mistook Dmitri's interest in the palace for amazement rather than sadness.

"This was just for one family?" asked Dmitri, imagining what reaction Iurii Nekrasov, his alter-ego industrial worker, would have to such extravagant surroundings.

"And now it is a people's rest home when Comrade Stalin is not visiting, "explained Poskrebyshev. "You see how we have made the possessions of the 'former people' benefit all of mankind?" Dmitri thought back to the state of decrepitude the town of Yalta was now in, and the malnourished condition of its inhabitants that he'd witnessed there. He left Poskrebyshev's question unanswered.

"So, it is agreed, then? You shall be barracked here for the next month, Iurii Stepanovich," said Poskrebyshev. "I think you will find it to be a most magnificent experience."

Whilst disgusted with himself for not making an attempt on Stalin's life, there was some satisfaction knowing the photo of him standing shoulder-to-shoulder next to Stalin would be noticed by Fëdor, or someone who recognised the true identity of the Kiev winch operator, and that would result in the most violent of internal recriminations. Perhaps even Stalin would be told who'd really shaken his hand and feel a shiver of fear at the closeness to his own death from that moment.

"Thank you, comrade," said Dmitri. "Your offer will be a magnificent experience indeed."

Dmitri had to find the White Baron. And he would use his new role as Red Army soldier to do so.

This was definitely a risk, but also perhaps his best opportunity.

XVI

DMITRI LOOKED at himself in the full-length mirror.

He should have been amused. Here he was, a Romanov prince dressed in the uniform of a Red Army soldier, having infiltrated the 'palace' guard of Stalin himself.

He straightened the peak of his broadcloth *budenovka* – a soft felt pointed hat - on the front of which was a red star. He ran a finger under the vertical collar of his ill-fitting khaki tunic. He fastened Iurii Nekrasov's cartridge belt in place.

But there was nothing comical or entertaining about this unusual moment. His bizarre image was being reflected in the mirror that his friend, the tsarevich, had once seen himself in.

It was through an obscene twist of fate that Dmitri, as Iurii Stepanovich Nekrasov, had been billeted with other soldiers in the room that had once been Alexei's bedroom. On his overnight visits to the palace this had also been Dmitri's room, one his friend had insisted on sharing with his distant cousin.

In this bedroom he and Alexei had planned practical jokes on the four grand duchesses, or OTMA as Alexei called his sisters, using their initials. In this room Alexei had been nursed through the agonies of his illness. In this room Dmitri and the tsarevich had stayed up late into the night playing games of Robbers' Rummy; Dmitri was the only person who didn't let the heir to the Russian throne win.

Everywhere Dmitri saw the ghosts of the people he'd once loved.

Now this was the room where obscenities about the imperial family had been graffitied on the wood panelled walls. Windows had been broken. Walls were bare of the pictures and religious icons that once cluttered them. Floors had been stripped of their rugs and were now caked in mud from the soldiers' boots.

He was determined to make the most of what was left of the day and find the White Baron quickly. He did not want to have to stay overnight in the room that now haunted him with memories too upsetting to dwell on. Fëdor would soon realise who Iurii Nekrasov really was, so he didn't have time to indulge in memories of happier times.

On his tunic he'd stitched the rectangular insignia given to him, showing his new service category as K7. This piece of rectangular cloth was his chance.

"Comrades," began Dmitri as he addressed the other men in the bedroom. "There is a nest of counter-revolutionary conspirators here in Yalta." He glanced across at the man in the leather jacket whom he'd been told was the unit's Party commissar, and through whom all military decisions had to be checked. The young bespectacled man nodded, so Dmitri continued, "Let's smash open that nest."

"How?" one soldier asked. He was half-drunk and showed little enthusiasm for yet another political speech.

"By finding the man I suspect to be at its centre," said Dmitri. A few of the soldiers sat up. "They call him the White Baron, but to us he is a traitor."

GENERAL BARON Konstantin Nikolaevich Izvolsky didn't recognise Dmitri, but the prince hadn't expected him to. They'd last met at an event in the South of France a couple of years before. The circumstances of their reunion were somewhat different to that previous meeting.

The White Army general, known as the White Baron, was dressed in rags being held together more by hope than actual thread. There were signs of physical mistreatment to his face and in his awkward gait. The injuries looked freshly made. The general has resisted being brought to the palace by Dmitri's Red Army troops.

Dmitri placed a wooden chair in the middle of the room. They were using what had once been the adjutant's room next to the tsar's study on the upper floor of the palace. Dmitri requested this room for the interrogation. He told the soldiers it was because there was no escape through a window to a balcony, having thoroughly reconnoitred the former palace to, supposedly, find such a room.

The general was forced into the chair.

Dmitri paced around him in a circle. The Red Army soldiers watched. Dmitri had to convince them he was genuine.

"Who else is in your nest of counter-revolutionaries?" he asked of the general.

The general raised his chin and replied, "There is no such thing, as I -"

A hard slap across the face from Dmitri silenced the old man. The two soldiers also in the room smiled and stepped forward, they each had clenched fists. They looked to Dmitri for permission, proving to him that in just a few hours he'd already gained their trust. He understood what they wanted and nodded his approval.

Dmitri looked out of the window at the Orthodox cross that was still on top of the church dome just outside. He heard the general's cries of pain. He wanted to stop it but knew this was necessary.

When he turned around the general was on the floor, taking kicks from the two young soldiers.

"Comrades, go and have a drink to celebrate," said Dmitri. "I'll wait with the prisoner."

"A drink, comrade?" asked one of the men.

Dmitri stepped into the adjoining room that had once been his godfather's study. This was still being used as such by one of the senior officers. He found a half full bottle of Cointreau, perhaps leftover from the tsar's cellar. It was covered in a layer of dust and unlikely to be missed by the current office's occupant.

He took a swig from it and handed the remainder to one of the two soldiers.

"Enjoy yourselves," he said. "You've earned it today."

The soldiers were hesitant. Dmitri took a second drink, and this seemed to reassure the soldiers, who left with the bottle. Dmitri closed the door to the corridor and waited a few minutes to ensure no one was coming back.

"It's very good to see you again, General," said Dmitri. He tried to lift the general back onto the chair, but the old man pushed him away and sat down himself. He winced in pain.

"You dogs all look the same to me," said the old man. His body tensed, expecting another beating. "So what, you've interrogated me before?"

Dmitri leant in close and whispered in the general's ear in French, "Only if you consider me asking you to move your car outside Aux Dames de France in Cannes two years ago as an interrogation."

Dmitri stood up, removed his hat, and watched as the general's eyes searched for something familiar in the face in front of him.

"My God," said the general as the pieces of his memory finally fell into place.

The general, a former Chevalier Guard, tried to stand up to bring himself to attention. Dmitri lightly pressed his shoulders down. From a seated position, the general saluted the great-grandson of a tsar. Dmitri returned the salute, and then extended his hand forwards in a gesture of greeting more familiar to him.

"I'm sorry about that rough stuff, General," said Dmitri. "I hope you understand it was necessary. Are you badly hurt?"

"I've survived much worse several times over, Your Highness." The general's expression remained one of confusion. "But how -"

"It will take too long to explain, General," interrupted Dmitri. "But I think it's fair to say we haven't got much time before they realise who I really am."

"Thank you for coming, Your Highness. I can't believe it." The general wiped a tear from his glassy eyes with a shaking hand. "I hadn't imagined you'd attempt such a journey yourself. You honour the country with the presence of a Romanov prince once more on Russian soil."

"General, I'm not sure my presence should be welcomed. My being here endangers many people."

"I know why you're here," said the general.

"That will save us time then," replied Dmitri. "Are you ready to go? I have enough money to pay some Tatar smugglers for assistance in getting a boat. I'll have to convince the soldiers I'm taking you for interrogation elsewhere."

"Go?" The general looked confused.

"Yes, to Istanbul, and then Manchuria. The White Armies are gathering and will only fight with you in command. I was under the impression that previous messengers with a similar plan had been sent away by you."

"I've received no such emissary, sir."

"I've been told you were suspicious of them because of the traps being set by the OGPU."

"Sir, since I was captured six months ago, I have never made any secret of my intentions towards the Soviets. I'm not one of those who mouth the slogans just to survive. They force me to sell matches at the station like a peasant, and mobile patrols monitor me throughout the day. Every few weeks I'm taken in for interrogation, which is their euphemism for torture." Dmitri noticed the old man's arms and legs, and even his head, were shaking as if an electric current was passing through his frail body.

"So you've really had no such approach to aid your own escape before today?" Dmitri was becoming confused by Tao Chen's misinformation.

"None, nor would I accept one. I'm ashamed by my cowardice in leaving with Wrangel's evacuation. At least here, I've been able to help the sabotage efforts."

"But you said you knew why I was here?" asked Dmitri. "If not to escape, then what?"

"To rescue your sister."

XVII

BEFORE DMITRI could ask the general anything further, two men entered the adjacent room – the tsar's former study.

"Comrade, I don't care to hear you excuses any longer," said one man. "Consider this a matter for the Red Army from now on."

"But comrade, this is clearly an OGPU matter," replied the other.

Dmitri realised he had to make his presence in the adjoining room known, otherwise it would look as if he was hiding. He pulled the felt hat down low on his forehead and stepped into the doorway.

Upon recognising Fëdor Dmitri's instinct was to turn away, but he knew he couldn't.

"Who are you?" asked the other man. On his tunic was the insignia indicating a K14 service category, which Dmitri knew used to be equivalent to a field commander. The other detail about this second man was that he used to be Dmitri's family chauffeur before the Revolution.

"Well?" asked the man who Dmitri now recognised to be Gennady Bunin.

Dmitri had to answer the question. Not speaking was only drawing more attention to himself.

"I'm Iurii Nekrasov," said Dmitri with as much conviction as his surprised voice could muster.

"What are you doing here?" asked Bunin. Fëdor had stepped over to the large windows to look out towards the Black Sea, fortunately keeping his back to Dmitri.

"I'm interrogating a prisoner," said Dmitri. He was confident the former chauffeur, not having seen Dmitri since he was a teenager, would be unlikely to recognise him. Fëdor on the other hand would not be so easy to deceive. Dmitri needed to get out of the study before Fëdor turned around. He gestured into the adjutant's room.

Gennady took the bait and walked over to the doorway.

"Oh him," he said, seeing the White Baron in a chair with blood on his face.

"Bastard!" exclaimed the White Baron.

Gennady rushed forward and kicked the chair from under the old man, who crashed to the floor in pain.

"He won't tell you anything," said Gennady to Dmitri, "but don't let that stop you, comrade!" He laughed as he slapped Dmitri jokingly on the arm.

Gennady closed the door to the office as he left.

Dmitri helped the general back onto the chair then crept to the office door and pressed his ear against the wooden panel.

"The Romanov playboy is definitely coming to Yalta," said Fëdor. "He's most likely already here."

"I'm sure he is," replied Gennady.

Dmitri held his breath and tensed his body in case the door was about to be flung open.

"What's more, I can tell you where he'll be going," added Gennady.

"How can you be so sure, comrade?" asked Fëdor.

"Because I have his sister at the Swallow's Nest."

"Where?" asked Fëdor.

"It's a villa I'm using along the coast," said Gennady.

"She should be brought here, where there are more troops, and where we can guard her," insisted Fëdor.

"Comrade!" Gennady laughed loudly. "I can assure you the Swallow's Nest is quite impregnable. While you've been chasing this Romanov dog around Europe, I've been waiting for him to come to me."

"I have authority here, comrade," said Fëdor.

"Maybe," replied Gennady. "But I have the bait."

Dmitri heard them leave through the door that used to lead to the tsar and tsarina's bedroom and dressing rooms. He then beat his forehead against the door in disbelief and grief.

Bunin had been the family's chauffeur, and his wife, Valentina, their laundress. The Bunins had been with Dmitri's branch of the Romanov's since Dmitri's early childhood. Valentina had always been a difficult, acerbic woman, but Gennady had been like an older brother to both Dmitri and Anna. Dmitri had ridden on Gennady's muscular shoulders as a boy and had played hide and seek with him. He had even been visited by Gennady at his bedside when unwell, and told fairy-tales to help the young prince get to sleep.

Could Anna really be alive? And could Gennady really be her gaoler? Both circumstances seemed too fantastic to be believable.

"HE'S QUITE right," said the general, having had the overheard conversation relayed to him by Dmitri. "Swallow's Nest is impossible to get to," he added. "It hangs over a cliff with only a narrow path on the other side by which to approach it."

"Regardless, General, I must get there," said Dmitri. "If Anna is really alive."

"I'm sure of it," said the general. "I'd heard she'd been returned to Yalta some weeks ago. Rumours had reached us in the town that the princess was alive and in the Crimea. More definitive confirmation came when it was revealed in the local press that she'd been brought here after spending nearly fifteen years in labour camps."

"Perhaps Gennady is protecting her," suggested Dmitri. "Maybe, like me, he is just pretending to be a Soviet loyalist?"

The general shook his head.

"She is their maid," he said. "And I'm told she's kept in conditions even the peasants in the town would have found difficult to endure. I've heard about her being subjected to cruel humiliations in front of visiting Soviet and Red Army officials."

"Can this really be true?" asked Dmitri. His elation at having his sister resurrected had been crushed just as quickly with a visceral grief.

"Gennady himself confirmed it, boasting about his new maid around Yalta." The general fixed his eyes on Dmitri's. "You must keep that anger for revenge under control for a few more hours yet," the general warned. "We will help you rescue the princess."

"We?" asked Dmitri.

"I have friends in low places," advised the old man. "Do you remember Koreiz?"

"The Yusupov Palace?"

"Yes. It's an asylum now, mostly filled with former nobles. They will help us."

"A bunch of lunatics? Are you serious!" Dmitri was on the edge of explosion.

"It's full of sane people, sir, in hiding. Surely you can see that the insanity is outside, around us now." The general turned Dmitri around to face him once again.

"Keep your head, sir. This is what I was trained for. When I sent word about the princess, I had expected an army to arrive." He held Dmitri at arms-length and added, "But I suppose you'll have to do."

"Is there really a way?" asked Dmitri.

"Your godfather trained me well, Your Highness. And your current uniform gives me an idea." The general looked pensive, then added, "I have a plan."

THE GENERAL had given Dmitri several preparatory errands. These tasks were made almost impossible due to the disbelief of his sister being alive and the need to see her for himself before he could accept it. His thoughts were consumed by the intense desire to get her to safety, and the fiery maddening need to mete out the cruelest of attacks on the former chauffeur and his wife.

He was nervous leaving the general behind at the palace under guard. The old man, knowing he would receive a further working over, nevertheless told Dmitri to go. The tasks were necessary, and the general knew he had to remain a prisoner to keep suspicion away from Dmitri.

There were no other soldiers in the tsarevich's former bedroom and where Dmitri now collected the rest of the money he'd hidden earlier.

He left the palace by the steps that were attached to this room.

He ran his hand underneath the stone balustrade and found the grooves where he and the tsarevich had carved their names as children. They'd done so when Alexei was unwell. Seeing the tsarevich out of bed, Derevenko, Alexei's personal bodyguard, had rushed outside and stopped the boys before they'd finished their task. Alexei had finished carving his own nickname of Lyosha, but

Dmitri had only written the Mit- of his before they were stopped.

Dmitri looked around and, seeing nobody looking across, he crouched down pretending to tie his boot laces. He picked up a sharp stone and scratched the -ya to what he'd begun writing so many years before. It felt appropriate to complete something he'd started with his friend, a boy who was never allowed to become a man as Dmitri had.

"Leaving us already?" asked Poskrebyshev. He'd been smoking a cigarette at the back of the small church. Dmitri worried that he might have been seen defacing the balustrade.

"I left some things at the sanitorium," replied Dmitri.

"We'll send someone to collect them for you," suggested Poskrebyshev.

"Comrade, with respect, that would be like having someone clean my boots for me," said Dmitri. "That would be a relapse into Tsarist military abuses."

"You're giving me a lesson in proletarian class-consciousness, comrade?" asked Poskrebyshev. His voice didn't sound confrontational.

"I suppose so, comrade," replied Dmitri.

"Then I was right to choose you, Iurii Stepanovich." Poskrebyshev chuckled. "But it isn't safe to go alone. There are counter-revolutionaries crawling around the town. And I'm sure we can find a vehicle to save you the walk, if that won't offend your proletarian sensibilities too much?"

Being Iurii Nekrasov was beginning to drain Dmitri's stock of communist phrases with which to reassure his enemy operatives that he was who he pretended to be.

THE DOCTOR at the sanitorium looked petrified.

He hadn't expected anyone to be in his office, much less a Red Army officer pointing the doctor's own revolver from his desk drawer at him.

"I'm not here to shoot you," said Dmitri.

"The smuggler from earlier?" asked the doctor as his memory caught up with him and the fear began to lessen.

"Perhaps," replied Dmitri. "Or maybe, as this uniform and the soldiers waiting outside would suggest, I'm something else." He lowered the revolver.

"What are you doing here?" asked the doctor.

"I need a boat," said Dmitri. "And I need it to be waiting for me at the Koreiz pier at sunrise, and with charts of the Black Sea." He didn't have time to play games.

"Absolutely not," said the doctor.

"Perhaps you'd like to explain how you top up your medical salary to the OGPU?" asked Dmitri.

"It would seem, *comrade*, that you'd have some explaining to do also," replied the doctor, emphasising the sarcasm of his voice.

"Can you really take that risk, doctor?" asked Dmitri. "Can what I ask for be arranged?"

The doctor studied Dmitri's expression, trying to assess its sincerity.

"Maybe," said the doctor.

"And with this." Dmitri placed the remainder of his money on the doctor's desk.

"Perhaps."

"Yes, or no?" insisted Dmitri.

The doctor picked up the bundle of money to estimate the amount, and replied, "Yes."

"If the boat is not there," began Dmitri, "I shan't hesitate to -"

"It will be," interrupted the doctor. "Because you have more to lose than I do by betraying me."

"Trust doesn't come cheap," suggested Dmitri.

"This buys you a boat," replied the doctor. "It doesn't buy you trust."

IF THE doctor betrayed him, or was arrested, then Dmitri would be left stranded inside Russia with no means left for him to buy his or his sister's escape. But there was no other way out of Russia.

The soldiers drove an anxious Dmitri back to Livadia. The pace of changes to Tao Chen's original mission was accelerating, carelessly so. Dmitri fidgeted with anxiety, picking at the torn leather seat.

"Stop the car," ordered Dmitri.

"Comrade?" asked the driver. The vehicle came to a jolting halt.

Dmitri considered his options. What if the general and the doctor were part of a trap? Dmitri considered going straight to the Swallow's Nest now and, with the two soldiers in the car, pretend he had enquiries to make with Gennady. He could perhaps free Anna on his own.

"Comrade?" asked the other soldier.

But Gennady would likely recognise Dmitri now. He was waiting for the Romanov prince to go to the villa on the hill. And the boat wouldn't be ready until the morning. There would be no escape route until then.

Had Tao Chen been misled, he wondered.

Dmitri had known Tao for years. He'd undertaken several missions for him, and had complete trust in the Chinaman. He'd never been deceived by Tao before. Dmitri considered whether Tao Chen had known about his sister and used the White Baron as a rouse, or if the Hongmen had also been misinformed.

He'd learnt to deal calmly with criminals, spies, thieves. He never let the cool, debonair demeanour be compromised. But Tao Chen knew, as not many others did, the almost incapacitating strength of the personal tragedy his mother and sister's deaths had on him. Knowing this, Tao Chen would perhaps be sensible enough to realise Dmitri, if told the real motivation for his being sent back to Russia, would have been unable to keep control of himself.

Unlike the doctor, Dmitri had to trust others.

"Drive on," said Dmitri, adding, "Back to Livadia."

XVIII

OVER THE last few years Dmitri's illicit romances and the occasional devious reclamation of the Romanov treasures had found him in many tight spots. These moments had taught him how to keep control of his anxiety. If he'd let every jolt of fear, panic, and 'what if' scenario overwhelm him, he'd have been crippled by inaction; such clear-headedness was required again now. His sister needed him.

There was only a glimmer of moonlight coming through the un-curtained window to light the room.

As Dmitri got dressed into his Red Army uniform the soldier in the camp bed next to him woke.

"Comrade?" asked the soldier.

"It's my turn to guard the prisoner," whispered Dmitri.

Satisfied by the explanation, his neighbour went back to sleep.

Dmitri worked quickly and quietly, gathering together bits of uniform from the other soldiers' kit. He checked up and down the corridor, then returned to collect the clothes. He tied these in a bundle and hid them in what used to be the tsarina's oratory, which was at the bottom of the staircase.

It felt strange to be walking through the palace when it was so quiet. It was a powerful experience, as if Dmitri was now reconnecting with the building. A brokenness that was always with him had a brief respite, as if something were trying to heal itself inside him.

He allowed himself to soak up the memories of happy times here, and the Dmitri he had once been had the briefest of returns to life. He ran his hand along the wood panelling of the banister and ascended slowly step by step.

As he approached the tsar's former study Dmitri lightly ran his fingers over the door handles that the imperial family had also once touched.

Parts of the palace had remained intact, but not enough. And so much else was different now. Dmitri had changed. The family he knew so well who had lived here had been murdered. The country that was once his home was not so anymore. It's true, thought Dmitri, you can't ever go back.

This was now a place of something and someone else. Not a home. The bones of the building were the same, but the life had been stripped from them. Livadia was a corpse, and he'd paid his respects. He now had his sister to rescue, and for that Dmitri needed a clear head.

IT HAD been an horrendous act of brutality.

One of the general's eyes had swollen shut. The rest of his face was bruised and bleeding. He was barely conscious.

The Red Army soldier still had the bloodied wooden chair leg that he'd been using in his hand.

Dmitri couldn't react to the fury he felt.

"Comrade, has the prisoner confessed?" asked Dmitri. He wanted to take the makeshift weapon and break the Red Army soldier's neck with it, but instead he stepped over the shaking body of the general to show his indifference to the beating.

"I haven't asked him any questions, comrade," joked the soldier. "And I don't think he can answer any now!" He laughed.

Dmitri forced a smile.

"Well, go and get some rest," said Dmitri. "I shall guard the prisoner until morning."

"He won't give you much trouble," joked the soldier.

"You made it easier for me then, comrade, thanks," replied Dmitri.

He waited for the soldier to walk down the stairs at the end of the corridor. He shut the door to the former adjutant's room. He also checked that the adjoining study was empty. Only then did he rush to the general.

"Here," said Dmitri, tipping a bottle of vodka to the general's lips to try and revive him. The old man groaned as Dmitri cradled him on the floor. "This is monstrous," added Dmitri. "You should have told them about me."

"Never," replied the general in a whisper. He opened the eye that hadn't closed with swelling.

"I need to get you somewhere safe," said Dmitri.

"It looks worse than it is," said the general as he tried to stand up.

"Absolute nonsense," insisted Dmitri. "You need a doctor."

"What I need, sir," mumbled the general through lips that were split and bleeding, "is to help save your sister."

"It will kill you, General."

"Unfortunately, I doubt it," said the old man. "But I would rather die fighting."

Dmitri understood. And he needed the general to help save Anna.

"Do you think you can walk?" asked Dmitri.

The general nodded and pushed Dmitri away to prove that he was strong enough.

"We need to get you cleaned up," said Dmitri. He walked across the corridor and through what used to be the tsarina's dressing room into what had been her bathroom. Both were now being used for storage, but water still flowed from the tap, so Dmitri was able to help wash the general's face. The old man didn't even flinch as his wounds were cleaned.

"There are too many guards that way," said Dmitri, returning to the bathroom having checked the main corridor.

"Stalin is sleeping in the room at the end," said the general. "I heard the soldier's talking."

"That used to be Marie and Anastasia's bedroom," said Dmitri. An anger returned with heat and pace. He wanted to cleanse that room even if he could no longer protect its former occupants.

"There are too many of them," said the general, seeing in Dmitri's expression what the younger man was thinking. "And your sister is more important, Your Highness," he added.

They crept back towards the stairs. Dmitri walked on ahead and signalled for the general to struggle behind when it was clear. Dmitri collected the bundle of uniforms, one of which he gave to Izvolsky to change into. They left by the first door and edged out of the palace through the Italian courtyard.

Every step seemed to echo loudly, too loudly.

From the archway Dmitri could see the impossibility of their situation. Pairs of Red Army soldiers circled the exterior of the palace. They were only meters apart. He and the general waited, but at no point was there a clear run across to the treeline, even if the general could run. Dmitri could perhaps make up an excuse to be wandering around in the middle of the night, but even in a uniform the general was too obviously suspicious.

"It seems you must go on without me," whispered the general.

Dmitri thought for a moment. An idea came to him; a suddenly remembered advantage that he had over the Communists "Perhaps not," he whispered to himself.

They kept their bodies pressed to the wall, hidden by the darkness of the columned inner colonnades and went back inside the building.

Fortunately, the former billiard room was still being used as such for those times when the palace was used as a sanatorium. The general leant against the billiard table for a rest as Dmitri edged around the room. He tapped lightly on the wooden panels of the wall.

One of the panels made a hollow sound. Dmitri pushed against it and the panel popped out from the wall.

"My goodness!" whispered the general.

"I wasn't supposed to know about this," said Dmitri, "but Alexei and I found it open one day by accident."

"A passage?" asked the general. Dmitri nodded. "Where to?"

"To safety," said Dmitri, adding, "if you can make it?"

"I can," said the general.

THEY MADE their way slowly across the countryside from the exit of the secret passage to the coastal path. The general was unsteady and trying to disguise the pain he was in, but unsuccessfully so.

The Tsar's Path, renamed Sunny Path by the Soviets, followed the coast along the edge of the mountains. It was almost five hundred feet up from the sea. Designed for those in the Crimea being treated for tuberculosis who would struggle with steep dips and inclines, the path was almost perfectly horizontal. It stretched for four miles.

Dmitri knew the sculptures, exotic plants, and pathways down to resorts and beaches well. He had walked, run, and ridden along it many times in his youth.

After twenty minutes they reached their destination, the former Yusupov palace, now turned into an asylum.

"Wait here, sir," said the general.

"I can help," said Dmitri. "You're not well enough."

"Wait here," repeated the general with some irritation; he was unused to repeating himself.

"Absolutely not," insisted Dmitri. "I'll make it an order if I have to, General."

"We can climb through the fence down the right-hand path," suggested the general.

"And why would two Red Army soldiers be crawling through a gap in the fence, General?" asked Dmitri. He tugged at the military tunic. "Follow me, but try to stay in the shadows."

They approached the guardhouse by the main gate.

"We're here to relieve you, comrade," announced Dmitri to the sentry.

"I've only been here twenty minutes," replied the soldier.

"And you're complaining?" asked Dmitri quickly. General Izvolsky tried to stifle a cough, but he couldn't catch his breath because of the earlier beating and the long walk. The coughing became painful, and he doubled over.

"Is he alright?" asked the sentry. "Seems a bit old for the army." He started to approach Izvolsky, but Dmitri stood in his way and offered the sentry a cigarette whilst ignoring the general, who was still struggling to breathe.

"He's a former imperial army officer," said Dmitri, adding, "someone in the Party thought it a good idea for him to learn what life for the ordinary soldier is really like.

And my punishment is doing this sentry duty whilst having to look after the old fool."

"That seems very unfair," said the sentry, taking the cigarette offered, which Dmitri lit.

"If he dies, then at least I only have to look after myself tonight, eh?" joked Dmitri. "Get in the guard house, dog!" barked Dmitri to the general, who followed the instruction, wiping spots of blood from his mouth with his sleeve.

"Are you sure you're supposed to take *this* post?" asked the sentry.

"You can stay and look after him if you prefer," suggested Dmitri. "I could do with some more sleep." He started to walk back towards the footpath.

"No," said the sentry. "I think I'll leave you to it."

"Thought you might," said Dmitri, returning to the gatehouse as the sentry hurried off before the possibility of a mistake having been made was realised.

"How are you?" asked Dmitri of the general once the sentry had passed out of sight and hearing. The general waved him away as he gulped air and tried to control his breathing. "You'd better stay here in case anyone comes. Where are these friends of yours?"

"No," insisted the general through short breaths. "I'll go."

"You're in no fit state."

The general forced himself to stand up straight. He gave one loud cough.

"I'm well enough, sir. I know these men. They trust me, and I can find them and bring them here quickly."

"But –"

"I must insist, sir," interrupted the general. "You can see it is the sensible way forward."

THE FAINTEST glow of sunrise could be detected on the horizon.

"Your Highness," whispered General Izvolsky. Dmitri stepped out of the guardhouse.

Almost immediately other men began to arrive. The general called them to him. Each man greeted Dmitri with disbelief that a Romanov had returned to Russia, and excitement at being able to serve the dynasty once again.

After the last man had arrived for duty, and with the rising sun providing them with light to see each other more clearly by, the White Baron assembled them to explain his plan. They were all former imperial military officers, though wouldn't be recognised as such in their current condition. Their expressions revealed an unbreakable spirit, even if their clothes and physical condition betrayed a serious state of neglect and hardship.

Since the revolutions, many had been inmates of labour camps similar to those Dmitri had spent two years in, or had been frequent visitors to cell 8 at the Butyrka Prison. Weeks, months, or sometimes years at a time these men had spent the last decade and a half never knowing when they would next be arrested and sent away. Most had been forced to witness their families and friends persecuted and accused of false crimes. Many of such never returned from their internment. A letter might be received informing them their relative was no longer allowed communication privileges. Most realised that meant they were dead.

These former aristocrats were phantoms of the imperial past trapped in the Soviet present, but the here-and-now had just given them a new purpose. Princess Anna Andreovna Romanova, the daughter of a grand duke, who was himself the cousin of their murdered tsar, had been resurrected and needed their help. She could have been the sister, wife, or daughter of any of these men; her rescue would be symbolic and defiant. They had lived the last few years only for the brief happy moments that could be salvaged from the wasteland their lives had become since the revolutions. Today's mission promised to be one such occasion.

The group of seven men formed up, forcing their postures into military positions which, whilst instinctively in their muscle memory, caused bones made weak by maltreatment to ache. Even the White Baron, the great General Izvolsky himself, looked to Dmitri for leadership.

The young Russian prince had never served in the Imperial Army, being only sixteen at the time of the February Revolution in 1917, but he had grown up amongst military procedure in the royal palaces, and so military men were familiar to him. Whilst the general was the tactical commander that day, Prince Dmitri Andreevich Romanov was their commander-in-chief. The thirty-two-year-old playboy had to take on the role in place of their murdered tsar.

"It's neither money nor titles that make you noble," said Dmitri. Standing next to the general, he addressed the ramshackle unit of volunteers. A couple were aged only a few years older than himself, whilst others were contemporaries of his father, or even older. "My godfather, the late tsar, would be very proud to know men such as yourselves, having suffered the indignities you have these past years, would still parade in his name on an occasion such as this, knowing the risks and the hostile battlefield we are operating in."

Some of the men stiffened their posture even more, regardless of the pain their hunched backs would suffer.

Dmitri continued, "I cannot promise you victory but, in answering the call to be here, I can assure you, in this hopeless position, of honour." He took out the cross from under his Red Army uniform and held it up. "I don't need to warn you of what awaits us, but may God grant us the strength and wisdom to fight, to endure, and to survive."

Where the words had come from, Dmitri could not be sure. He had been moved by the sight of these men, the living dead, coming to help rescue his sister, despite knowing the extreme danger. After fifteen years of humiliation and misery, their spirits were intact, and he had somehow found the words to prove himself worthy to them for their sacrifice. Even the White Baron was moved by Dmitri's speech. He saluted his commander-in-chief, immediately followed by the rest of the men. Dmitri returned their gesture of respect.

One of the men started to sing in a hushed tone, "Strong, sovereign, reign for glory, for our glory." Everyone joined in with the old national anthem at a similar whisper, perhaps the first time it had been heard sung in Russia since the Revolution, "Reign to make foes fear. God save the tsar."

The White Baron stood the unit at ease. He gathered them around in a closer group to explain the plan, keen to get moving in case any early morning walkers should appear.

He explained that Anna was with Gennady and his wife further along the coastal path at the Swallow's Nest, a small neo-Gothic villa perched precariously on top of the Aurora cliff. The tumultuous Black Sea crashed against rocks one hundred and thirty feet directly below the wrap-around observation deck.

The general explained the advantages and disadvantages of the building's strategic position. Being on the promontory, there was only a narrow approach from the rocky mountain path. This meant they would be seen approaching, but it also limited the ability of the Soviet guards to get reinforcements quickly. The unit would use natural cover of rocks, trees and shrubs to approach undetected as far as possible. Upon discovery, the three youngest men would approach. Being dressed in the stolen Red Army uniforms, they would try to get as close as possible and pretend to be reinforcements to guard the princess.

If this failed, or once the first three had gained access successfully, the remaining men would form themselves into a second unit and charge in an attack.

The general conducted a stocktake of their armaments; it made for a sorry assortment. Dmitri had taken three revolvers at the palace that had been easy to remove without waking their owners. Otherwise all they had were improvised weapons made from everyday objects. Broom sticks, broken glass bottles, cutlery, as well as pillowcases and socks with heavy items such as an ashtray inside. It would have to make do.

One man had an old tin can with a serrated edge which, when Dmitri questioned it's use, he moved towards the groin of the man next to him and made a twisting motion; the very thought of its effectiveness made Dmitri wince more than had it been a high-calibre rifle. The general ordered each man to fill his pockets with sand or gravel, instructing them to throw this in the faces of their enemy when close enough to disorientate them. Such preparations reminded Dmitri that, regardless of one's inferior tactical position, the mind and its creativity is always the best weapon.

The men broke into their two groups, and the first got dressed in the stolen uniforms Dmitri had reclaimed from the bushes where he'd hidden them earlier. These men took the revolvers. They would rendezvous near the Swallow's Nest. Each man accepted this; not a single divided heart about what they were going to do was present amongst the group of 'former people' that morning.

The general took Dmitri to one side. With him was the bundle one of the men had arrived with. The general unwrapped it.

"Climbing equipment?" asked Dmitri, inspecting the hemp ropes, knife-blade pitons, a rock hammer, carabiners, and a pair of boots fixed with tricouni nails on the soles.

"It's kept for those here on holiday. Do you know how to use this equipment, sir?" asked the general.

"It's been a couple of years since I was last climbing," said Dmitri. "I'm sure it'll come back to me. But why?"

"Because I need you to scale the cliff on the other side of Swallow's Nest." The general paused, expecting the young prince to offer some exclamation of surprise or expression of reservation; there was none. Dmitri listened attentively for the rest of his briefing. "We can't possibly win from the frontal attack, we're just a distraction to allow you to get in, remove the princess, and leave, undetected ideally."

"That's suicide for you and your men," said Dmitri. "I must come with *you*."

"If you do, we shall all fail," said the general. "This is war, Your Highness."

"But how will I even leave?" asked Dmitri.

"Back the way you came, down the rope, assuming the princess is in a condition to manage it. That's why you'll need to fix ropes rather than attempt a free climb."

"I understand," said Dmitri. "You'd better have this then." Dmitri passed his own Red Army revolver to the general.

"No." The White Baron shook his head. "You'll need that to fight your way out if you're discovered in the building."

"It will be close quarters, so I can use some of these," suggested Dmitri holding up the metal pitons. "At least with the revolver, you might kill a couple of their soldiers on the approach." The general could see the logic of Dmitri's argument. He took the gun. "How will I know when you're ready?" asked Dmitri, trying to concentrate on the operational aspects of the mission rather than the strategic goal of rescuing his sister, which would only cloud his judgement with worry and doubt.

"I'll work to your pace," suggested the general. "Approach from the eastern side, I think that'll be slightly easier for you anyway. I'll have a man watching, and we'll move forwards when you're in position at the top."

"Good luck," said Dmitri, "and thank you. There should be a boat waiting for us at the Koreiz mooring. Tell your men to head there afterwards."

"Don't wait for us," said the general. "Once your sister is safe and you reach the boat, set off. And good luck, Your Highness." The general saluted, this was returned by Dmitri, then the two men shook hands. Dmitri wanted to say more, but there wasn't time, and he couldn't think of any words that would accurately convey what needed to be said.

Each hurried off to approach Swallow's Nest from different sides.

XIX

AS A younger man Dmitri had spent nearly a year in the Alps learning German, skiing, and mountaineering.

One of his teachers in all three pursuits had been George Ingle Finch, an Australian by birth, who'd been mentioned in dispatches at Mons, and a man who refused to conform. He'd reached twenty-seven thousand three hundred meters on the North Ridge during the 1922 Everest expedition with Mallory and Bruce.

A year later, when Dmitri met him, Finch was ticking off first ascents for many of the mountains in the Alpine range. Finch was tough, exceptionally brave, indifferent to comfort and social niceties, and someone who lived for the moment. Dmitri found, in his unorthodox teacher, a kindred spirit. The young Russian prince hoped those lessons from nearly a decade before would come back to him now.

He scrambled across the sea-splashed rocks, occasionally checking upwards to make sure nobody from the fairy-tale castle jutting out from the mountains was looking down. Once at the base of the one-hundred-and-thirty-foot Aurora cliff Dmitri organised his equipment. He changed into the nailed boots that didn't quite fit but were thankfully too tight rather than too loose. He scanned the rock face to plot his route.

With one end of the hemp rope tied around his waist, and dusting his hands with rock chalk to soak up the moisture caused by nerves, Dmitri started his ascent.

The lower portion of the rock face had a smooth surface, making it hard to find fingerholds. His instinct was to rush, knowing his sister was at the top, but the voice of Finch filled his head as he climbed, forcing Dmitri to remember the principles he'd been taught. Even on such a short climb, energy had to be conserved, especially as Dmitri had not eaten or rested properly for some time. Incorrect balance would result in unnecessary weight being thrown to his arms instead of the legs, this would waste energy and tire him out quickly.

After a few minutes, Dmitri felt the skill coming back to him, and a rhythm developing with smooth unhurried movements. The boots were old, but their weight encouraged him to keep his heels down, assisting the toe tricounis to bite into the rock firmly. Once or twice Dmitri leant his upper body into the rock and paid the price for the mistake by being thrown off balance, losing sight of his foot placements. It went against every instinct to lean backwards slightly, but this made for an easier climb.

Every placement had to be tested before taking any weight. Reaches had to be no higher than eye level. Only one of his four limbs could be free at any time - the 'three points of attachment' rule was something Finch had impressed upon his young Russian student time and time again back in 1923. 'Never make a move that can't be reversed' he'd instructed, equating climbing to chess, where the player always had to think several moves ahead.

At a small ledge Dmitri hammered a piton into the rock and attached the rope for a first belay. He continued up. An arête jutting out enabled him to traverse horizontally to an easier section. The rock began to smooth out again, at points he only had a two-finger hold, in a tendu, where the fingers were almost extended in an open hand position and the load applied from the tension in his forearm muscles.

With legs stemmed widely apart in footholds, Dmitri felt himself somewhat stuck. He knew there were now three anchors in the rock which secured his rope, but the lack of obvious holds above him resulted in a paralysis. His legs strained under the tension. Before he could stop it, both feet cut loose from the rock.

His fingers held on.

They wouldn't hold his whole weight for long.

Now Dmitri allowed himself to think of his sister and all that she'd likely endured over the last twelve years, feeling abandoned by her family, and forced to suffer every kind of indignity at the hands of the Bolsheviks. He took control of his fear and calmly let his feet find their former places, jamming the nails of the boots into the rock. The easing of strain on his arms and hands gave him the opportunity to move them to try and make the only possible hold he could see, albeit an over-reach.

The fingers of his left hand caught the edge. He knew he didn't have a good purchase on it, but he committed his weight anyway. The fingers slipped. Disengaging from the rock face completely, his body plunged quickly.

He fell but didn't scream. He expected disaster.

The rope around his waist took the tension, as did the anchor points.

The fibres of the rope strained, but they held.

He crashed back against the rock face and immediately grabbed for a hold; the hemp ropes had been known to snap quite frequently and, at the height he'd reached, he'd either die or be crippled on the rocks below if disaster struck.

Finch had often ordered his students to peel off from the rock face deliberately, insisting that knowing what it felt like to fall, and how to recover from failure, was just as important as knowing how to avoid such an occurrence through skill and practice. Dmitri's heart was pounding but, because of Finch's teaching, he was accustomed to the feeling of falling, and recovered his composure quickly. He made a fist and jammed this into a crack, twisting it in place to make a secure jam with which to get the other three limbs into safe contact with the rock. If he slipped now, his left hand would likely be ripped clean off.

The manoeuvre worked, and he recovered his footing.

The next section required even more technical skill, which Dmitri was pleased to discover he could still remember. A well-executed gaston, a grip with the thumb down and elbow at a horizontal angle in a reverse side-pull, enabled him to navigate a tricky obstruction. He scaled another section of rock, one that had no holds, by laybacking - holding the vertical edge with both hands and walking up on the outcrop with his body against the smooth surface.

He nearly lost it again further up, when being forced to have all four limbs in a straight line, resulting in him swinging to one side like a barn door on a hinge. A quickly placed foot stopped the impact and saved his position. After a difficult roof, where he once again had to break a Finch rule, and find footholds blindly, he emerged by a clump of green shrubs that were clinging to life in a most inhospitable place.

Under cover of these bushes he made sure his latest anchor was solidly in place, checked his rope was still snag free, and that the other equipment was in good order. Dmitri could catch his breath for a moment and shake out his tired limbs.

The next, and final section, would be easier as it was on an incline, almost providing ready-made steps. He attached more anchor pitons as he continued up. He would now be in hearing distance of any guards patrolling the Swallow's Nest observation deck above him, so he used a piece of fabric from his shirt sleeve to muffle the sound of the hammer. From this point, the White Baron's look-out would know to signal for the rag-tag battalion of former officers to start their quiet advance, trying to get as close to the compound undetected as they could.

When within reaching distance of the balustrade, Dmitri quickly, but carefully organised the ropes ready for a fast descent. He slid the remaining knife-blade pitons into the waistband of his trousers, and cleared his thoughts, readying himself for his own attack. Having trained with the Hongmen, Tao Chen was right that Dmitri's skills were the equivalent to several men, but it required a clear head. To fight as successfully as his training allowed, he couldn't let the emotional reaction when first seeing his sister compromise his effectiveness. This would be hard, if not impossible, to do. He had to prepare to see her again and be ready to ignore everything he would feel in order to keep alert.

He visualised the techniques Tao Chen's men had taught him. He mapped out the compound above him, with the Soviet OGPU and Red Army personnel armed and expecting an assault. He played out contingencies in his mind. He remembered the sensation of being injured, the advice that, even if shot, to keep fighting, as death was the only other alternative. And he waited for the sounds of the White Baron's first platoon to be discovered and break cover in their attack.

After having been rescued from the labour camp in Siberia by the Hongmen twelve years before, Dmitri had received his combat training at an unknown location, assumed to be somewhere in China. The nineteen-year-old Russian prince had been taught by two grandmasters, one barely five feet tall with long grey hair reaching down his back, the other a bear of a man. One had the eyes of an owl, the other a body of stone. Despite their physical differences, both had the same relaxed alertness; always calm but ready. Between them, all four elements were made evident: the grounded stability of earth, the fluid adaptability of water, the energy and determination of fire, and the intellectual freedom of wind.

Along with other recruits, Dmitri had learnt the moves of unarmed combat. The strikes, blocks, punches, and kicks took repetition day after day to learn, until the mechanics had become part of him, moving into the skin, muscle and bones of his body. Onto the mechanics were layered the techniques, understanding about positioning, use of energy, sensitivity, and reflexes. The finesse was taught through practice until the students understood that brief is beautiful, that quickly releasing the force applied after a strike is as important as its application. No energy could be wasted, that was for the opponent who, through such tension, would tire quickly.

The Confucian principle of Chung Yung, combining definite principles with flexibility, doing enough and then stopping, formed part of everything the students did. Mastery meant finding the exact sweet spot, knowing where principles had to be maintained but where flexibility was needed; too much of one, and all would be lost.

After all that had happened to him during and since the revolutions, Dmitri had gradually learnt to control the anger and bitterness he'd arrived at the training camp with. Initially he just wanted to train, to improve, for revenge. By the completion of his studies, he wanted to help, to serve. At the highest level of his training he was blindfolded and would fight opponents who could see. He would rely on using sensitivity, feeling his opponent switch their energy, knowing then where to strike. It was not a learning process, but a return to nature, to rely on the instincts of an animal; it was unlearning.

During this final test with the Hongmen, Dmitri spent weeks away from the school in a remote region. He endured trials of earth, fire, wind and water, to deeply understand and know how to use them. Standing naked under a waterfall, his skin feeling as though it was being torn off as the pressure of the torrent suffocated him, Dmitri learnt how to clear and focus his mind and to harness pain. Starved, exhausted, delirious, and injured, Dmitri successfully returned from his test as a weapon.

Through the trials he'd learnt that his dominant element was earth; it gave him certainty, confidence, and tenacity, but could, if not controlled, lead him to stubbornness and resistance to change. Dmitri used his training to adapt himself properly to the other elements, to embrace his stability and use the knowledge of the wind, the power of fire, and the emotion of water to feel truly connected.

It was that training, a moral enlightenment, that he harnessed now. This was not going to be street fighting, but a correct use of force to preserve and prolong life - to save his sister.

There was a sound above Dmitri of people running. This was immediately followed by gun fire and shouting. The first attack must have been discovered, and the all-out assault had commenced.

Dmitri crawled up the last rock. He launched himself over the balustrade and landed on the observation deck. Before the first guard to hear Dmitri had even turned around, the Russian prince was upon him. With one quick neck strike using the edge of an open hand, the guard's artery had been crushed, forcing an increase in blood pressure to his brain, which knocked him out. Dmitri picked up the gun and delivered one clear shot to the guard's head, which exploded across the white stone paving.

Another guard immediately had Dmitri in a choke from behind, a grip with such force that the Russian prince would be unconscious in seconds if he panicked or scrambled uselessly at the attacker's strong arms. His training taught him that a small movement can neutralise a mighty force, so Dmitri grabbed the little finger of the guard's right hand and snapped it back. The distraction of pain eased the guard's chokehold, allowing Dmitri to deliver an elbow strike. He also kicked down on his assaulter's shin. Both moves separated the two men. With the gun still in his hand, Dmitri fired at the guard. Only one bullet had been left in the chamber. One bullet proved to be enough.

Two Red Army soldiers came running around the corner of the building to investigate the noise. Dmitri ran at them shouting for help. The confusion caused by Dmitri's call for assistance, aided by him still wearing the Red Army uniform of a unit commander, provided enough of a delay for him to deliver a launching knee strike to one soldier. As Dmitri stamped down on the top of the joint, ripping the kneecap away, this first soldier bent over in excruciating pain, and was easily thrown over the balustrade to the sea one-hundred-and-fifty feet below.

The second soldier fumbled for his revolver. This allowed Dmitri to deliver a *biu sau*, to his eyes, concentrating the power in just Dmitri's fingertips, rather than wasting energy on a tensed arm. The soldier collapsed but delivered a fast kick to Dmitri's groin. With them both now on the floor, Dmitri managed to hook his leg on the soldier's throat and bend his knee to force the soldier's body down. Dmitri lifted his hips, and snapped the soldier's right arm back, dislocating it.

As the Russian prince was standing up someone rushed out of the building and put Dmitri into a headlock. This opponent knew how to fight, and kept his victim to the side, knowing Dmitri would be able to use his free hands to punch if in front. However, Dmitri had been taught the power of the unexpected. With his left hand he reached through the attacker's legs from behind and, taking a firm grasp on his genitals, pulled violently downwards.

Both opponents were on the floor, and in significant pain, one from a dislocated arm, the other from damaged testicles.

The soldier with the dislocated arm saw his revolver lying on the paving just out of reach. Dmitri saw it too, but it was further away from him. It would be a mistake to both go for the gun, as the soldier would get there first. Instead, as the soldier stretched forwards, Dmitri used the only object that was within his reach, the man with the injured groin, and launched him at the soldier who, pulling the trigger too quickly, shot his colleague. A well-thrown piton by Dmitri killed the last soldier.

The sound of fighting from the mountains continued, but inside the building was quiet. Dmitri closed the door behind him and paused to assess the new threat environment. He had a gun, but as soon as he used it, his location would be betrayed. He inhaled forcibly through his nose, held the breath for a few seconds, then released the air through his mouth; this loosened his muscles and kept him fluid.

The nail-soled hiking boots would make for a less than stealthy approach, so he took these off along with his socks to give himself more grip on the floor. Walking slowly, heel-to-toe, maintaining the relaxed alertness of his training, he crept barefoot along the hallway. Dmitri had a gun in one hand and a piton in the other.

Gennady rushed out of an open doorway, knocking the weapons out of Dmitri's hands.

Dmitri saw the flicker of recognition on Gennady's face as the two grappled.

Now, and in a different context, the former chauffeur recognised the Romanov features in the face of the Red Army soldier he'd spoken to earlier at Livadia.

But Dmitri was no longer the privileged teenage aristocrat that Gennady had known fifteen years before. Dmitri lifted his back foot. The move felt like a fall. It was so unnatural that students of the Hongmen found it difficult to execute, but such a 'fall' is faster to carry out than a step backwards. Such a move harnessed the quick fluidity of water, like a retreating wave. It freed him from Gennady's grasp, bringing the former chauffeur off balance.

The two men fought, moving back and forth along the corridor. Dmitri relied on his superior skill. The strikes, parries, blocks and counter strikes had been repeated thousands of times during incessant drills with the Hongmen. They were instinctive. He relaxed, used force correctly, doing enough, then stopping. He was conserving his energy whilst Gennady was wasting his. Dmitri's strikes combined a soft approach with a hard contact, and soft recovery; no power was wasted. But Gennady was no ordinary soldier or OGPU guard fighting just because he'd been told to. If Dmitri felt he had the power of moral righteousness on his side, Gennady felt a similar strength. One man was fighting to save his sister, the other was fighting to defeat the object of his hatred.

An explosion outside shook the building. Plaster and dust filled the hallway, separating the two men fighting. Dmitri crouched defensively. When the dust cleared, Gennady had gone, as had the gun.

With a small metal piton in each hand, Dmitri searched the rooms.

Someone approached him quickly from behind. Dmitri turned just in time.

He used the pitons to slash each wrist as the woman's fists came towards him. He side-stepped quickly to plunge one of the knives into his attacker's neck; these were the three most vulnerable points.

Dmitri recognised the face of Valentina, Gennady's wife, and the family's former laundress. She died quickly; her hate-filled eyes still open after her last breath had escaped.

The stairs led to two bedrooms. Dmitri found Gennady in the room on the seaward side of the ornate castle folly. The former chauffeur had Anna in a chokehold. A gun barrel pointed to her temple and a gag was tied around her mouth. As Dmitri stepped further into the room, Gennady stepped back so that he was almost leaning against the large French-windows that looked out to the Black Sea. He pressed the barrel of the gun firmly to the princess's head. Dmitri stopped where he was; there was no way he would be able to cross the large room before Gennady could pull the trigger. He had no pitons left to throw.

"I'm glad you get to see this," hissed Gennady through a clenched jaw. "She's been a good maid but will make a better sacrifice."

Dmitri tried to push out of his mind the emotions fighting to overwhelm him at seeing his sister, the sibling he'd grieved the death of, for the first time in so many years. She looked exactly like their mother, albeit less well kept, but then Dmitri was hardly the figure of health with his roughly shaved head, tired eyes, and ragged clothing.

"Was your life with us really that bad?" asked Dmitri.

"Why don't you choose to stay, become my chauffeur, and see for yourself," replied the man dressed in the uniform of the Red Army. He had a cruelty that made him unrecognisable from the kindly young man Dmitri remembered him to have once been. Dmitri wondered whether that malice had always been there, supressed, or was it the result of life under the Bolsheviks. "If you do, I won't kill your sister. You can both serve me and my wife."

"Valentina's dead." There was some satisfaction in telling Gennady this, but Dmitri hoped it would also get Gennady angry. Angry people make mistakes.

"So, you won't stay voluntarily then?" asked Gennady. He convinced himself that Dmitri was bluffing about his wife.

"No thanks," said Dmitri. "I've tasted enough Communism already. It's like cheap vodka." Dmitri smiled. "Very cheap."

A flicker in Anna's expression suggested she was trying to communicate something to her brother. Did she have a plan, or was she saying goodbye, he wondered.

"Well then," said Gennady. "You'll have to remain as a prisoner. But first, say goodbye to your sister."

Dmitri knew Gennady now expected him to rush forward, even though such a move would be entirely futile. Even if the gun jammed, Gennady could easily throw Anna through the French-windows and be ready to fight Dmitri by the time he'd crossed the room.

Brother looked at sister, trying to judge what each other's expression suggested.

Whether he ran across the room, or stayed where he was and did nothing, his sister would be shot. Above all else Gennady wanted Dmitri to see his sister killed in front of him. The Hongmen had taught Dmitri to do the unexpected, so he turned and ran out of the room.

Anna felt the slack in Gennady's arm as her brother fled unexpectedly, denying Gennady the audience he wanted. Her captor was distracted by the confusion this created. It was her only chance. She made sure her feet had a firm grip on the polished wooden floor, then threw her meagre weight backwards towards the windows. The force jolted Gennady's arm. He fired a shot, but it missed completely.

As they moved backwards, Anna reached out to her side. Her fingers touched the wooden window frame, and she grasped with all her strength, braking her motion. Gennady continued backwards. He crashed through the window and fell to the concrete paving of the observation deck below.

"Annochka!" Dmitri had her in his arms before her knees buckled.

"Mitya!" She'd yanked the gag away from her mouth. "I can't believe you're here."

"We need to go," he instructed. All he wanted to do was hold her, promise everything would be all right, and make sure she was real. But they had no time, and he'd prepared himself to resist these natural brotherly urges upon finding Anna. "Can you run?" he asked. Her body was little more than skin and bones; he would carry her if need be.

"I just pushed a man through a window, Mitya," she said, "I can certainly run." Dmitri was reminded that Anna had always been the tougher of the siblings.

The fight at the front of Swallow's Nest continued to keep the soldiers and OGPU officers occupied. Dmitri stopped to pick up the climbing boots. He was alert to danger as he lifted his skeletal sister over the balustrade.

"Put these on," he urged, helping Anna into the overlarge boots, and tying them as tightly as he could.

"Down there?" she asked disbelievingly.

"If you can make it," replied Dmitri. His sister shrugged her acceptance of the circumstances and the challenge. Dmitri fed the double rope through Anna's legs, looping behind one thigh, across the chest, over a shoulder and diagonally across her back. "Keep hold of this with your rear hand," he instructed, "this is your brake. Keep your other hand forward on the rope for balance. Off you go."

"But Mitya, what about you?"

"I'll be right behind you, but if anything goes wrong, there's a boat at the Koreiz mooring. Now get moving!"

"Where are you going?" she asked. Dmitri had jumped back over the balustrade.

"To signal the others," he called back. He wanted to stay with his sister but had a duty to the men fighting on his behalf.

He ran around the building, taking a rifle off a dead soldier as he did so. He fired into the backs of those soldiers defending the access path from the White Baron's attack. He caught the eye of one of the former Imperial Army officers in the distance and waved, hoping the signal would be understood.

The Red Army soldiers, knowing now there was an insecure rear flank, divided themselves up to cover the new threat.

The White Baron's small band of old men dispersed away from the villa, causing confusion as the Red Army soldiers tried to decide whether to give chase or to investigate the man dressed in one of their uniforms shooting at them from the terrace of the villa.

Only the White Baron ran forward as his men fled. His approach decided the minds of the soldiers who all converged on him, the easy target. This gave his retreating men and Dmitri a head start.

This was the White Baron's last stand, and he was soon surrounded. Dmitri couldn't get to him. The general raised his arms in surrender, but his fists were still clenched in defiance. Four Red Army soldiers stepped forward to restrain him. The general then looked across towards the cliffs where Dmitri was standing, trying to determine how best to help the old general. With one hand the general saluted the Russian prince, in the other he unclenched his fingers to reveal a hand grenade without its pin.

The Soviet soldiers turned to see to whom the general was saluting, in doing so they weren't quick enough to react to what was in the old man's other hand.

The explosion scattered shell fragments and body parts through a cloud of smoke.

Dmitri held his salute to a man no longer where he had been standing. Another hero gone, thought the Romanov prince.

There was no time for a graceful abseil. Dmitri would have to test whether the dulfersitz technique taught to him by Finch was robust enough for the required speed.

As he made it down the first section to the cover of the trees, voices could be heard up by the Swallow's Nest. When Dmitri broke cover to rappel down the rest of the rock face, he would easily be seen. Anna was already at the bottom, so the rope was slack. He glanced out through the cover of the bushes. Soldiers were on the observation deck, but it didn't appear they'd seen the rope.

Dmitri grabbed the rope, took a breath, and ran. He launched himself off the outcrop and onto the vertical rock face below. His bare feet, soft through years of easy living, scrambled for a decent footing. He ran the rope through his hands so fast that the skin on his palms was shredded.

The voices from above grew louder and shots were fired, but Dmitri was already out of range. What he couldn't see, but knew would be happening, was the rope tied to the balustrade being cut.

He bounced his feet off the rock face and threaded the rope quickly through his sore hands. He glanced down periodically to find the easiest route, then let his legs swing left and right to follow that descending pathway to safety.

Once, twice, three times his ripped feet lost their position and his shoulder smashed against the rock face, but he reconnected, leant back, and continued the descent, expecting the rope to give way when cut, and for his body to plummet onto the jagged rocks below.

He felt the sudden slackness as the rope was indeed cut, which once again made him lose his positioning. Luckily, the rope snagged on one of the other anchors that were, so far, holding.

With thirty feet to go, the pitons started to come loose under the full weight of Dmitri's body, firing themselves out of the rock one by one. The rope slackened and jolted, but Dmitri focussed, ignored the pain in his soles and palms, and continued. The last few feet became a free fall. He hit the ground, landing fortuitously on the sand between two rocks that would otherwise have killed him. The entire rope fell on top of him.

"Mitya!" Anna splashed sea water over his face. He was disorientated, but conscious. Anna ripped the sleeves from her shabby stained top and wrapped each one around her brother's damaged hands. She loosened the laces of his army boots, which had been left at the bottom of the cliff and slipped these on his bloodied feet.

"We need to go," he mumbled.

Anna made good progress over the rocks, but the nail-soled climbing boots were a hinderance once they were on flat ground, so she discarded these and ran barefoot. There was no need for caution as the alarm would already have been raised all over Yalta by now; speed was their only resource.

People walking to and from work, and patients from the sanatoriums, were also on the path, but didn't hinder the two people sprinting past them. Perhaps they knew this was an escape and were pleased. Every step was agony for Dmitri, but he'd learnt through his mountain training with the Hongmen that pain was just a warning, a signal, not a disablement. His feet would still move if compelled to do so, despite the agony, so he ran for his survival.

Anna tired quickly. Dmitri carried her the remaining distance to Koreiz, formerly known as the Yusupov Palace; she weighed almost nothing.

They made it to the jetty, only to find there was no boat waiting for them to escape from Russia.

XX

THE JETTY at the Yusupov Palace had been where the dowager empress and other senior members of the imperial family had departed aboard a British dreadnought in April 1919. Dmitri's father had left Russia aboard that British ship, a ship Dmitri's mother should have been on.

This was where the escape boat should have been left for Dmitri.

Three of the former Imperial Army officers arrived, each out of breath.

"Is it just you three?" asked Dmitri.

"Yes, I think so," clarified one of the officers. "It was chaotic."

"I'm afraid there's no boat," said Dmitri. "And I have no other escape plan."

"But Mitya, there is a boat," said Anna. She'd walked to the end of the wooden jetty and had come back to join the group on shore. "Out in the sea, there's a small boat at anchor."

"I doubt that's for us, Annochka," replied Dmitri dismissively; he was trying to formulate another plan.

"Whether it's for us or not," interjected one of the three officers, "I'd rather drown trying to get to it than be arrested and go back to that." He gestured behind himself to Yalta.

Every inch of the coastline would soon be crowded with Red Army and the OGPU. Dmitri looked from each man to the other, and then at his sister. She nodded her agreement.

Each escapee quickly undressed down to their underwear, then ran along the jetty and dived into the water.

Dmitri was a strong swimmer, but he stayed with his sister and the three men, all of whom struggled with the exertion. Their bodies were not used to such hard exercise, and they'd just fought a difficult battle at Swallow's Nest. The salty water made Dmitri's torn hands and feet sting, but he tried to ignore the pain.

As they swam, the boat seemed much further away than it had appeared when they were on the jetty. But the prospect of escape carried the group onwards. The three officers were not young men, but each of them found his own pace and persevered. The sea was calm, but the morning's late summer sun was strong.

After a long swim, the group spread out in the water. If there were armed Bolsheviks on board, at least with some space between them the escapees would be harder to hit. Dmitri put on a sprinting swim when he was close enough and scrambled aboard. He was prepared for a fight, but the twenty-five-foot yacht was unmanned. There were charts of the Black Sea, and some provisions. He wondered if this was the vessel which had been arranged, and it's positioning far out from the cove was thought safer than at the jetty.

Anna and the three men were helped on board, collapsing with exhaustion once on the boat. Dmitri looked for any other boats that might be coming in pursuit; so far there were none. The craft was a motorboat, but with masts, so could be put to sail also. Dmitri was at best an amateur sailor, at worst, the Russian prince was clueless about what to do with a boat that was anything other than a dinghy.

"I can help," said one of the three officers.

"You know about boats?" asked Dmitri.

"I was a Captain First Rank with the Baltic Fleet of the Imperial Russian Navy during the war," he replied, finding whatever reserves of energy he could to stand up and survey the ship's equipment and layout. "But I'll need your help, sir." He'd barely finished speaking before the others were on their feet, including Anna. All of them were ready to do whatever was needed. Their pale, emaciated bodies were marked with scars both old and new, and bruises.

"Mitya, I think there's someone in the water," said Anna. Without a telescope, it was difficult to tell if this was a person and, if so, whether they were a friend or foe. "Do we go back?" she asked. The four men looked from one to the other; they were all now one small step into freedom, and so far, they liked the feel of it.

"We go back," instructed Dmitri, "just in case he's one of ours."

"And if he's not?" asked one of the officers.

"Then we make damn sure to run him down."

THE SWIMMER was the oldest of the former Imperial Army officers.

As they dragged his wheezing body onboard, a gathering of Red Army soldiers had made it down to the shoreline and were firing shots at the boat. They were out of range, so the bullets kicked up water about thirty feet short of their target, but the fugitives had revealed their means of escape from Russia. Their advantage had been lost.

The former Imperial Navy officer, Captain Shatrov, shouted instructions to his tired but willing crew. There was no working radio, nor any weapons in the boat. Their only chance was to outmanoeuvre whatever craft might be sent in pursuit from the Soviet small ships in Yalta, or the larger Black Sea fleet in Sevastopol.

Despite not yet being safe, it felt good to be making progress away from Russia, and with his sister, thought Dmitri, as he obeyed Captain Shatrov's commands. The captain gave simple instructions to get them free of the headland and out into the sea proper; meanwhile, he was studying the charts and trying to plot a course to safety. Being Mercator charts, the shortest distance between two points was not necessarily a straight line, so the captain was calculating using latitude and longitude points converted into nautical miles. It had been many years since the fifty-year old former Imperial Navy captain had been at sea, let alone plotting a course.

They were a crew of six, but after the exhausting swim, only Dmitri and Captain Shatrov had yet recovered their senses. Anna was taking care of the elderly straggler, former General Count Lukashin, in the cabin. The remaining two middle-aged former Imperial Army officers were gathering their wits on deck and trying to help as much as they were able to.

Dmitri struggled to control the rudder properly. At maximum knots, his inexperienced manoeuvres were too hard, so the water pressure when the rudder was off the centreline kept knocking the tiller out of his hand and slowing them down. So far there were no boats in pursuit, and the coastline with the Swallow's Nest promontory was reducing in the distance behind their boat. The dark blue sea surrounding them gave Dmitri a sense of security, despite his difficulty handling the boat.

"Even at a decent cruising speed, and following a direct route, it will take us over twenty-four hours to reach Istanbul," said the captain. "That is also where the Soviets will expect us to go."

"It sounds like you might have an alternative plan," said Dmitri.

"If we change course, we can cut across the Black Sea at its narrowest point to the northern Turkish coast. It will take much less time."

"Once we're on foreign soil, do you think we'll be safe?" asked Anna.

"It gives us more options," replied Dmitri. "We can contact the émigré Russian All-Military Union in Istanbul and ask for their assistance."

"Is that agreed, then?" asked the navy captain. Each crew member, including his sister, turned to Dmitri for a decision. The protocol was being respected that the Russian prince was still their commander-in-chief in place of a tsar.

"It is," said Dmitri.

"I suggest we put to sail and spare the motor for when we really need it." No one offered dissent to Captain Shatrov's recommendation. "I hope you're all quick learners. Princess Anna Andreovna, perhaps you'd be more comfortable in the cabin." The captain was being respectful to Anna, but he received an indignant look of horror from her.

"Captain, I haven't been a princess for fifteen years, and I was only a child then." She held up her rough bony hands. "These know very well what hard work feels like. I have every intention of being as useful as any man aboard." The captain looked across at Dmitri, but the Russian prince shrugged and smiled. Even when she was a teenage princess, Anna had a stubborn precocity. The Bolsheviks had failed to knock that out of her it seemed.

Captain Shatrov took the helm. The remaining five crew members, including the elderly General Count Lukashin, who'd also refused the offer of rest in the cabin, followed the instructions given. All hatches were closed to avoid someone accidentally falling through, and the boat was turned head-to-wind, so the sails didn't fill with air before fully raised. The main sail and headsails were untied from their booms, the halyards were attached to their winches and cranked up to get tension in the lines. These were cleated off and tied up.

When at the Nikolayev Naval Academy as a cadet, Shatrov had studied fluid mechanics, so he understood very well how to get the most out of the boat. Airflow being faster over the leeward rather than windward side of the sheet, the captain positioned the vessel to accelerate the airflow, which reduced pressure, and formed a vacuum to suck the boat forwards. By presenting the curved surface of the sail sheet to the wind and holding it at the best possible angle, the captain maximised the vacuum effect and, therefore, the forward motion.

The crew of half-naked, barefoot, bedraggled, damp, former nobles and imperial officers carried out their tasks with enthusiasm and discipline. Very quickly, the boat was operating efficiently, and its crew moving around the vessel in a dance choreographed by the captain at the helm.

To keep the optimum speed, the captain had to watch for luffing as the sails started to flap around. He then increased the tension in the lines to maintain the optimum angle. There was a risk of over-sheeting and stalling-out, so the captain brought the boat closer to the wind to see how significant the luff was, then bear away by one or two degrees to get back on the critical angle. A less experienced sailor would have let the wind set the boat's course.

The sensation of sea travel, despite the hurried nature of their current voyage, was exhilarating. The skimming of waves against the hardwood hull that had been made years before by a master craftsman, the smell of rope, varnish, and salt air made Swallow's Nest already seem like only a couple of miles in distance, but a lifetime in impact away. For Captain Shatrov he was himself again: tolerant, decisive in his manoeuvres, and calm under pressure. The humiliations of the Soviet yoke were being rinsed clean by the splash of the waves. Nevertheless, this was an escape, not a cruise. It was war.

The Bolshevik ships were first spotted by the captain, who had eyes trained for the oceans. The distant specks didn't remain as such for long. Within a short amount of time, everyone on board could clearly see the silhouettes of two decent-sized ships under steam in pursuit. As the escapees' boat was crossing established shipping lanes in an unorthodox dash across the water at its narrowest point, any vessel on a similar course could only be following them.

Rushing carelessly to the headsail, following an instruction given by Captain Shatrov, Dmitri's injured foot caught on a splinter of wood, his wounds reopened, and he slipped on the blood. Before his bandaged hands could get purchase on any of the fixtures, he was in the water and quickly being left in the boat's wake. As the choppy water hit his face, he gasped involuntarily. The muscles in his windpipe contracted to stop any water getting into the lungs, and Dmitri found that he couldn't breathe. His chest felt as if it was trapped in a vice, and his heart rate slowed dramatically. He hoped the boat would maintain its course and leave him, knowing any rescue attempt would hinder their chance of out running the Soviets. Anna must escape, he thought.

The captain had no intention of leaving anyone behind. He executed an emergency stop, bringing the boat hard on the wind and tacking so the headsail was sheeted to the windward side. He jibbed the boat around and back to Dmitri. The stern was pitching, so those on board reached over the side with the intention of scooping up their overboard crew member. Dmitri was in a state of confusion and couldn't focus enough to catch the rope being thrown down to him. One of the former imperial officers didn't hesitate. He jumped into the water and looped the tie-line around the Russian prince's waist. Both men were hauled on board, but the ship had lost a significant amount of time and had come to a complete stop.

The Soviet ships were gaining on their little wooden yacht.

Whether in Russian territorial waters or not, there was nothing to stop the Soviets either sinking the yacht with all hands onboard or capturing the crew of absconders.

Anna took Dmitri into the cabin. The other crew members followed the captain's instructions to get them back underway.

The captain's owl-like eyes saw another ship on the horizon ahead of them. The Soviet ships would be unlikely to take any offensive action against the small yacht if there were witnesses, assuming the ship up ahead was not also a Soviet vessel diverted in their direction for a pincer movement. It was their only chance. The captain adjusted their course towards the new ship.

The Soviet ships were moments away from reaching firing distance, if sinking the yacht was their plan. Captain Shatrov had maintained a good speed, and his yacht was now in clear sight of the vessel approaching towards their bow. The Soviets would still be able to catch the yacht and force a surrender, or hold them until the other ship was out of sight, so the captain decided to attempt a tricky manoeuvre and cross the other ship's path, to come up on its port side and try to get their attention for help.

The Soviet ships would be too large, and too late to intercept the yacht if it were on the port side of the approaching vessel.

The captain brought the yacht to bear away a few degrees to build up speed. He shouted instructions to his amateur crew and swung the boat into the wind. The sail started to backwind, and the crew member nearest was told to let the sheet go as it blew across the boat. Once across, it was homed to a new tack as fast and hard as possible. At the helm, the captain came out of the turn just before it was completed to allow the boat to settle on its new course, and not oversteer itself.

He'd tacked successfully and was now on the port side of the approaching ship, which would come between them and the Soviet vessels.

If the approaching ship was also Soviet then all would be lost, so too would it be if the ship carried on past them, thinking they were incompetent sailors on a confusing course. Against all instinct to keep moving, the captain ordered both sails lowered quickly.

Dmitri had recovered from his fall overboard. He was on deck with Anna to hear the captain's plan. With no radio equipment to send a distress signal, they would have to rely on manual signs. All crew members were told to stand facing the approaching ship, and continuously raise and lower their outstretched arms to each side. The captain himself smashed the wall mirror in the cabin and used a fragment of it to catch the sun and signal the approaching ship for help.

The Soviet ships dropped back slightly.

Those on board the yacht continued to wave their arms in formation as the other ship approached. It was a fishing trawler. It hadn't reduced its speed.

They all scanned the vessel anxiously, looking for any insignia, hoping not to see a red and white flag with familiar hammer and sickle motif.

As she waved her tired arms, tears of hope fell down Anna's cheeks.

XXI

ENTRY TO the Bosphorus had seemed like the gates of heaven themselves when the Turkish fishing trawler delivered its supplementary cargo of six Russian runaways to Istanbul.

The trawler's captain had been reluctant to help, but the condition of the yacht's occupants was such that he agreed to take them to Istanbul. The escapees accepted they would be handed over to Turkish customs officials, as none of them had any official papers. Dmitri had left the false papers relating to Iurii Nekrasov with the clothes he'd abandoned in Yalta.

Threats made over the radio to the trawler's captain from the Soviet ships had fallen on deaf ears. They had been told to make diplomatic representations to the Turkish authorities in Istanbul if, as claimed, the rescued passengers were wanted criminals. The Turkish captain was clear that the yacht had been outside Russian territorial water, even if only by a fraction, when found.

Never had six people seemed so pleased to be placed under arrest when handed over to the customs officials at Istanbul. The only sour note was that Anna was separated from the men, but the several hours aboard the Turkish trawler, during which they were kindly given some spare clothes and decent food, had given brother and sister an opportunity, at last, to start repairing the wounds of their separation. This made being split up again even more difficult when in port at Istanbul. Dmitri feared the Soviets would be able to bribe and cajole Turkish officials into handing her back over to them while Dmitri was locked up separately with the other men.

As immigration prisoners with no identity papers, they were held at Kiz Kulesi, a small fortress on an islet previously used to guard the mouth of the Bosphorus at the Marmara Sea. In its past the building had been a lighthouse, signalling station, quarantine ward, and was now being used as a customs control point. Being surrounded by water it was thought safe from escape but, for Dmitri, he was glad of the choice of detention facility as it also prevented unauthorised capture from the Soviets.

Dmitri was permitted to send a message to the émigré office of the Russian All-Military Union in Istanbul, making it clear that Princess Anna Andreovna Romanova was amongst those being held. His own rakish reputation as a playboy could lead to the mistaken belief that he'd been arrested for some sexual misdemeanour. It wouldn't be the first time over the last few years that émigré Russians with influence had been called upon to get him out of a scrape. But the mention of a princess long assumed to be dead would certainly motivate the local émigré community to make urgent enquiries.

"You have a visitor," announced one of the Turkish officials.

Dmitri hadn't expected it to be the person who arrived at the cell door. The youngish, nondescript face of the man from the flight across Europe, who'd joined at Strasbourg, could have been an easy one to forget, but

Dmitri had an excellent memory for both faces and names.

Dmitri's heart sank. He remembered Aubrey had said this man had assaulted him in Tangiers. He'd also boarded the flight with Fëdor.

"I suppose it's time I introduce myself properly," he said to Dmitri through the rusty bars. He was speaking French rather than Russian, but this didn't necessarily mean he wasn't an educated Soviet.

"I'm not sure I want to hear who you are," replied Dmitri. His voice was heavy with hostility.

"My name is Captain Emile-Jacques Brossard. I'm with *le Deuxiéme Bureau*. Paris asked me to protect you. I believe your great aunt applied some considerable pressure to my commanding officer."

"That sounds like her," said Dmitri.

Emile-Jacques showed Dmitri identification confirming what he'd said. He then offered a hand for Dmitri to shake. The Russian hesitated, but he had no one else to trust. Dmitri shook the Frenchman's hand, and said, "Well, you could have told me earlier. I flew a bloody plane out of Budapest in the middle of the night to get away from you! Can you break us out of here, Captain?"

"The paperwork's being processed now. The Turkish authorities will release you into French custody. We should have passports ready for you all by tomorrow, so you can leave Istanbul."

"My sister's here somewhere," said Dmitri.

"She's waiting for you all downstairs," replied Emile-Jacques.

"And the Soviets?" asked Dmitri. He was still cautious. "Our departure from Russia wasn't exactly discreet."

"I understand the Soviets have made representations to the Turkish authorities, but the French ambassador in Ankara has made things quite clear that he is your guardian angel. The Turks have taken his side on the matter."

"Well, please pass on our thanks to His Excellency."

"You can do that yourselves," replied the French spy. "He's coming here to host a lunch for you all tomorrow."

"I hardly think we're attired for a diplomatic reception," said Dmitri.

"Well, let's get you to your hotel, and perhaps we can find a decent tailor."

BY FERRY, and then horse-drawn phaeton, the unkempt Russian fugitives were conveyed to the Pera Palace hotel.

The arrival of the six bedraggled new guests turned every head in the reception lounge. Emile-Jacques hurried them through to the rooms he'd been instructed by the consul-general to take on behalf of the Russians. The foreign journalists who'd been taking tea in the salon waiting for a story to cross their path hurried to the manager's office to find out more information about the bizarre arrivals. The four men were doubled-up in twin rooms, but Dmitri politely declined the offer for him and his sister to be separated in different suites; they took a third twin room as neither wanted to be alone.

After Emile-Jacques had left to update the consul-general, the Romanov siblings were visited by local tailors with some ready-to-wear clothes. Dmitri made a quick selection and left his sister to have the clothes adjusted to her near-emaciated figure.

"Annochka, you look so much like Mama," said Dmitri, returning to their room and finding his sister transformed. She was dressed in an aqua-blue silk frock with white mousseline de soie frills at the collar and sleeves. Her long hair had been cut into a fashionably short style. A single tear escaped and slid down her left cheek. Dmitri rushed to her, but she pushed him away.

She looked at her brother with an unkind expression, one of mistrust. He understood.

"You're not alone anymore," he said. He stepped closer to her slowly, as one might when trying not to frighten a wild animal.

"Oh, Mitya!" She rushed into his arms. Her body shook against his as fifteen years' worth of tears burst free. "Never leave me again," she sobbed. She'd dreamt of seeing him again, but never imagined it would be possible.

Each time he eased his grip, expecting his sister to speak and dry her tears, she succumbed to a fresh wave of crying. He eventually laid his sister down on the bed once the tears stopped. The crying had exhausted her. Dmitri pulled the armchair next to the bed, so he could hold her hand while she eased herself out of the agitation that had so suddenly but understandably overwhelmed her.

When they'd last seen each other, being separated at the prison camp east of Moscow, he had been a young man of seventeen, and she a girl of fifteen; they'd assumed at the time their separation would be brief. Even though his sister was still only in her late twenties, the fifteen hard years since had aged her, and she resembled almost identically their mother as Dmitri last remembered her. Dmitri felt as if he was watching a ghost lying on the bed in front of him.

Anna seemed to have calmed, but whenever Dmitri moved, she tightened her grip on his hand, and wouldn't let him go. He didn't mind; he'd hold her hand for the next fifteen years if that's what it took to help her recover.

Anna's demand that he never leave her again had a trace of animosity to it, and he didn't blame her for that. When told years before that his sister was dead, and by more than one reliable source, Dmitri had spiralled through the emotions of grief, hatred towards the

Bolsheviks, and deep sorrow that his beautiful sister had not lived to be a woman. But he had been in a labour camp at the time, and the conditions endured for those two years of his internment had numbed some of the enormity of the grief for him.

Realising now that his sister had been alive all this time, while he had more recently been enjoying the life of a playboy émigré, gave him a greater sense of sorrow and guilt than anything experienced before. He shuddered to imagine what that fifteen-year-old girl had gone through, waiting year after year for someone to rescue her, or at least for some confirmation that she hadn't been forgotten. He couldn't forgive himself for giving up on her just because people had told him she was dead when he'd never seen her corpse himself. It was a personal disgrace and dishonour that he felt now like a void in his gut that wouldn't go away.

Since her rescue at Swallow's Nest and their escape to Turkey, Anna had shown a familiar sense of strength and defiance. This was an independence of character that had already been present in her as a child, but which had been toughened with the years of hardship and loneliness under the Bolsheviks. Lying on the bed, her eyes bloodshot and her cheeks flushed bright red, she now looked to Dmitri like a helpless bird with a damaged wing.

Brother and sister were meeting each other for the first time as man and woman, he a well-dressed playboy and she a refugee from hell itself. Half a lifetime and a completely different existence now separated them. Each would have to get used to their new role as sibling on different terms, but that would take time.

Once Anna's hand had slackened when she finally succumbed to sleep, Dmitri crept around the room tidying things up from the clothes fitting. He wanted to remain close in case his sister woke up. He scribbled down a brief telegram to be sent to the grand duchess in Paris, asking her to ensure newspapers were kept away from his father, in case any reports of Anna's survival and rescue should feature. The re-introduction of father and daughter would have to be done sensitively, and in person.

Confident that Anna was in a deep-enough sleep, and wouldn't need him, Dmitri quietly closed the door and went to hand the telegram to the reception desk.

Dmitri stopped for one drink on the terrace of the hotel and puffed on a Montecristo No.4 to let his thoughts settle before returning to his sister.

"I don't believe it!" exclaimed a middle-aged Englishman. He'd recognised Dmitri and rushed over.

"Major Willoughby isn't it?" asked Dmitri. His manner was lukewarm.

"Tangier, exactly, old boy! The El Minzah Hotel. Had to leave there in a bit of a rush I'm afraid, spot of trouble with the sultan." Willoughby sat down at the prince's table without having been invited. He waved for the waiter to bring a fresh round of drinks for them both.

"So I'd heard," replied Dmitri. He turned away to look across the terrace as the sun set behind the vista of Istanbul, dotted with minarets, and divided by the waterways of the Bosphorus Strait and Golden Horn. He'd found Willoughby to be a pompous blowhard in Tangier and was in even less of a mind-set to accommodate the self-important blustering fool now. "Please excuse me," said Dmitri standing to leave, just as the waiter brought the new drinks over.

"But, old chap, I thought we might…" Willoughby's voice trailed away as the Russian prince paced out of hearing puffing on his cigar and stepping back into the hotel.

Dmitri almost didn't recognise his four fellow refugees from Russia as he paced through the restaurant. Scrubbed clean, smartly dressed in dinner suits, and now revived by a decent meal, no one would believe the conditions they'd been living under up until the previous day. It was only by the dark circles around their sunken eyes, and the rough skin on their hands that a close observer would detect something amiss with the picture of four middle-aged men of means enjoying a decent supper together. Dmitri remained standing, but indulged himself with a scoop of caviar, as he acknowledged the thanks of the men and promised to see them for breakfast.

Anna's new dress was lying neatly on the armchair when Dmitri returned to their room, but she was back in bed and asleep.

He got changed for bed himself but couldn't rest.

They were out of Russia, but it would only be once they were back in Paris that he would consider them to be safe, and the rescue mission accomplished. The idea of a lunch party with the consul-general the following day seemed just about the last thing he wanted to do. It was not appropriate for his sister in her condition but, if that got them the passports and tickets to Paris, then Dmitri promised himself that he'd try to make the best of it.

XXII

IT WAS a new day in Istanbul. Dmitri convinced his reluctant sister to venture out into the city with him for the morning. She'd been hidden away in Russia for enough years already, he told her with a cheeky smile. There would be plenty of time for reflection but trying to push aside any morose feelings was a better therapy for now, he thought, for both of them.

He wanted to visit the émigré Russian HQ to thank them for helping with *le Deuxième Bureau*, and to find out more about the Soviet reaction to the escape, but he knew Anna needed a break from other Russians, regardless of whether Red or White.

Anna managed to eat some breakfast, but picked at the food as if it was the first time she'd ever seen fresh bread, eggs, or preserves.

'It beats bark soup', he joked. Anna smiled. He'd reminded her that, even if for only two years, he had also been in a labour camp, and had some small understanding of her experiences.

He'd dressed in a pair of airy plus-fours and a clean shirt. Anna had chosen a pair of blue and white checked wide-legged slacks, a striped jersey, open-toed sandals, and a knitted beret from the small selection of clothes brought over the previous evening. It was the least feminine outfit available to her. Dmitri knew Sable would take Anna under her wing in Paris and show his sister how to dress like the woman she now was.

Dmitri tipped the lift boy with some of the cash Emile-Jacques had given him. Anna looked horrified at what she considered extravagance; such small details reminded Dmitri just how much of a recovery Anna would need before she felt settled in the new life of freedom.

Emile-Jacques had left a message at reception that he would call at midday to escort them over to the consul-general's residence. The other four escapees had already left for an excursion in the city by the time Dmitri and his sister made it down to the reception area.

His bandaged feet were still sore, but he wanted to get his sister out of the hotel to relieve the sombreness of her current state of mind. Dmitri decided that a quick trip to the Grand Bazaar would be something pleasant for them to do for an hour or so. His sister could choose something to buy for herself. It would be the first such nonessential thing she'd probably ever bought.

Istanbul was somewhere Dmitri had visited before but didn't know well. Being a strategic point for trade, the city had passed through the hands of the Persians, Greeks, Romans, Venetians, and Ottomans, and had its name changed three times. As a Romanov, Dmitri felt a sympathy for this city of siege and survival. Despite the decay and neglect suffered since the capital was moved to Ankara, the city had undeniable character, and generous locals who gave it a vibrancy which Dmitri hoped would invigorate his sister.

They crossed the water to the old city where the sound of muezzins competing in their calls to prayer, and the irregular narrow streets, conjured images of the ancient orient. Anna nibbled on some syrup-drenched baklava bought from a street vendor. Dmitri could tell she was trying to force herself to enjoy the experience. She still wasn't able to relax or to trust the world around her, regardless of how different it seemed from the Soviet labour camps. Despite not being guilty of a crime, she had still been a prisoner. Her brother reminded himself of this each time she flinched at the touch of his hand on her arm, or sudden loud noises.

The Grand Bazaar was, because of the constant hum of activity, more settling to Anna than the irregular street sounds outside. They followed a narrow lane and were soon in the heart of the covered maze of market traders selling anything from jewellery to clothes, from carpets to metal work, and huge selections of spices that filled the passageways with a distinct smoky scent. It was a chaotic labyrinth that made those inside it feel part of something that was alive. Dmitri hoped this would invigorate Anna and at least distract her for an hour or so before the difficult consular lunch.

"By Jove! We meet again!" Major Willoughby darted out from one of the passages, as Dmitri and Anna browsed along one of the main thoroughfares. "The fates are pushing us together, eh?" He took off his hat and gave a small bow towards Anna, forcing Dmitri to introduce them. Willoughby, a flabby man, if not quite fat, had wet patches on his blue shirt, a balding head dotted with sweat, and a moustache that looked damp, and needed neatening up. He was horribly out-of-place.

"Major Willoughby, let me introduce my sister, Her Highness Princess Anna Andreovna of Russia."

"Just Anna," whispered his sister as a correction, it was the only name she now recognised as her own.

"Very pleased to meet you, Your Highness," said Willoughby. "You both look as lost as I am. It's all terribly muddling."

"That's part of the fun," suggested Dmitri, being deliberately contrary. Anna seemed nonplussed by the Englishman's presence, but Dmitri was keen for their brief acquaintance not to be mistaken as friendship. "Good day, Major," he said, in the tone of a dismissal. He led Anna off towards the drinking fountain up ahead.

"Now this looks familiar," said Willoughby, appearing once again, apparently not having taken the hint.

"We're going to browse the carpets," said Dmitri.

"Oh, I'll have a basin of that. I've a dotty old Aunt in Harrogate who would love a rug from Constantinople." Willoughby tried to take a drink from the fountain, but the flow was more forceful than expected and it soaked his whole face instead. Anna gave a small laugh; it was the first time she'd done so since the reunion with her brother.

"Bloody Turkish plumbing," joked Willoughby, drying his face with a handkerchief. "I say, you don't mind if we chum up together do you? At least until we're out of this damn maze?"

"Well, actually, Major, my sister and I were..." Dmitri started to make an excuse.

"That's fine," interrupted Anna. She walked over to a row of shops selling hats of every variety on the opposite alleyway.

"A new hat, what a good idea!" bellowed Willoughby. "That's even better for Auntie Gladys. She'd look great in a Fez!" Willoughby joined Anna by the hats. Dmitri followed.

Dmitri turned his back just for a minute to try on a hat. When he turned around to get Anna's opinion on the headwear, she had gone, as had Willoughby.

Having promised himself the night before that he'd never leave his sister again, here, only the following day, that promise had been broken. Dmitri had been bargaining with a trader trying to get the best price on a

Panama hat to protect his still-shaved scalp from the sun. He'd been distracted for just a few moments.

He checked for his sister in the shops and stalls in the area, pushing away the hat seller he'd been bartering with. He was sure that Anna and Willoughby had just gone on ahead.

Not finding them, he started to panic a little more.

Each trader he spoke to with a description of her and Willoughby ignored him and tried to start a negotiation for their wares. He found his way back to the fountain and stood on tiptoe to peer down each of the thoroughfares that radiated off from it. He couldn't see either Anna or Willoughby.

He had to take control of himself and keep the wave of dread in check. Nothing untoward could have happened, he assured himself. It was difficult enough for him to navigate around the labyrinth, never mind for Soviet agents intent on kidnapping. And Willoughby would have raised the alarm to Dmitri.

Dismissing the possibility of anything underhand having happened, he was still uneasy, knowing that his sister was very fragile. Upon finding her brother gone, she might have some sort of breakdown as she had the evening before when crying uncontrollably into his shoulder. Willoughby didn't seem the sort to be able to handle a weeping female.

Handing over the full price for the Panama hat, Dmitri went back to the fountain and raised the hat high in the air at the end of his long arm. It was a signal that Anna could follow, if she was wandering lost along the avenues of trade looking for him.

After several minutes, and with two aching arms, there was still no sign of his sister or the Englishman. Dmitri gathered his navigational wits about him and searched each of the thoroughfares, passageways, alcoves, and warehouses. He frequently returned to the fountain.

The frustration and worry turned to panic when his extensive search resulted in nothing.

A Turkish police officer he found, who spoke a small amount of English, refused to take Dmitri's concern seriously, advising him that foreigners are always getting lost in the market, and that they turn up back at their hotels.

In leaving the Grand Bazaar, Dmitri felt as if he was abandoning his sister all over again. But his efforts at finding her and Willoughby there had been a waste of time. He hoped Willoughby might have escorted her back to the hotel, or at least that Dmitri could enlist the support of Emile-Jacques and the French to raise her disappearance with the Turkish police.

He ran up the hill to the hotel from the ferry crossing terminal. He no longer cared about his painful feet. He touched the cross around his neck and prayed that his sister would be sipping tea on the terrace with Willoughby when he got there.

She was not at the hotel. Not on the terrace, not in their room, and no message had been left at reception.

"Everything all right?" asked Emile-Jacques with a smile as he approached Dmitri at the reception desk. He had a tray with two tall glasses of raki on. The look on Dmitri's face told the French spy something was seriously wrong.

"Anna's missing," blurted out Dmitri. He took one of the glasses and gulped at the aniseed infused grape spirit.

"Where? From the room?" asked the Frenchman.

"We went to the Grand Bazaar. I turned away for a second, and she and Willoughby had gone." At Dmitri's mention of the Englishman's name, Emile-Jacques' expression suddenly became one of concern. He also took a sip of the raki.

"Willoughby, you say?" he asked.

"Yes, he's just some buffoon of an Englishman I met in Tangier who attached himself to us earlier today."

"Do you know him well? Willoughby?"

"He's not important," said Dmitri. "You must contact the police here and get a description of Anna circulated. She's wearing slacks, a stripped jersey and a beret."

"Please, sir, I need to be clear. How do you know Willoughby?"

"To hell with him! It's Anna that we need to find."

"His name's not Willoughby," declared the captain. Dmitri's blood turned to ice in his veins before the Frenchman had finished the sentence. "He's a Bolshevik spy."

"But he can't be," replied Dmitri. "He's a damn fool of an Englishman if ever I saw one."

"Oh, he is English," said Emile-Jacques. "In fact, he is an actor. His real name is Basil Calloway. Major Willoughby is one of his creations."

"Bit of a stretch, from ham actor to Bolshevik spy wouldn't you say?" asked Dmitri. He didn't believe the Frenchman. He didn't want it to be true.

"As I understand it," explained Emile-Jacques, "the acting roles dried up when he started sermonising communist rhetoric to the repertory companies. The Bolsheviks recruited him in London about ten years ago."

"And I took her shopping, of all the damned stupid things to do." Dmitri cursed himself for not being more suspicious of Willoughby.

"There's no need to –"

"Do you know where they've taken Anna?" interrupted Dmitri. "What do we do?" There were more questions coming into Dmitri's head than the French spy could answer quickly enough.

"Since Trotsky was exiled to an island near here three years ago the city has attracted Bolshevik assassins. But Trotsky is always surrounded by his own protection."

"Assassins! By God, we must find Anna, Emile. Where would they have gone, to a ship? Can your ambassador blockade the port somehow?"

"I suggest we stay here."

"Absolutely not!" exclaimed Dmitri.

"I'll make some calls to get others from the Bureau, and some sympathetic Turkish officials to pull the necessary strings."

"I can't just sit here," exclaimed Dmitri. "You must know where they frequent. Anything, however tenuous."

"The ambassador would not want us to lose you too. Please remain here with me," urged Emile-Jacques.

"No," insisted Dmitri. "Good God man, she's my sister."

Emile-Jacques looked to the ceiling trying to settle the conflict in his mind. Losing one of the Romanov's would be embarrassing to explain to the ambassador, losing both would be career-ending. But he had two younger sisters back in France, and he knew how slow the Turkish authorities would be to search the ports. He led Dmitri by the shoulder to a quiet corner of the lobby.

"Take this." Emile-Jacques discreetly handed his revolver to the Russian prince. "I've heard rumours that they use Galata Tower. But be careful. Just stay outside and watch. I'll follow once I've raised the alarm to all those I can get involved in this search."

Dmitri was running towards the hotel exit before Emile-Jacques had finished speaking.

THE LARGE stone cylinder of Galata Tower rose nearly seventy meters above the districts situated north of the Golden Horn. This made it easy to find. It was also only a short distance away from Dmitri's hotel.

Dmitri cut his way through the ramshackle houses that had been built against the crumbled ramparts of the former medieval fortress, of which the tower itself was the only feature which remained intact. He'd run all the way from the hotel, but now moved cautiously, hoping to surprise the Bolsheviks, if they indeed had Anna trapped inside. Even if she wasn't here, Dmitri was ready to beat the necessary information out of whomever he found.

'One of ours, ten of theirs' had been something the Soviet guards repeated when Dmitri was in the prison camp after the Revolution. When the camp became overcrowded with aristocrats, soldiers, landowning peasants, and those from the intelligentsia who'd criticised their new masters, the guards were paid ten roubles for each execution carried out to relieve the congestion. Ten prisoners were shot for every Bolshevik they received reports of having been killed in the aftermath of the uprising. Dmitri repeated their mantra to himself now.

No matter the odds, he would use the training received from the Hongmen to save his sister; one of his, ten of theirs.

The tower was set to one side in a small town square. He moved around to get a clear view of the only entrance, which was up a short flight of stairs. One of the heavy iron doors then opened, so Dmitri ducked into a nearby alcove.

Gennady came out. His leg was in a brace up to his hip, requiring the use of sticks to walk. He leant against the metal balustrade at the top of the stairs and lit a cigarette. Fëdor and the Englishman calling himself Willoughby joined Gennady.

Dmitri wasn't close enough to hear what was being said, but Gennady was clearly not pleased with his henchmen, whose body-language was both apologetic and nervous. Seeing these men here, Dmitri was sure his sister would be inside. He was disappointed that Gennady hadn't been killed by the fall from the window at

Swallow's Nest, but the broken bones sustained by Anna's push were clearly causing him difficulty. With any luck, thought Dmitri, the former chauffeur might be left with a permanent limp as a reminder of the Romanovs he'd once worked for.

A car pulled up at the bottom of the steps. If Anna was brought out, Dmitri would have to make a charge for it and hope that his sister, as before, could help free herself while he fought and distracted her captors.

He gripped Emile-Jacques' revolver tightly.

More angry gestures and words were exchanged between Gennady and Fëdor while the Englishman stepped away to avoid the confrontation. As Gennady hobbled down the steps to the waiting car, he angrily brushed aside the offer of help from Willoughby. Fëdor watched the Red Army commander and Englishman drive away, before returning inside the tower.

There was no further reconnaissance Dmitri could carry out. There was only one entrance or exit, thick stone walls leading up to a double-tier of windows and a wrap-around walkway at the top of the huge structure. As impenetrable as it seemed, he would have to go in, armed just with the revolver and six bullets. He checked the gun to make sure the chamber was full. He then dashed across the square to the Tower.

The metal door had been left open. He listened for the sounds of voices inside the ground floor. This wasn't a military post, nor an official diplomatic Soviet one, so armed guards inside the entrance would be unlikely. This was a secret site for Bolshevik spies, so any accidental visitor would have to think this was a Turkish-run building. Having been a sentry tower, astronomical observatory, prison, and fire watchtower over the centuries, the Tower could easily pass as something other than it currently was.

With the revolver tucked under his shirt, Dmitri wandered in casually. He found a Turkish woman sitting behind a reception desk. He'd have preferred it to be a man acting as decoy, but this was war.

"Excuse me, sir, this isn't for tourists," she said. Her warning in English was repeated in French to make sure she'd been understood. Dressed in plus-fours and a Panama hat, Dmitri looked the part of sightseer quite well.

"I'm not a tourist," replied Dmitri in Russian, trying to pretend he was with the Bolsheviks. The female receptionist nodded her understanding. Dmitri noted that it would seem strange to any genuinely innocent visitor that a Turkish receptionist would also understand English, French and Russian fluently. She smiled, and reached across the desk to the candlestick telephone, ready to announce him as a visitor to whoever was on the other end of the line.

'One of mine, ten of theirs' Dmitri repeated to himself.

He thrust his weight violently against the desk, which smashed into the woman sitting behind it. The force thrust her head back, cracking it against the turquoise tiles on the wall behind. Her body slid to the floor, leaving a streak of blood down the ceramics.

Dmitri couldn't risk her waking up and raising the alarm before he'd found Anna. He rushed forwards, looped his belt around the neck of the unconscious woman, and pulled it tight. He maintained the pressure until he was sure she was dead.

Dmitri crept up the staircase to the next floor. There were three young Russian men playing cards. With his fingers ready to grab the revolver and shoot all three, he decided to try the same approach as with the receptionist. The men might assume he would only have got this far if the decoy sentry had allowed him up the stairs. He nodded to the men, took out a packet of cigarettes, and asked for a light. His expensive brand appealed to the card players.

"Comrade Bunin?" asked Dmitri. The mention of Gennady would confirm that Dmitri was supposed to be there. He gestured to the next upper platform stairwell. One of the men shrugged. All three returned to their game.

So far, so good, thought Dmitri. He just hoped Anna wasn't on the top floor; his luck was sure to run out eventually.

The second floor was a radio room with lots of equipment, but no one manning it; presumably, that was the job of one of the men downstairs playing cards with his colleagues. There was a heavy door which closed across the stairwell he'd just ascended. By good luck, there was a key in the lock, which he turned after closing the door. He slipped the key into his pocket. Worrying about how best to egress from the building would require a different plan, if he made it that far. The radio equipment was likely to be the crown jewel of the spy station and having it on his side of the locked door might prove useful, he thought.

The next stairwell, leading to the third floor, was narrow, brick lined, and required him to stoop his six-foot-tall frame to get up it.

The third floor was a kitchen. There was a young man of similar age to those encountered downstairs. He was making coffee when Dmitri appeared silently through the stairwell arch. Dmitri tried the same approach as before. He smiled and walked purposefully, but non-threateningly, over to the man as if he were meant to be there.

"Turkish coffee?" asked Dmitri as he came alongside the Soviet agent, sliding an empty cup along with him.

As the man filled the cup, Dmitri saw the flicker of intention to attack in the man's eyes. This was an almost imperceptible change in expression which the Hongmen had trained Dmitri not only to recognise, but to instinctively act against when seen, without delay. Dmitri was such a successful fighter because he'd learnt to react to his instincts.

As Dmitri launched the cup of hot coffee in the Soviet's face, he also grabbed a forearm, swung the man around, and clasped his other hand over the man's mouth. These movements were so fast and so smooth, that the Soviet agent's mouth was covered before any sound of distress had escaped. Dmitri kicked the man to his knees and uncovered his mouth only long enough to use both hands to grab his skull, push his neck to one side, and then twist his head sideways in a powerful move that snapped the spinal cord.

Dmitri stepped over the corpse of the Bolshevik. He continued up the next flight of stairs, ready to continue the fight in this nest of villains.

There were unoccupied camp beds on the next floor, so he continued up further.

He was almost at the top.

He took out his revolver.

Anna was sitting in a chair. She wasn't tied up. Presumably having a tower full of Soviet agents preventing any escape through the only exit door was considered sufficient security. Fëdor was standing on the other side of the room, and both men made eye contact at the same time.

Dmitri fired first.

It was only because Fëdor was standing next to an open window that he was able to save himself. As Dmitri fired, the Soviet dived out onto the wrap-around balcony behind the thick stone wall. The bullet hit his arm rather than his head or body.

"Get downstairs!" shouted Dmitri to his sister. He grabbed her thin arm and pushed her towards the stairwell that led down to the dormitory. He had no intention of following her yet.

A circular room with many windows was a difficult position to attack from; it was easier to be defensive. Dmitri stepped out onto the exterior balcony. He could move in a clockwise or anti-clockwise direction, either running head-on into Fëdor or chasing him around in circles. His training came back to him: pause, breathe, discern the threat.

He would wait for Fëdor to cross in front of one of the windows.

There was no movement.

With access to the radio blocked by the locked door, even if the three agents on the first floor had heard the gun shot, they would not be able to provide, or call for, reinforcements. That gave Dmitri an advantage. He could wait, Fëdor could not.

Dmitri returned inside the circular room. He pressed his back to the stone wall. He didn't blink. He watched the windows near where Fëdor had exited, waiting for a flicker of movement. He felt like a snake lying in the grass, immovable, waiting for its prey to make a mistake.

He heard vehicles screeching to a halt below the Tower. If these were Bolshevik agents, who had somehow been alerted to the siege, it would be impossible to get Anna out safely until Emile-Jacques arrived with the Turkish police.

Dmitri reassessed the threat and decided he couldn't play the long game and wait.

He had five bullets left, but he didn't need them all. Steadying himself in a solid shooting stance, he fired a round into the floor, and shouted in pretend agony to make Fëdor think the other Bolshevik spies were coming up the stairs as part of a rescue.

The figure of Fëdor ran across a window to his left. Dmitri's arms, loose but strong, with the revolver suspended at the end of them, swung to follow the movement.

Fëdor dashed across the next window, and the one that followed.

Dmitri aimed the sight of his revolver at the next gap in the wall, anticipating the trajectory of his target; this was just like a boar hunt, he thought.

In the half a second it took for Fëdor to cross from one stone shield to the next, Dmitri's gun found its target. The bullet struck. The force threw Fëdor's body sideways, hitting the railing. The gun in Fëdor's hand fell to the floor.

Dmitri watched as Fëdor thrust his arms up to protect his head from another shot, but this threw his body off balance even further. The bolts of the rusty railing creaked with the strain of the body pressing against them. As the fixings broke free from the crumbling masonry, Fëdor's upper body fell backwards, carrying the rest of him over the ledge with the railing.

"Please!" exclaimed Fëdor. His fingertips were clinging to the ledge when Dmitri cautiously approached. The bullet wound in Fëdor's upper arm was too painful, and the fingers on his right hand fell away. He would soon fall.

"Help me," sobbed the Bolshevik assassin. He glanced downwards at the people in the town square seventy feet below him. When his head turned back to face Dmitri his expression was one of abject fear. The four fingers of his left hand were straining to keep him from a death-fall.

"Beg me," said Dmitri. He leant against the ledge.

"I beg you," replied the Soviet. "Please, Your Highness, show mercy."

"That's better, Fëdor," said Dmitri. He lit one of the two cigarettes he was holding. He saw an expression of hope in the eyes of the dangling man, which is what he'd wanted to see. He held the cigarette towards Fëdor, as if offering it to him.

"No?" said Dmitri, seeing the confusion and hatred beginning to reappear in Fëdor's expression. "You're probably right. These Turkish ones are foul." He flicked the lit cigarette at Fëdor, who instinctively jerked his head to miss the projectile. This sudden movement made his fingers slip a fraction.

"Careful," warned Dmitri. He tucked the other cigarette behind his ear. "I'll give you exactly the same amount of mercy your comrades showed to my mother, Grand Duchess Xenia Nicolaevna of Russia." He picked up Fëdor's revolver by the barrel and smashed the grip down heavily on Fëdor's white-tipped fingers.

It was satisfying for Dmitri to see the realisation of imminent death in Fëdor's eyes as the fingers that could not withstand the repeated beating from the revolver's butt released their grip on the stone ledge.

Fëdor fell.

Dmitri smiled as he listened to the cry of fear for the two seconds it took for the Bolshevik assassin to reach his death on the ground below.

Dmitri edged cautiously forwards to peer over the ledge, worried in case rifle shots might meet his curious glance if those who'd arrived were Bolsheviks.

The Turkish police were congregating around the bloodied, twisted corpse of Fëdor. Dmitri recognised Emile-Jacques amongst the gathering crowd.

ANNA WAS waiting in the radio room, armed with a home-made weapon, and ready to strike whoever emerged from the stairwell above. Luckily, she paused long enough to recognise her brother.

"Mitya!" She cried with relief, collapsing into his arms. Whatever strength she'd summoned for the anticipated fight had drained her reserves, such that they were. Dmitri caught her and helped her into a chair.

"Are you hurt, Annochka?" he asked, looking for signs of injury. She shook her head; even replying had become too much effort.

The banging on the locked door, made her tense with fear, so Dmitri thrust the revolver into her hand to give her a feeling of safety and control.

He tore the last few pages out of the journal lying open next to the transmitter and thrust these into his pocket; these would be passed to the émigré White Army, if he survived. He started to drag the heavy equipment across the floor, to barricade the door from the Bolsheviks trapped between him and the police outside. Dmitri and his sister could then wait for the Turks to force a surrender from the three ensnared Bolshevik spies.

Before he could get the transmitter equipment in place, the door burst off its hinges.

Anna raised the gun. Her eyes were wide with fear. Dmitri was just able to grab her arm and deflect the shot into the door of a nearby wooden cabinet.

Emile-Jacques ran in with several Turkish police officers.

"Are you both alright?" he asked whilst scanning the room for Bolshevik agents. Instead he found Dmitri and his shaking sister.

"My dear fellow!" said Dmitri, realising they were safe. "I think it's about time for lunch." He took the cigarette he'd earlier tucked behind his ear and clasped it between his lips. He patted his trouser pockets looking for a lighter, then asked casually, "Has anyone got a match?"

XXIII

THE TRAIN journey to Paris on French diplomatic passports, had given Dmitri and his sister time to talk. They were able to start building a bridge over the gap of fifteen years that separated them. With every mile the train progressed westwards, and with each new border they crossed, Anna cleansed herself further of the stain on her soul that the decade-and-a-half of labour camp cruelty had left.

When they reached their destination at the Gare de l'Est in Paris, Anna's nerves were still jittery, but she was able to hide this fragility when in public. Both brother and sister suffered with nightmares, reliving traumas in their sleep that were too unpleasant to think about when awake.

During the journey Dmitri had prepared his sister for the meeting with their father, trying to manage her expectations. He knew it would be a new grief for his still-fragile sister to deal with. The father she'd known, the strong man she'd dreamt about meeting once again, had gone. In his place, Anna would meet just the shell of Grand Duke Andrei, a man who could not provide her with the comfort and support she needed so desperately.

She'd known about her mother's death for many years. But she'd imagined her father as he had once been, and waiting in exile for news of his daughter. On the train from Istanbul, Dmitri had explained that their father's body had escaped from Russia, but his mind had been left behind.

Had it been too cruel to tell Anna about their father, he thought? Should he have told her he'd died, and let his sister deal with just one grief? Was he cursing her with the promise of habitual heartbreak each time she would now visit their father, something Dmitri also experienced?

When the royal Russian siblings descended the steps of the Orient Express in Paris, they were able to put on a good show for the press who'd gathered there to greet them. The return of a Russian princess was quite a story.

One journalist, someone lurking at the back of the group trying unsuccessfully not to be seen, caught Dmitri's attention.

"I read your article on the train," said Dmitri. "You made me sound like a hero."

"It was a feeble attempt at an apology in print," said Aubrey. "Now, in person, please accept my apologies." He held out a hand.

"I suppose it doesn't matter now," said Dmitri.

"If I'd know your sister was -"

"Please don't," interrupted Dmitri. "Whilst I wouldn't necessarily trust you again, I'll say this, you're not too bad a journalist." He shook Aubrey's hand.

"Again, I'm sorry, Your Highness."

"Let's consider the matter settled, Bones," replied Dmitri. He saw Anna almost paralysed with fear as the journalists barraged her with questions. "We have to make tracks, gentlemen, please excuse us."

DMITRI HELD Anna's cold shaking hand during the taxi ride to the sanatorium, and along the corridor to their father.

The frail white-haired old man Anna saw across the room, staring vacantly out of the window, was not her father. When she'd last seen him, he'd been astride a powerful horse riding through the snow with her at the palace in Tsarskoe Selo. A week later her parents had left wintry Petrograd for the warmth of the Crimea. Three weeks later the February Revolution had forced the tsar's abdication, and she and her brother found themselves trapped in Petrograd. Anna had been separated from her father since then. Fifteen years distance felt like several lifetimes.

Anna remained in the doorway. Her heart was racing. She was unable to move across the room. The hope she'd long had of feeling her father's strong arms around her once more, had been the morsel of a promise that had enabled her to survive the labour camps. It was obvious to her now that the old man sitting in the chair would be unable to embrace her.

If she left the room, without making eye contact, thought Anna, she could maintain the fantasy, and perhaps the hope that her father was still alive, in the fullest sense of what she understood that to mean. But it was a selfish thought, and she was not a selfish person. She needed her father as he had been, but the patient at the sanatorium needed her more.

Anna pressed her body against her brother's. He clasped her ice-cold hand and walked with her across the room.

Anna knelt in front of the old man she barely recognised and forced herself to smile, not wanting him to see her sadness even though her heart was breaking. With her free hand, she took hold of the bony, loose-skinned hand of her father. The nurse had positioned this as usual on top of the blanket across his knees. With their hands linked, what was left of this branch of the Romanov family formed a chain. It was a reunion neither sibling had ever thought would happen.

"Papa," whispered Anna. She crouched closer to her father.

Then it happened.

Grand Duke Andrei turned his head fractionally towards the gentle female voice that had called him papa. It was the first voluntary reaction Dmitri had seen his father make in over a dozen years of catatonia.

Anna looked to her brother to check whether this was anything significant. Dmitri smiled at her encouragingly.

"Papa?" she repeated.

The old man's eyes focussed on the face of the woman speaking to him and calling him by a name in a tone which seemed familiar to him. What remained of his mind searched for meaning.

The grand duke's face changed. An expression emerged, as it hadn't done in so many years.

Dmitri and Anna watched as a tear broke free, and slowly navigated its way down the craggy pale skin of their father's face.

"Oh, papa, papa, papa," cried Anna, breaking her hand free from her brother's. She wrapped her arms around her father's emaciated shoulders. Dmitri saw that where one tear had leaked out of his father's eyes, a stream now flowed.

Anna released him and sat on the floor on the opposite side to her brother. Andrei's head turned to find her. He opened his mouth, and a slack jaw tried to form sounds.

"Is it really you?" he asked. These were the first words spoken, croaked through long-dormant vocal cords, since the grand duke had asked the British captain aboard the dreadnought leaving the Crimea what had happened to his wife.

"It's me, papa, yes it's really me," replied Anna, sobbing.

Dmitri had been holding his breath, and now filled his lungs.

Their father had returned.

XXIV

IT WAS just before midday when Dmitri woke up.

As they hadn't got back from the jazz club until five o'clock in the morning, he was still tired. He glanced across at the two naked women in the bed next to him, and smiled to himself; it had been a good night. It was a perfect re-introduction to society after his travails in South-East Europe.

He eased himself gently out of the bed, trying not to disturb his two companions. Slipping on his underwear, he rummaged in the side pocket of his dinner jacket to find the paste copy of the sapphire bracelet which had once belonged to his mother, and which the usual colleague in the Marais jewellery district had made for him.

Trying not to even breathe too loudly, he returned to the bed. He delicately pulled back the sheet, and located the left wrist of the Scandinavian princess, who had slept wedged between him and Sable. With careful, but fluid and consistent movements Dmitri undid the clasp of the genuine bracelet. The Nordic royal had proudly boasted the night before about purchasing the item for next-to-nothing from a man she'd met in Italy. Dmitri now started to slide this treasure off her wrist.

The princess moved, bringing her arm in closer to her body, making it less accessible. He had to gently loop the fake bracelet around her wrist, but it was difficult to connect the two ends and fix the clasp. After the second attempt, Sable's hand reached over and held the bracelet in place on her companion's wrist, allowing Dmitri to use both hands to secure it in place.

He waited a few seconds to make sure the princess was still asleep and hadn't noticed the switch taking place. When he was happy that the task was successfully complete, Dmitri scooped up his clothes and shoes from the pile which had been so frantically cast aside the night before. He padded around to the other side of the bed, leant down and kissed Sable. She smiled, keeping her eyes closed, and turned away to resume her sleep.

Fortunately, a taxi was idling outside the entrance of Sable's apartment block on the Champs-Élysées. Dmitri gave the address of the grand duchess' chateau in the Bois and collapsed in the back seat. He was hung-over and exhausted from the night before, but happily so.

He hoped Count Mishukov would help him sneak in without alerting the grand duchess.

With the return of his family, Dmitri knew he would have to make more stable living arrangements. He couldn't consider returning to Tangier now, but nor could he live under the restrictive hospitality of the grand duchess, who expected her guests to align their daily activities with her long-established routine.

Anna had asked to stay at the sanatorium as she needed the clinical care it offered to aid her own recovery, and she wanted to be close to their father as he made fresh steps each day out of the void he'd been trapped in for so many years. When they were both discharged

Dmitri would have to plan for their future. He was pleased there was a future now.

Dmitri puffed casually on a cigarette, having now restocked with his special blend of Syrian leaf from his tobacconist. He took a quick swig from the silver-plated and calfskin Berluti hip flask given to him as a present by the wife of a prominent British politician. He closed his eyes to let the motion of the Renault taxi sooth his pounding head.

But Dmitri was not asleep. There was something which disturbed him more than just the thumping headache, a feeling he couldn't explain at first, then it came to him.

He recognised the taxi driver. There had been something peculiar about his expression when Dmitri got in. The driver was too pleased to see Dmitri; it had been an unusual reaction for a cabbie to have, even if he recognised Dmitri from the newspapers.

Dmitri adjusted himself on the seat so that he could open his eyes just enough to get a better view of the driver.

The recognition chilled his blood.

He'd slimmed down slightly, the bushy moustache had been removed, and the greying hair dyed black, but the taxi driver was undeniably Basil Calloway, or Major Willoughby, or whatever name the English actor-turned-Bolshevik spy was currently going by.

The option of attack was considered, but quickly dismissed by Dmitri. As much as he wanted revenge on the Englishman who'd abducted his sister, thrusting himself forwards and grabbing the steering wheel would likely kill them both. His priority had to be escape, as he now had a sister and father to look after. Emile-Jacques and *le Deuxiéme Bureau* could coordinate the search and capture Calloway, but Dmitri had to survive in order to alert them.

The car was keeping up a decent speed, despite it being the middle of the morning in the city centre.

Dmitri used his combat training to consider how best to extricate himself from the moving taxi. He groaned in mock discomfort and sidled over to the pavement side of the vehicle. This was part of his preparation.

To escape, Dmitri would need two things to happen: for the traffic to become more congested and slow down the taxi, if not stop it altogether; and for the route to take them along a grass-lined boulevard to soften his leap to safety.

The jump had to be made at an angle in the opposite direction to the vehicle's motion to throw the velocity of his body in reverse and avoid getting run over by the rear wheels of the taxi as he landed. The landing needed to be on his shoulder. His body had to be tucked in a ball to keep his head safe and able to roll out of the jump more easily.

After a few minutes, the conditions he'd hoped for emerged as the vehicle slowed slightly along a grass-verged avenue.

Dmitri took a deep breath.

He raised his body up, opened his eyes, and smiled directly at the driver. The Englishman's expression showed surprise at the sudden reaction of the prince, and at the obvious recognition of the passenger he'd likely thought duped by is latest disguise.

Before Calloway could make the car react to what was about to happen, Dmitri winked at the actor, wrenched the door open, and jumped.

The ground came upon him harder than he'd expected.

He flicked his foot off the hard surface as soon as his shoulder made contact with the grass verge, forcing his body into a roll to limit the impact.

After a couple of painful seconds his body stopped tumbling. His dinner suit was torn to shreds, exposing scarred and bloodied skin beneath. But Dmitri was alive.

The taxi came to a screeching stop. The rear red lights remained illuminated, showing Calloway was keeping his foot on the brake pedal, trying to decide what to do. After a few seconds, and as a crowd rushed to Dmitri's aid, the red lights turned off. The taxi pulled back out into the moving traffic away from the excited scene behind it.

As people fussed around him, Dmitri uncurled from the ball he'd tucked himself into for the jump.

Every muscle, bone, and nerve in his body was on fire, but every limb seemed to be in working order, and his skull was intact.

The Russian prince stood up, pushed his shoulders back, buttoned up his ripped tuxedo jacket, brushed down the front of his torn evening trousers, and ran a finger across his pencil-thin moustache.

He checked that the taxi wasn't returning in his direction, and promised himself that he would see Basil Calloway again.

He smiled at his audience, who looked on in disbelief that the man had survived the fall.

"Blasted taxi drivers," he said, addressing the open-mouthed crowd. "So that's what happens when you don't tip."

Dmitri Romanov will return in "Torchlight in Berlin."

Ingram Content Group UK Ltd.
Milton Keynes UK
UKHW041129210423
420562UK00001B/160